SoulShares

Mantled in Mist

Book Six

Rory Ni Coileain

For more information contact:
Riverdale Avenue Books
5676 Riverdale Avenue
Riverdale, NY 10471.

www.riverdaleavebooks.com

Design by www.formatting4U.com
Cover by Insatiable Fantasy Designs Inc.

Digital ISBN: 9781626012486
Print ISBN 9781626012493

First Edition January 2016

Prologue

July 17, 1913 (human reckoning)
The Realm

I should just do it. What am I waiting for?

Fiachra glanced nervously around the grotto. There was no place for anyone to be hiding, in the little granite cave or its spring-fed pool. As if anyone would stop him from doing what he planned, or even cared what he did.

A gold-wing whistled at him from its perch in the old oak outside the grotto's entrance. *#fLY fLY fLY fLY aWAY#*

The bird's prescience would be eerie, if gold-wings knew any other song. Not that he was actually going to fly away. But vanishing to the point where not even a Fade-hound could find him came close.

It was ironic, though, that the grotto was guarded by an oak. Considering that oaks were the source of all his problems. There were dark-haired Fae in other Demesnes—Earth and Water, especially. But none of them were as reviled as the few tanned, dark-haired Fae of the Demesne of Air, whose gift for languages was rumored to have allowed them to consort with the

1

feral *Gille Dubh*, the Dark Men of the oaks, back in the lost times before the Sundering of the Fae and human worlds.

Fiachra had had enough. Enough of the taunts, the scorn. He had always challenged the ones who tormented his mother, and his sister, in the decades since he had come into his birthright of magick. But if he called out every Fae who considered hurling blood insults at him personally a form of sport, he'd have every House in the Demesne howling after him. Enough.

He ran his hand idly over the slab of stone on which he sat. It had served as a table, and a throne, and many other things, years ago when he and his sister Kiara spent their days playing here. Even the other Fae children had refused to waste their time on the *sule-ainme*, 'animal-eyed' children. Fitting, that he'd decided to come back here to end the whole idiotic charade.

Needless to say, he didn't plan to give the *bodlaig* the satisfaction of ending his own life, or seeking out the fabled Pattern and exiling himself. No, he planned to walk among the ones who scorned him for many centuries to come, Faded to invisibility. Having the last laugh, a thousand times over.

He had been warned about what he was about to do, more times than he could count or remember. Fading from one place to appear instantly in another was something any Fae past his birthright could do with ease, channeling and spending only the smallest part of the magick within him. But Fading and staying Faded was another matter. A master mage could do it and still hope to return to corporeality. But a commoner like Fiachra? He would be trapped forever, his teachers and his mother had solemnly warned. Invisible and incorporeal.

Perfect.

The gold-wing fell blessedly silent at last. Even the breeze stilled, and the late afternoon sunlight slanting into the grotto seemed thick enough to touch. The trickling of the spring that fed the little pool echoed in the stillness.

Fiachra looked down from his stone seat into the water, and his reflection looked back at him, distorted by the ripples. He could just make out the wavy black hair, dark amber faceted eyes, and warm brown skin that had earned him so much ridicule. *One last look.* Mirrors were traps for Faded Fae, drawing them in with no hope of escape. His teachers had never said whether water would do the same thing. No doubt they trusted their warnings had been sufficient to ensure Fiachra would never be tempted to find out the truth for himself.

Small things gleamed at the bottom of the pool. Coins, crystals, beautiful stones. He and Kiara had tossed them there when they were small, tokens to seal wishes. Wishes had been their substitute for magick then, before they came into their own power. The grotto had magick of its own, the magick of stone and water, and sometimes their wishes had worked.

But Fiachra was no longer a child, and no wish could give him what he longed for. He sought a final word, but no word came to him. There was no one to speak to, anyway, nothing but the gold-wing. And the damned oak.

Fiachra Faded, and disappeared.

Chapter One

It had taken Fiachra a full day, and most of the night, to cross the clearing surrounding the small round stone tower. This was, for him, making good time. It was also one of the many things no one had seen fit to warn him about, him or anyone else imbecilic enough to do what he had done more than a hundred years ago.

There was no chance of missing the tower in the darkness. Very little was ever truly dark to a disembodied Fae, as it turned out. Magick was like light to him, all the shades and variations of elemental magick and living magick. Everything in the Realm was painted in unspeakably beautiful light. Especially during the last few months, when a sudden blossoming of living magick had made him realize how dim and dreary the last decades had been by comparison.

He'd stopped giving a damn about any of it, though, around 99 years ago. There was no pleasure in being able to roam at will unseen when it took all of his will to travel in a season the distance of a day's ride in the body, and no value at all to the last laugh when he was the only one who heard it.

4

There were few things capable of killing a Fae. Fiachra was beginning to think loneliness had a place on that short list.

It was time to do what he should have done in the first place.

The tower of the Pattern wasn't what Fiachra had expected. He'd thought it would be larger, certainly. More impressive. Not a simple cylinder of gray stone with a crenellated top, set in the center of a greensward, as if the surrounding trees dared not come too close. Although there was something strange about the magick binding the tower's stones—not elemental, and not living, at least not in the way the other magick in the Realm was alive. It glowed like bound moonlight, bright even in the moonlight bathing the clearing.

Fiachra hoped the peculiar magick wouldn't be the first thing he'd encountered capable of keeping him out of something he wanted to get into.

Almost close enough now to touch the weathered stone, he heard voices.

"We are stretched too thin, Aine." A deep male voice, oddly accented, shivering with overtones of power yet somehow hollow.

"Cuinn an Dearmad was meant to channel the ley energy alone." This voice was a female's, cool, with the same accent and power, but more substance. "How is it that a thousand and more of you—of *us*—cannot manage it together?"

Fiachra touched the stone. To his astonishment, he could feel the strange magick, as he'd felt nothing else in a century.

"Cuinn's place was carefully prepared. As much

as we could prepare anything, with our foreknowledge crippled as it was. The rest of us... we have our functions, our duties, but channeling this power was never meant to be among them."

Fiachra tensed and forced himself forward. Power slid like cool blades through what would have been his body if he'd had one, a sensation that would have made him gasp if he could.

"Are any of the threads breaking? Is that why we sense magick escaping the Realm?"

Fiachra stopped, halfway through the wall, staring. The inside of the tower was a single chamber, open to the sky, lit with torches of a fey fire in sconces wrought of what could only be truesilver. A red-haired female knelt on the floor of polished and glittering stone, the long sleeves and skirts of a billowing lilac gown pooling around her like water. She faced a male, likewise kneeling, his dark hair touched with white, with skin fair as milk, in robes embroidered like something out of an ancient illuminated manuscript. And Fiachra could see the far wall of the chamber through him.

"No. Together we hold, but like a net we are stretching, beginning to separate." The male raised one hand to his temple, wincing as if something pained him. "Already the threads holding our bodies have started to part from the threads holding our souls."

The threads holding our bodies...?

The female nodded slowly. "You diffuse the ley energy into the Realm, instead of sending it through one great conduit."

"Exactly. And we prepared only to prevent anything from coming to the Realm from the human world. We never intended to allow anything through from that side—certainly not all the ley energy required to fuel the Realm!" Even hollow, the insubstantial male's voice stung.

"Peace, Dúlánc." The female frowned in thought. "I will go to our old sanctuary in Caerfionn and see if there is any help in the records we left behind. Though I hate to leave this place unguarded."

Leave it. Leave it now. Not that this pair could see him, or hinder him. But he wanted to investigate, and he wanted to do it in peace. To see if the glitter was in fact the storied Pattern, and to try to find out what the male meant about threads holding bodies.

"This place did well enough when you shared the Pattern with us." The male smiled for the first time since Fiachra had entered the tower. "But we are glad you choose to stay and keep watch."

The female laughed, a charming sound. Though Fiachra had mostly forgotten what it felt like to be charmed. "I believe it's safe to say that there was no one else both available and qualified for the position."

"You talk like Cuinn." Again the smile flared, then dimmed. "You should go, sister. This will be no safe place soon."

The female nodded. "I will return as quickly as I can. With good news, I hope." The color drained from her form, leaving her a lovely ghost of herself; the ghost, too, swiftly dissipated, and the male figure sank into the floor as the eldritch torchlight faded to darkness. All perfectly choreographed, all exquisitely beautiful.

Fiachra sighed, or something like it. It was always painful for him to watch someone else Fade.

But after this many years, the pain was easily dismissed, and he drifted out into the center of the chamber. He had not come all this way to listen to mages, living or ghostly. Even the greatest living mage, Conall Dary, had been unable to see or help him, in the frantic years just after his mistake. No, the Pattern was what he had come all this way to see, and to surrender to.

He turned his attention downward.

He stared.

What he had thought was black stone was clear crystal, shot through with a complex pattern of lines and arcs and whorls that thrummed with a visible pulse. Some of the lines were a silver polished to an impossible bluish sheen, others a blue so brilliant as to be nearly silver. The lines, the threads, hung frozen in crystal; frozen, yet never the same, from one moment to the next.

And between the brilliant lines, Fiachra looked down into a sky full of stars.

A sudden gust of wind whirled around the roofless chamber. Fiachra ignored it, still gazing raptly at the floor. Wind touched him no more than any other corporeal thing.

"...the threads holding our bodies have started to part from the threads holding our souls," the male had said. Which lines were bodies and which were souls? And could he reach them? He tried to will himself down, through the floor.

Nothing happened.

The wind pushed him to one side, into a pool of light. Moonlight.

Not possible.

8

Fiachra looked up. A small round window in one wall of the tower perfectly framed the full moon.

The crystal floor fell away beneath him, leaving only the brilliant lines and the stars beneath them.

The wind whipped itself to a gale, a fury. It drove him down, into the lines.

The silver-blue lines were blades keen enough to slice through a Fae as incorporeal as the impossible wind. Their touch was an agony he had never imagined. He clung to a blue-silver thread, huddled around it. Or he would have if he could.

The pitiless wind sieved Fiachra through the Pattern, his howl one with the wind.

***

Something scratchy-soft cushioned Fiachra's cheek. The unexpected sensation startled him awake.

I was asleep.

My eyes were closed.

I have eyes.

He was lying on grass. Rough, wiry grass. Liberally scattered with small stones, judging by the way the ground felt against his very naked skin. Groaning, he pushed himself up, and winced as a stone dug into his elbow. It was night, a night far blacker than he was used to, though a Fae's keen senses were more than adequate to allow him to see the silent forest surrounding him, a full moon visible between the branches of the overhanging trees. And to see his own very pale bare legs. Hands. Arms.

This isn't my body. It can't be. A thrill raced through him, setting nearly invisible blond hairs

9

standing on end up and down his arms. He would give just about anything for a mirror, if he had anything to give or anyone to give it to.

On that thought, he felt a stirring he hadn't known in a century—magick, welling up in him, in a current stronger than he'd ever experienced. And, obedient to his thought, the air in front of him solidified and silvered, a perfect mirror.

I've never been able to do that before, either...

Long blond hair tangled and tumbled around his face. Gem-irised eyes he suspected would be a light blue or green in daylight peered out from under brows slightly darker than his hair. His nose was proud, his cheekbones high, his lips full and soft-looking.

No one would have mocked this face. No one ever would.

Something moved in the mirror, something behind him.

Fiachra gaped as a figure emerged from the tree behind him. A naked, tanned-dark male with wild shoulder-length black hair took form from the wood and stared down at him.

SLAIDAR. A whisper came from the leaves over his head, a hiss of leaf against leaf. *Magick-thief.*

Where did you come from? The male's voice was similar to that of the leaves, but angrier. And both were perfectly understandable, thanks to the gift of languages common to Fae of the Demesne of Air.

He was lying under an oak tree. Not just any oak tree—a *darag.* And the feral creature had to be its pet *Gille Dubh.* It was almost enough to persuade Fiachra to go against thousands of years of Fae tradition and start believing in gods, because someone was

10

definitely laughing his, her, or its divine ass off at his expense.

"I haven't stolen anything." Fiachra lurched to his feet, fighting dizziness as he brushed away clinging acorns—not stones, as he'd originally thought. He wasn't telling the whole truth, given that the owner of his new body was probably more than a little angry at having lost it, but there was no reason to go shouting that particular truth to the local flora.

It speaks. The *Gille Dubh* wasn't even looking at Fiachra, he was looking up into the branches of the tree. *Do you understand it?*

YES. IT PROTESTS ITS INNOCENCE. PERHAPS IT THINKS WE HAVE FORGOTTEN.

It made a certain amount of sense that the tree was smarter than its pet.

Let me teach it how easy it is to forget death.

Even after close to a hundred years of disembodiment, Fiachra recognized a murderous gaze when he saw one. And even if he'd been inclined to forget, the cold fury with which the *Gille Dubh* regarded him would have been all the reminder he needed.

PEACE, COINNEACH. The ancient oak didn't sound peaceful, it sounded ready to kick Fiachra's arse from here—wherever 'here' was—to next fair's-day noon. **IT WILL DISAPPEAR.**

The tree's hissing whisper sounded just implacable enough to make Fiachra consider disappearing without arboreal assistance. "I'll be going now—"

For an instant, there was something taller about the *Gille Dubh*, taller and darker and infinitely more

11

menacing. *If my line carried enough of their blood to let me do that, no Fae would ever have given me shit twice.*

Whispers rose again, like the wind, where there was no wind. *If I may not kill it, then send it far away*, the *Gille Dubh* whispered, like a curse. *Some place where magick has returned but there are none of us to be tainted by it.* The male spat at Fiachra's feet.

Fiachra stirred the leaves on which the spittle had fallen with a toe. "I was expecting sap."

Apparently the *Gille Dubh* understood his tone of voice, if not his words, because his fists bunched at his sides and a low growl rumbled up from his chest. Which would have been sexy as hell, coming from a Fae. Fiachra could almost credit the old stories about his supposedly mixed bloodline, except for the persistent legend that the tree men had only been interested in males.

BETTER SHALL BE DONE. IT SHALL BE BOTH SENT AWAY AND TIME-SLIPPED. Fiachra got the distinct impression the *darag* was smiling. **WHEN IT WILL LAND IS NOT A THING I CAN CONTROL. AND I CANNOT SAY I AM SORRY.**

"What the bleeding ulcerated hell are you—"

Chapter Two

August 9, 2013
Washington, D.C.

Peri tried to relax back into the plastic chair. It wasn't really made for relaxing in, though; the only way to sit in it was to slouch, in a posture that showed off a hell of a lot of leg and pretty much screamed *fuck me*.

A low chuckle came from across the tiny waiting area. A man who looked like Idris Elba's younger brother was draped across an identical chair, right under the plasma screen that cycled through the price list for all the forms of massage theoretically offered at Big Boy Massage. Peri knew he could handle the shiatsu and could fake Thai, but in the unlikely event a client wanted anything else on the menu, he was screwed.

Which was, of course, the idea.

"You must be the new guy." Idris Junior's voice was even sexier than his smile. "Don't worry, we don't stay in the chairs long once things get busy."

Peri nodded. "Boss explained the system to me yesterday when he hired me." And what a job interview that had been, with Peri still kitted out as Falcon and carrying his stiletto heels because he hadn't wanted to run up the stairs from Purgatory in them. "Three boys working at once, max, with the fourth out here to keep an eye on the screen." Big Boy Massage had four small massage rooms opening off the waiting area, one for the boss' exclusive use when he was around and three for business, two of which were presently occupied. And each of the massage tables had a kick switch built into one leg that would light up a telltale in one corner of the plasma screen if the masseur was in trouble with a client. Lochlann Doran wanted his boys to have each other's backs.

Safety in numbers. That was how it was supposed to work, right?

Except when the one who has your back is a coward.

Long-Dark-and-Chiseled nodded, then treated Peri to the sight of a luxurious stretch, all the way from fingers interlaced overhead to bare toes pointed and curled hard, the mesh muscle shirt and leather shorts in between doing little to deter speculation about what lay beneath. And leaving Peri feeling decidedly underdeveloped by comparison. Though he doubted his companion could rock a mermaid hemline the way he himself could.

"Relax while you can, baby, pace yourself." God, Peri could listen to that voice all night. "Something tells me it's gonna be a long night—"

The street door opened, closed.

Sweet six-pound-nine-ounce baby Jesus.

Peri sat straight up in the loathsome plastic chair, ignoring the way his ass complained, and stared. The newly-arrived client had to be at least 6'5". The first things he noticed were eyes that reminded him of

14

pictures he'd seen of glacier ice, an uncanny shade of blue. Looking into those eyes felt like grabbing onto a bare electrical wire, and when the guy shifted his gaze to Idris the Younger, Peri wanted nothing more than to grab the wire again.

But at least now he could look at the rest of the guy without anyone noticing him going slack-jawed and stupid. The client—*my client, please God, I promise to be good for as long as I can stand it, just let him pick me*—had hair so blond it was almost white, just long enough to show a little wave, and wore a denim jacket over a plain faded blue T-shirt and cut-off shorts.

Now the Adonis in denim was studying the menu. Peri caught himself holding his breath.

"Do you do shiatsu?"

He's looking at me.

"Sure do."

The blond's smile, and his trace of an Irish accent, combined to make Peri's shorts feel much too tight. "Anything else?"

"We can talk about that once we get started." The standard answer. Letting a john comparison shop in the lobby used up valuable time. Besides, Peri wanted to whisper the specials into this guy's ear.

"Sounds good to me."

Peri unfolded himself from the torture chair, and grinned as his co-worker gave him a surreptitious thumbs-up. *Don't wait up*, he wanted to say.

He turned to *oh my GOD he's tall*. His own 5'8" frame was just right for Falcon's five-inch stilettos, but looking up at 6'5" without them was going to give him a pain in the neck.

Good thing he wouldn't be looking up much longer. Unless it was while he was lying on his back. That he could handle.

"Which room?" The blond's hand closed gently around Peri's upper arm.

Not protocol. But Peri was doing a whole lot of not caring about protocol, as a shiver ran the whole length of his body, driven by a shot of energy from that touch. The shot paid very special attention to his heart, which was suddenly hammering double-time. And his groin, which was also pounding, but in a very different way. *What the hell?*

"This way." He was surprised he could speak. He concentrated on leading the blond to the empty massage room without tripping over his own feet, and on closing the door without sagging against it and trying to get his breath back.

I think I'm losing my mind. First night in a new place, and I'm hyperventilating over Prince Charming.

By the time he trusted himself to look up again, the blond was sitting on the massage table, his sneakered feet just an inch or so from the floor. "Is this where I get naked?" His voice was surprisingly soft for a man his height, and there was an intimate quality to the softness that made Peri feel like he was being touched.

Which wasn't the way it was supposed to work in a place like this. He touched the customers. They only touched him when he let them. That was why he preferred working in massage parlors to freelancing. Most of the time.

"Not if all you want is shiatsu." The blond god

was sitting on the padded teak table with his knees apart, and Peri edged between them. Too close. But he wanted to be close. On his own terms. "So maybe it's time we talked about that."

"Maybe."

Just the hint of a smile touched perfect lips; this close, Peri could see stubble. It would be soft, he knew. This guy was a natural blond, nothing out of a bottle. He could think of a lot of places he wanted to get chafed.

"You're not a cop, right?"

Listening to the blond laugh was like knocking back really good sake. All you felt at first was the warm glow that spread out from your core, all the way to your fingertips. But you just knew that any second, your legs were going to give out on you.

"Do I look like a cop?" The blond glanced down. Peri did likewise, and was treated to the outline of an insistent erection straining against thin, worn denim. "More to the point, does *that* look like a cop?"

"Well, now that you mention it, I wouldn't mind a cavity search." Peri hated the glibness of the words, given that he knew how sincere he was. Some customers, he'd shout *hallelujah, come on, get happy* if all they wanted was a quick hand-job. This one...

This one he wanted to walk out of Big Boy Massage with and stroll hand in hand back to the apartment he was going to be able to pay the rent on this month thanks to Lochlann, order a pizza, and see how much of the Kama Sutra the two of them could get through by sunrise. Which was insane.

He dropped his hands to the blond's thighs, stroking gently, open-handed, savoring the way the

17

almost invisible hair tickled his palms. Then he closed his hands around thick wrists and drew large hands around and back, inviting them to cup his ass. Feeling just a little guilty, since technically he was stealing. Taking pleasure for himself before he was paid to give it. Though the blond looked as if he enjoyed it... unless that was just wishful thinking on Peri's part.

"How much for..." The blond frowned. "What's your name?"

"Huh?" The change of subject left Peri blinking. *No names, ever* might as well be inscribed over the door of this place, and every place like it he'd ever worked. "Why do you want to know?"

"I don't know. I just do."

Big hands ran lightly up and down Peri's arms. More touching. More of that indescribable sensation that made him want to laugh and moan and drop to his knees, surrender, lose himself. And that was even before he looked into those amazing blue eyes.

Eyes that really *saw* him. Eyes that held secrets and wanted to share them. Peri barely suppressed a shiver.

And the man wanted to know his name.

"Peri." The gentle touch was making him bold. Or stupid. Probably both. "And who are you?"

For a second, he wasn't sure if the smoking hot blond had heard him; his gaze had dropped, his eyes were on what his hands were doing, and he seemed perfectly happy to go on that way for a while. "Name's Fiachra," he murmured at last.

Peri was trying to think of a more intelligent comeback than *beautiful name*, when Fiachra touched him under his chin with a fingertip, tilted his head up, and looked into his eyes, and he stopped thinking altogether.

"You are so fucking beautiful," Fiachra whispered.

Peri blinked fast, catching the tears before they could do more than make his eyes sting a little. What he was was exotic. He knew it; he'd always known it. He had his Japanese father's dark almond-shaped eyes, and his father's glossy black hair, though peroxide and L'Oréal turned it to pale gold. His mother's Swedish ancestry had lightened his complexion and given him killer cheekbones and a slender body. Fucking beautiful. And fucking untouchable.

His beauty was his armor, these days. Whether other men hated or lusted, at least they did it from a distance. A safe distance.

He didn't deserve the jealousy he got. He knew that. But he didn't deserve the safety he had, either.

Maybe it was better if this one didn't see past the surface. Wanting to be seen, known, was dangerous.

Fiachra cupped Peri's jaw in the palm of his hand.

Peri couldn't breathe. *Maybe... maybe this time is different...*

The blond kissed him. Slowly at first. Gently, even. Almost reverently. But then the heat started building, and anything that might have resembled reverence vanished. Soft wet sounds, more intimate than sex. Gasps for breath. That sweet strange excitement, slowly intensifying. Peri found himself leaning in, Fiachra's thighs tightening to hold him. Hard cocks ground together as Fiachra shifted his weight forward; Peri would have cursed, but that would have required him to stop kissing, and there was no fucking way he was going to do that.

Different? Hell yes!

Hesitantly Peri slipped his arms around the other man's waist, under the denim jacket, spreading his hands out over the splendidly muscled back under the T-shirt. He felt Fiachra's breath catch, felt him stiffen.

"This is probably a bad idea." Fiachra didn't pull back far, only enough to let him whisper.

"Probably." Peri didn't pull away either.

Fiachra stole another quick, intense kiss. "No, I mean *really* bad."

Peri didn't want to hear another rejection. Not tonight. Not from this man. "Look, it's okay, we can keep it just biz." *I am such a liar*. He couldn't keep his hands still, they were roaming all over an acre or so of muscular back without any input from his brain. "How about I let you—"

His fingertips brushed something solid and metallic, shoved into the back of Fiachra's shorts. Handcuffs. The blond froze.

"Don't finish that offer, Peri." The blond didn't pull away. "You haven't said anything yet I'd have to arrest you for." Slowly he ran his thumb along Peri's cheekbone, traced it around the curve of his ear. "Especially if you actually do shiatsu."

"Got my certification two years ago." Peri was surprised at how even his voice was, and even more surprised at the tears stinging his eyes. It wasn't the thought of being arrested that hurt—the occasional night in jail was an occupational hazard for men like him—but the touches, the kisses, the promise of warm strength, had been nothing more than a setup. *That* hurt like fuck. Especially since he'd let himself think Fiachra really saw him. And since he hadn't been looking for the hurt this time.

Of course, Yukio and the others hadn't been looking to be hurt either. And look how that had worked out.

"Then we're good."

"I don't see how we can be good if you're a fucking cop sent here to bust me." Peri shoved the old pain down into the deep place where it lived in him, where it was supposed to fucking stay, and tried to step away, but Fiachra—*if that's what his name really is*—wouldn't let him. Not in a you're-under-arrest kind of way, but in a don't-make-me-let-go-yet kind of way. Which confused the hell out of Peri.

"I'm not going to bust you. Unless you insist. I don't want to." The grip of the blond's thighs eased a little, but now his fingers were laced through Peri's hair, and he still couldn't move.

Peri worked his hands between the two of them and shoved. Tried to shove. His body apparently refused to believe he really wanted to do anything so stupid.

"Please don't." The breath of Fiachra's plea was hot against his lips.

Fortunately, Peri's foot had more sense than the rest of him, and even as Fiachra kissed him again, hungry and open-mouthed, even as he kissed back—*I am such a fucking idiot*—he kicked the switch set into the table leg.

An idiot for kissing the blond in the first place? Or for trying to stop?

A sharp knock on the door was followed

immediately by the door swinging open, and a familiar bearded face in the doorway. "Trouble in here?"

Peri started to answer, but his throat closed tight around the words as Fiachra's expression went from naked hurt to... nothing at all. Blank, with chips of glacier ice for eyes.

"Nah. I was just leaving."

Fiachra pushed Peri back—not roughly, but with a sense of purpose and finality—and slid off the table.

Wait—

Fiachra pushed past Idris the Second and was gone, without a backward glance.

***

Wiping the last ten minutes or so of what had to be temporary insanity from his memory suddenly seemed like a very good idea to Fiachra, and the most efficient way to do that as far as he was concerned was to move on to his next assigned sting. There was a Metro station on the corner, and while he had a Fae's innate horror of enclosed conveyances, subway stations always had dark corners, private places from which he could Fade.

Next door to the papered-over front window of Big Boy Massage, he passed a display window, full of tattoo flash and objects apparently intended to be inserted through piercings. A hand-painted sign stood among the art, *Raging Art-On Tattoo and Piercing Parlor.*

Neither ink nor piercings had ever appealed to Fiachra, although that didn't stop him from admiring the art in passing. The idea of being inked or pierced made him uncomfortable. It felt like intentional defacement of something that didn't belong to him, namely his studly blond-god body.

17 years he'd been occupying this body, ever since the jumped-up weed had tossed him back in time and into the middle of New York's Central Park, and he still felt like a tenant. What of him was actually his own had been an open question from the moment of his transition. He'd kept the magickal gifts that were the birthright of the Demesne of Air—instant comprehension of languages, his own peculiar and rare gift of truthsight—but in coming through the Pattern he'd also picked up an almost frightening capacity to channel magick. If he'd ever had any clue what the hell he was doing, he had the innate potential to be a mage to rival Conall Dary, or even the ancient—and, Fiachra suspected, purely mythical—Loremasters.

A shame he hadn't picked up any extra powers of seduction. Surely the original owner of this piece of Fae perfection he was housed in could have persuaded Peri not to kick that switch.

Why do I still care? He's just a human.

A human more beautiful than any Fae, with a soft voice that reached right into Fiachra and started messing with his instincts. Hands that spoke a language all their own. And dark eyes that saw secrets, while hiding a pain too deep for even a truthseer to bring out into the light.

What had he seen? And what did a Fae care about a human's pain?

Set back from the street, a recess held several doors. One for the tattoo parlor, one with mailboxes and door-buzzers, one that looked like a darkened

23

storefront with board and flooring leaning against the window and against buckets of paint or plaster. And a flight of matte-black stairs led down below street level. A sign stood over the stairs, flickering dark red neon against a black background.

PURGATORY.

A name he'd already heard, in briefings both official and unofficial.

And a wordless voice, heard faintly from the other side of the black glass doors at the bottom of the stairs, like a Siren out of human legend and Fae reality.

Something moved at the bottom of the stairs. A swirling eddy of something insubstantial, not quite light and not quite magick, pouring out from under those glass doors. Something seductive, powerful, with a whispering song of its own. *What the fuck?*

<Ley energy,> a voice definitely not his own murmured in his thoughts. *<Too dangerous for you to risk alone. Allow me to assist you.>*

His focus broken, Fiachra stepped back from the stairs. "*Tá cúna saor in asc is'daoir,*" he muttered, not caring who heard.

Free aid is the dearest.

Even if it came from inside his own head.

Chapter Three

This was not supposed to fucking happen. None of it.

Fiachra sat on the splintered and scarred wooden bench, elbows resting on his bare thighs, hands hanging between his legs, staring into his open cubbyhole of a locker. Of all the bizarre twists his life in the human world had taken, tonight took home the Queen's Own Champion's token.

Peri.

Fae attitudes died hard. In the Realm, an offer of money in exchange for sex was one of the deadliest insults in the considerable *as'Faein* repertory of pejoratives. The word in the Fae language for 'whore,' *fracun*, literally meant 'use-value,' and implied that the one offering saw the other as nothing more than an object to be used to achieve pleasure. Several of the most memorable blood feuds in the history of the Fae race had started with that single word.

It didn't work that way in the human world, though. Peri wouldn't have seen an offer of money as an insult. Just business.

Peri. Shit.

Fiachra was anything but celibate. His first few years in the human world, spent mostly in making up for lost time after a couple of hundred years as a pariah and another century or so as a disembodied spirit, were mostly a very pleasant blur in his memory. But he'd never felt anything like the rush when he'd touched the exquisite blond Asian male.

His borrowed body knew magick when he felt it. Just not this kind of magick.

Magick. Don't even fucking get me started on—

"You're still here, Darkwood?"

He didn't turn at the sound of Russ Harding's voice. It was bad enough to be a Fae working for humans, but he'd learned to live with that over the years. Time in grade meant a lot, though, in the human police forces, and he'd been a detective in New York City a lot longer than his nominal supervisor had been one here in D.C. Every reminder of Harding's existence was figurative sand in the shorts Fiachra refused to wear.

"Took me a while to finish my end-of-shift paperwork." He reached into the locker and hooked his jeans out with two fingers. "It shouldn't take so long next time."

The words stuck in his throat. He couldn't afford to let there be a next time, not after what he'd learned tonight. News of Harding's quiet obsession had found its way to Fiachra's ears almost as soon as his transfer had gone through. *You're working D.C. Vice? Wait till Harding winds you up and aims you at his favorite nightclub.*

Right. Purgatory was Harding's favorite nightclub the way Jean Valjean was Javert's favorite criminal. His new co-workers had been glad to fill him in on the details. No one from Vice had ever been able to nail the triple-X gay club with the hotshot lawyer. Harding was convinced all it would take was the right cop. And he'd made it clear from the start that once Fiachra had gotten his feet under him, he was going to be the one to descend into Purgatory and shut it down.

After tonight, though, Fiachra knew he couldn't do it. Not just because as a Fae, he had less than no objection to what was rumored to go on at the bottom of those stairs, through the shining black glass doors. No, he couldn't shut the club down because he'd finally realized he'd been drawn to D.C. for the express purpose of finding it.

He shook out his jeans and drew them on, his mind racing. His borrowed body's magickal sense had picked up what had to be a Summoning, coming from somewhere in D.C., over a year ago. One hell of a Summoning, especially here in a world where the stories said the only magick an exiled Fae had was what he'd brought with him from the Realm. He'd resisted the pull as long as he could, but the longer he'd held out, the less it felt like a summons and the more it felt like a compulsion. So he'd transferred from New York, taken the first available opening for a detective in D.C., and it was just his hard luck that the opening had been in Vice and not Homicide.

More magick—the unexpected sleeting tingle of a protective ward against his skin—as he approached Big Boy Massage had been an early warning, though he'd shrugged it off at the time as an impossibility. But that swirling hypnotic not-quite-magick at the bottom of the stairs was obviously what the ward was there to guard.

And then there was the matter of that overly helpful inner voice, apparently awakened by whatever he'd seen at the bottom of the stairs. As if he had a shortage of things to worry about. The near certainty that he was about to encounter other Fae for the first time, courtesy of the Summoning, was a large enough pain in his ass all by itself. The possibility of repossession of his body by its original owner was an additional complication he could do without.

Not to mention the complications caused by dark almond-shaped eyes and the most kissable mouth in two worlds.

"Two good busts tonight—but I'm a little surprised you didn't score at Big Boy."

Fiachra stood, adjusting himself carefully to avoid the zipper of his jeans. He took his time about it before turning to face Harding. Who, it turned out, wasn't even looking at him; the detective was scrolling through Fiachra's report instead.

"Just bad luck. The guy I chose was legit. He even showed me his shiatsu certificate." The half-truth came easily—not that a lie would have been any more difficult—as Fiachra had no doubt Peri could have produced his certification. He could still recall the scent of the human's tears, his hurt, upon discovering his client was a cop. He'd thrown the fact of that certification back in Fiachra's face like a slap.

Which didn't make sense. Pissed off, sure, that was a normal response for masseurs and rent-boys following a close encounter with Vice. But Peri hadn't been pissed off, he'd been wounded.

Why the hell can't I get him out of my head? Tingle or no tingle, the breathtaking male was just another human. *I've no shortage of other things to worry about, after all.*

28

Harding snorted. Fiachra decided he didn't care for the sound. Just like he didn't care for being used to harass Peri—or any other human males trying to make a living out of any normal Fae's favorite pastime. "Look, Detective. I know you're doing me a favor, given that there's no room in Homicide right now and I needed to transfer. But..."

His brain abruptly caught up with his mouth—rear-ended it, so to speak. Fiachra's conversations with Harding since his arrival in D.C., seen through the lens of truthsight, had been enough to let him be reasonably sure his new boss wasn't a raving homophobe. But he couldn't answer for anyone further up the chain of command.

"Yes?" Harding was looking up from the tablet now, one eyebrow arched.

Ah, what the fuck. "I'd rather not work the massage parlors and the bathhouses and wherever the hell else D.C. Vice goes purely to make gay men miserable. That's not something I want to be a part of."

Harding touched the computer off and tucked it under his arm. "I can respect that, Darkwood. There are other places we can use you."

Fiachra sighed. "Thanks—"

"But I still need you for the Purgatory operation."

A'buil gnas le lom ar-gúl. The curse *as'Faein* was slightly more elegant than its English equivalent, *fuck me backwards.* "I've been meaning to ask you about that for a while now. What makes Purgatory so different from Flox or the Crimson Door? Or Four Jacks, for that matter?" All gay nightspots he'd been told Vice kept a careful eye on, but stayed mostly away from.

29

Harding shrugged. "History, for one thing. Maybe the main thing. When I transferred into the department two years ago, I swear the owner of Purgatory had half of Vice on his payroll. And nobody cared who knew it."

Fiachra nodded. In a lot of ways, human police were like the Royal Defense back in the Realm. Unpopular to begin with, and once the stench of corruption set in, there was no getting rid of it.

"Then LaRouche sold the place, and…"

"And?" Fiachra grabbed his T-shirt from his locker and pulled it over his head.

"The new owner put a stop to the payoffs. Said he didn't believe in doing business that way. But that doesn't mean he's cleaned the place up." Harding looked Fiachra up and down. "If you believe a quarter of the stories on the street, Purgatory makes a Roman orgy look like a fundamentalist revival. Though the few times I've been able to get an undercover cop in there past their bouncers, they haven't seen anything we'd shut down any other club for."

"So what's the—"

"The problem's the other shit. A lot of it." Harding looked back over his shoulder as a couple of uniforms came in from the garage, eager to finish their shifts, then returned his level gaze to Fiachra. "Granted, there are some things the new owner won't tolerate. Some dickhead from Virginia was trying to run an underage prostitution ring using Purgatory's bar for a front. Guaire found out about his operation the same time we did, but he moved faster than we could. We had to question the guy in his hospital room." A brief *so-not-sorry* smile lifted one corner of the detective's mouth.

Guaire? Fiachra tried not to look too interested. In the Realm, House Guaire of the Demesne of Earth had been known as the Cursed House for the last century and a half or so. Coincidence, that name linked to a place where the raw stuff of magick welled up out of the earth? Bloody fucking unlikely.

Harding didn't stop talking when Fiachra stopped listening. "But when it comes to things that don't bother him, Guaire doesn't lift a finger. And not much bothers him. Their old bouncer disappeared without a trace, and I swear he's glad of it. We nearly had an international incident last spring, the son of an African ambassador passed out on his way into the club and the bouncer wouldn't let the EMTs call the kid's family—"

"Probably because the 'kid' would have been imprisoned, or worse, when he got home, if his family found out he was gay."

"Yeah. Well." Harding cleared his throat. "Nothing we write up against the club sticks, which makes me more suspicious than anything else. The owner's husband is a partner in a connected K Street law firm, and he has a talent for making charges go away. God alone knows what he manages to make disappear before we get wind of anything." The set of the detective's jaw was grim. "With an establishment like Purgatory, what Vice sees is only the tip of the iceberg. And with a tip like this, that's one hell of an iceberg. You can count on it."

Fiachra smothered a yawn with the back of his hand, took his wallet and keys out of his locker, pocketed both, and closed the metal door. "Well, if the connected mouthpiece makes anything disappear before the middle of the afternoon, would you kindly leave a note on my voicemail? I've a date with my pillow, and it gets cross if it's kept waiting." He'd been told many times that he sounded Irish—small wonder, all the Celtic languages were descended from the Fae tongue—and that the effect was more pronounced when he was tired. Which he definitely was.

"Har har." Harding stepped back from the locker room door to let him pass, though.

"Tell you what," the Vice cop added as Fiachra passed. "I'll take you off the rotation for tonight. And while I figure out what else to do with you, you can go check out Purgatory."

"Aye aye, sir."

Fiachra shouldered his way through the crush of uniform changing shifts and let himself out of the precinct house. The morning was already humid, with the promise of heat. Nothing he couldn't handle, though, not after 17 years of the summertime canyons of Manhattan.

Yes. The strange voice was back, an eager whisper. *Take us to Purgatory.*

Chapter Four

"Kevin Almstead." Kevin leaned back in his soft leather chair, loosening his tie with the hand that wasn't holding the phone.

"Kevin? Lochlann. Is this a bad time?"

"No, I'm between meetings." The lawyer craned his neck so he could see out into the hallway. "No one's in sight, if you'd rather talk face to face."

"Good idea."

As Kevin set the phone back in its cradle, Lochlann appeared on the far side of his desk. First a watercolor sketch of himself, swiftly adding color and substance, the other end of Fading.

"That was fast—you want to get the door?"

Lochlann laughed softly and gestured, and the heavy office door swung shut. He dropped into the chair opposite Kevin's desk, glancing around at the sleek blond Scandinavian furniture, sheer curtains, crystal accent pieces, plush pale beige carpet

"You've redecorated. Again."

Kevin waved a hand. "It probably won't be the last time. There has to be some decorating scheme that makes it easier to forget Art O'Halloran died in here."

"You have a point."

Lochlann's gaze strayed, and Kevin knew what the Fae healer was looking at—the framed picture sitting on the bookshelf behind his desk. A snapshot from his wedding; his father had been holding the camera, and Tiernan looked ever so slightly worried he was about to be cut out of the herd, brought down, hamstrung, and dragged back to the cave to feed a hungry pride. Kevin found it incredibly endearing. His father found it hilarious.

"So what can I do for you?"

"I'm not sure, actually." Lochlann scratched a cheek thoughtfully, a nail rasping against his morning's dark growth of beard. Fae tended to be blond or red-haired, and Lochlann was the only SoulShare in the D.C. contingent whose five o'clock shadow ever came close to rivaling Kevin's own. "My newest masseur had a run-in with Vice last night."

"You need me to make a call?" Kevin reached into an inside pocket of his suit and pulled out his cell phone. The calls he made on behalf of Purgatory and Big Boy didn't belong on the office phones.

"Not really. At least, not your usual call. Peri found out the guy was a cop by accident, he said. And he didn't get arrested."

"Peri?" Kevin arched a brow and set the phone on the desk. "You mean Terry?"

"No, but I can see where that may get confusing eventually." 'Terry' was, of course, Terrence Miller, Josh LaFontaine's business partner at Raging Art-On, at least until he and Garrett Templar got their exercise and dance studio next door to it up and running. "You've probably seen Peri Katsura at Purgatory, he's there as Falcon two or three nights a week. The drop dead gorgeous Asian drag queen," he added in apparent response to Kevin's blank look.

"Oh!" Kevin felt himself turning red. Most of the queens who hung out at Purgatory gave 'fierce' a whole new level of meaning. Forces of nature, the lot of them. He remembered Falcon, though. Falcon was different. He'd dated women exclusively before meeting his SoulShare—granted, not a lot of women, law school and being an eager young associate didn't leave a lot of time for that sort of thing unless you wanted to date other law students or associates who kept your same batshit crazy hours—and he'd originally wondered how such a stunningly beautiful, quiet, demure woman could have gotten so incredibly fucking lost as to find herself in Purgatory's fabled cock pit. "I didn't know his real name."

"Well, Peri isn't exactly his real name." Lochlann chuckled. "I doubt he's willing to go by his real name to clear up the confusion, but I'll let him tell you that story himself if he wants to. And my concern is that I don't recognize the cop he described, and I thought I knew everyone in Vice."

"You think the guy might be a shakedown artist?"

"It's happened before, though not at Big Boy. Yet."

Kevin nodded. There were times it amused him to see how seriously Lochlann took his role as massage parlor proprietor. But it made sense, from a Fae perspective. Lochlann wanted a place where he could do his own healing work if he chose—the male gave a wicked massage, and Kevin's touch of bursitis, left over from his college wrestling days, was gone as if it had never existed—and if D.C.'s gay community wanted a staff of willing and limber gentlemen to see them through the lonely nights, a Fae had no problem with providing that service. Lochlann did insist, though, that his employees be reasonably proficient in at least one therapeutic practice, just in case anyone asked.

"I can make a few calls, see what I can find out. Although most of my contacts are in the United States Attorney's office—I have Russ Harding's number, but I'm guessing you don't want me calling him directly on this one."

"You guess correctly." Lochlann tapped his chin thoughtfully. "Assuming the guy from Vice was using his real name, Peri says his name was Fiachra."

Kevin's eyebrow went right back up. "That almost sounds Fae."

"Or Irish." Lochlann grinned. "Remember, when you hear approaching hoof beats, your first thought probably shouldn't be zebras. And I can't imagine a Fae working for Vice."

"As to your first point, Purgatory is what they call in physics a strange attractor. I wouldn't bat an eyelash if a herd of zebras came charging up 18th Street." Kevin reached for his cell phone again. "But I concede your second point." He unlocked the phone and started thumbing through his contacts. "I'll see if I can get Vijay to give me a straight answer. Though it's close enough to lunch time that I may have a hard time getting through to him right away."

"No rush. I told Peri to let me know if he sees the guy again, but I doubt they'd send him back to the same place so soon. If ever—the way Peri described the guy, he's not very forgettable." Lochlann smirked.

"The word 'god' was thrown around a lot on the phone, both as a descriptor and in the phrase 'oh my fucking God'."

Kevin couldn't help laughing. "Well, I've never talked to Peri, but I can't imagine anything like that ever coming out of Falcon's mouth."

"No, they're very different personalities." Grinning, Lochlann got to his feet. "I'll leave you to it, Garrett's liable to be awake any minute and he's promised me a real Southern breakfast."

"Never keep a chef waiting. And always thank him properly." Kevin winked. "I'll understand if I get your voicemail later."

The Fae's self-satisfied expression as he Faded drew one last chuckle from Kevin as he turned his attention back to his phone. *Been a while since I offered to make my steak au poivre.*

Chapter Five

The sunlight felt like tiny hot needles pricking Peri's eyeballs. And that was even before he opened his eyes.

I did not *cry myself to sleep.*

Hell of a lot of good denial did him.

He groaned and rolled onto his stomach, groping for the pillow he'd pushed aside in his sleep, intending to put it over his head. The act of rolling, unfortunately, pinned an impressive case of waking wood between himself and the sheets in a position that was going to be painful in a few seconds.

Good.

The pillow didn't really help much. It made everything darker, but darker just made it easier for him to replay the few minutes from last night that he'd be much happier if he could selectively erase.

He would be happier. Really. It just complicated everything, when he could feel those strong thighs closing around him, those hands on his arms, shoulders... those kisses, Jesus, he could still taste every one of them.

Yeah, his cock hurt. Didn't change anything, though. He rolled again, keeping the pillow over his face. He wasn't ready to face the afternoon yet.

Hopefully it was afternoon. He'd had a hard enough time falling asleep—it had been well after sunrise when he'd finally lost consciousness—if it was any time before noon, he was going to...

... what, go back to sleep? Like that was going to happen.

He'd had three customers after Fiachra left. One hand job, one BJ, and one full-service who had left him unable to sit in the torture device his boss laughingly called a chair for half an hour afterward. None of them had done a damned thing to get the towering blond out of his head.

The towering blond cop. Fuckitall.

He'd given up hoping for a guy who would sweep him off his feet and take him away from the life he'd settled for, so long ago he'd gotten tired of finding it ironic that he'd gotten tired of the cliché. Fiachra wasn't his knight in shining armor, or even his sugar daddy in worn-out denim.

Fiachra had seen through the so-fucking-beautiful package that was Peri, though. Peri was as sure of that as he'd ever been of anything. And he'd been fine with walking away from what he saw.

Knowing all that didn't keep Peri's thoughts from wandering, though. Or his hands. Thumbs, fingers, teasing the blunt head of his cock as if he had every right to be getting off on thoughts of his own personal one-man S.W.A.T. team. Grimacing, he grabbed hold of fists-full of the sheet, to give his hands something else to do. This fit would pass. He just had to give it a minute.

More than a minute. *Hell.*

He had no business hoping for a rescuer. Hell, he

didn't have the balls to do something he'd need rescuing from. He'd gotten tired of trying to make sense out of that a long time ago, too. He wasn't even entitled to survivor guilt. Survivor guilt was for the ones who shared a risk, and somehow won the lottery and walked away from the danger, when someone else didn't. And he hadn't won any fucking lottery. Or lost one.

Yet.

You can't win if you don't play.

But there was something about Fiachra.

Damn it to hell.

Those kisses hadn't been a cop setting up a bust. He knew the difference. And he had yet to meet a lawman who could feign or force the kind of arousal it took to produce a hard-on like the one he'd seen. And scented. And even tasted, in those kisses.

To hell with the sheets. His hands were busy again, gripping tightly, cupping his sac, feeling the stubble. Teasing under the head of his cock with the side of his thumb.

There was a technique he used when a customer wanted him to show off, all long slow gliding strokes, ball play, tasting the clear drops that welled up one after another, tonguing his finger. Twisting and writhing, suffering beautifully.

Then there was what he did when he meant business. His own business.

He thrust up into his own tightly curled hand, eyes closed. Imagining Fiachra straddling him, spreading his ass cheeks wide and driving down and moaning faintly with the pleasure of being filled. Imagining what he, Peri, didn't deserve, couldn't have.

His breath came in short, harsh gasps, in time with the stabbing thrusts of his hips. Sweat trickled down his sides, down his neck, stung in his eyes. *So... good.*

If he hadn't gone exploring, hadn't found the damned handcuffs, maybe he could have had this for real. Or, more likely, given it to Fiachra. No one paid for the privilege of being fucked by a whore. But taking it would have been good too. *Son of a bitch.* He gripped tighter, groaning through clenched teeth.

Other hands were touching him. Caressing. Taking him out of himself. Even the memory of those few minutes was enough to bring him to a place he could never get to on his own. *So fucking good.*

It didn't even matter what his blond god looked like. It wasn't the hair, the face, the body, even the eyes that had him a heartbeat away from release. Fiachra's hands spoke a language, and his kisses made music of it. Telling him he was wanted. He, himself. Not the rent-boy, the masseur. Not even Falcon, the beautiful one who had never been touched by anything. Him. Peregrine Took Katsura.

I can enjoy him like this.
Because he'll never know.

Peri's back arched and his heels dug into the mattress. He refused to cry out as one thick ribbon of hot fluid after another coated his hand, as he wrung his now-slick and pulsing cock. This show wasn't for the neighbors.

It wasn't even for him, really.

It was a gift. To a man who would never know he'd received it.

Chapter Six

Nothing.

Fiachra wasn't sure whether he was disappointed or relieved. Whichever, there was nothing untoward going on at the bottom of the stairs leading down to the black glass doors of Purgatory. He still felt the pull, though. Nothing physical, just a powerful sense that he needed to be on the other side of those doors. Something down there was calling him.

Time to answer.

He started down the stairs, then slowed as the doors swung open and a gray-haired human male in disheveled business attire exited the club. His gait was unsteady and he held a little more tightly than necessary to the brass railing opposite Fiachra, but all the Fae's acutely sensitive nose picked up was excellent Scotch. And sex. A lot of sex.

Then the human was gone, and Fiachra was standing in front of the doors. Taking a deep breath, he pushed them open.

"I'm sorry, sir, I can't admit you."

Fiachra blinked. The way into the darkness within was blocked by a human male almost a foot shorter than he was, and nearly a foot wider. Broad shoulders and extremely well-developed biceps stretched a black T-shirt with a club logo past what he would have thought fabric and stitching could bear; the male was bald, and while his face wasn't unpleasant, it promised a great deal of unpleasantness should he ever become angry.

"Why not?" He didn't have to crane his neck to see past the bouncer, and while the club was busy, it certainly wasn't overcrowded.

"This is a private establishment, sir. Admission is at the discretion of the management."

Is this why Harding has never been able to get anyone in here? "There's no reason to—"

Then he saw it. Not quite light, not quite magick, curling over the floor inside the club like the smoke off dry ice.

Someone else saw it, too. *<Let me take care of the witless human.>*

Magick welled up in Fiachra, much more magick than he had ever channeled in the Realm. It rushed through him, past him, into the human. And the human blinked, shook his head, and stepped aside. "Enjoy your evening."

A useful trick when interrogating a suspect in a murder investigation, but he'd never thought he'd have to use it to get into a nightclub.

He'd never used it in the Realm. But until now, he'd always assumed it was his own gift, something awakened in the transit between the worlds.

Hey. Voice-in-my-head.

Silence.

Bod lofa dubh.

Hopefully he wasn't wishing *himself* a black

43

rotting dick. That would put a damper on the kinds of activities he'd enjoyed before falling asleep this morning. And again in the shower, upon waking. And... *oh, hell.* Any human hell, he wasn't picky. He could argue with a voice in his own head, stare off into space, blocking traffic into and out of Purgatory while he fantasized about a bewitching human...

Or he could find out who or what had called him here.

Fiachra stepped past the bouncer and into another world. Directly ahead of him, past what looked like a coatroom, was the club's bar, a curved length of pure black, backlit a sullen red, with a surface of glass. Light all the colors of fire flickered up from under the surface, illuminating everything sitting on the bar, and everyone leaning over it, with a glow like something out of Dante. Or maybe a Winterdark celebration in the Realm's Demesne of Fire. The strange cascading not-light seemed to have its source somewhere behind the bar, spilling out like the foam at the base of a waterfall, settling as it spread.

Off to the left, a few wide, shallow stairs led down to a dance floor spiked with gleaming poles, one of which was presently occupied by a young, long-haired Latin male wearing nothing but a pair of rubber palm-grips and a severely minimalist thong. Electronic music gave the floor a deep bass heartbeat; lights swept over the floor, picking out couples, faces, bodies, all without adding illumination to the rest of the club.

A few more steps, and Fiachra could see the rest of the club, the part that had been the focus of most of the write-up in Vice's dossier on Purgatory. Though that report certainly hadn't included even a fraction of what was going on in front of him. The cock pit was in fact a pit, irregularly shaped, sunken into the floor and filled with black leather furniture—chairs, benches, sofas, loveseats. Most of the furniture was occupied, by single males, couples, threesomes, moresomes. Fiachra could see three blowjobs in progress without needing to turn his head, or even move his eyes very much. A daisy chain of thoroughly inked bears occupied one of the sofas and spilled over onto the floor, grunting loudly enough for a Fae, at least, to be able to hear them even over the subsonics coming off the dance floor. A burly bare-chested gray-haired male frowned in concentration as he threaded corset laces through an elaborate set of piercings in a long-haired twink's back. Some of the couples, or groups, were so wrapped up in each other the rest of the club might as well not exist; some were on delicious flagrant display for anyone who cared to watch.

There were plenty who cared to watch, too. Almost as many humans stood around the edge of the pit as sported in it. And some wanted to get even closer. A drag queen—all Fiachra could see from where he stood was long dark hair and a spectacular sequined teal gown hugging a slender form—was perched on the arm of the sofa watching the bears at play, one dainty stiletto-heeled foot swinging back and forth like a pendulum.

All things considered, if Fae ever changed their collective mind and decided to believe in a blissful afterlife, the scene before Fiachra's eyes would almost certainly be found somewhere in it. Sex was an art form among the Fae, and Fiachra had always been an art enthusiast, to whatever extent his physicality permitted.

And Harding expected him to help shut Purgatory down? *No fornicating way.* Even leaving aside the whole issue of the Summoning that had originated from somewhere in the club, and ignoring the separate siren call of the pseudo-magickal energy welling up from behind the bar—

The drag queen startled, shoulders stiffening as if Fiachra's gaze were a physical touch right between her shoulder blades. Slowly she turned.

Fiachra stared, stunned, at wide dark almond-shaped eyes, impossible cheekbones, a perfect shining plum-colored mouth forming an oval of shock.

Peri?

He couldn't move. Couldn't think. Which was idiotic. In the time before the Sundering of the Fae and human worlds, thousands of years ago, the relationship between Fae and humans had been quite clear. The Fae seduced, played with, toyed with humans. Humans were prey, and Fae mostly benevolent predators.

No Fae had ever needed a human. Not the way he needed Peri. He'd spent the morning trying to pretend it was all sex. It wasn't. They were connected. Kisses, touches had set a hook, and the memory of pain in strange dark human eyes had channeled a purely human kind of magick.

And now this magick had a new form. One just as arousing, ensorcelling—

"Brodulein?"

The name was Fae, but it wasn't his. But it shattered the spell of the moment; Peri turned away, flushing, and Fiachra wheeled round to face the speaker, lips curling back in a very Fae snarl. "Who the hell are—"

Two Fae males stared at him, leather-clad, sex rolling off them both in waves Fiachra could feel against his skin. One had wavy dark-blond hair and faceted irises of a jade-green so pale they were almost white. The other wore his blond hair short, except for a forelock that curled over his forehead as if it expected to be grabbed. His eyes were blue topaz, and magnificent tattooed stars like those in a Royal's diadem swarmed around his nearly bare torso.

<Cuinn an Dearmad.> The voice in his head didn't sound happy. At all. *<And the lost Prince Royal of Fire, Rian Aodán.>*

Even the disembodied Fae Fiachra had been had heard the tale of the kidnapped princeling.

"I'm not Brodulein," he croaked. "But I don't think he likes you very much."

***

I take it you know him?

Cuinn was glad Rian was bespeaking him. He wasn't sure his voice was in working order at the moment. *I'd say yes, except that there's no fucking way this pestiferous bumbletwat can possibly be here.*

For someone who makes fun of Conall's vocabulary, you surely borrow a lot of it. Rian's smirk was too sexy by a factor of at least 12.

Don't make me hurt you. Cuinn wanted to pay some attention to that smirk, but unfortunately having a Loremaster dumped in his lap took precedence at the moment over what he wanted. *But if you could be a dear and go find Twinklebritches, I'll be happy to demonstrate the extent of my appreciation for your assistance later—Conall's containment channelings are a fuckload better than mine are. Just in case.*

I'll tell him you said so. Cuinn's bondmate slapped him gently on the ass and headed for the stairs, giving the newcomer a wide berth.

Said newcomer didn't seem to care much about either Cuinn or Rian. The errant Loremaster—for whom 'pestiferous bumbletwat' was as perfect a moniker as had ever been coined—was preoccupied with something going on in the cock pit. And it didn't take long to figure out what. Falcon slid off the arm of a sofa full of sweaty bears and hurried up out of the pit, shooting Brodulein an unreadable look before pushing her way through the customers and disappearing through the black glass doors just a minute behind Rian.

Cuinn tsked. "If you've pissed off Falcon, you're going to be in all kinds of trouble even before our resident mage gets here. The lady's popular."

How the fuck did a Loremaster get out of the Pattern? And why did it have to be this one?

***

It's going to be all right. It's all good.

No amount of positive self-talk could keep Peri's heart from racing as he climbed the stairs stopping halfway up to slip off his heels. He was still firmly in Falcon's headspace, and Falcon wasn't nearly as cool with the possibility of being arrested as Peri was. Nobody ever touched Falcon. That was what Falcon was for.

Maybe he didn't recognize me.

No, that wasn't going to work. He'd felt the blond god's gaze right between his shoulder blades, and when he'd turned around...

... he'd felt arms. Around him. Just like he hadn't been able to stop wanting to feel them last night. Like he'd imagined them this afternoon. Like he still wanted to feel them.

I'm losing my mind.

He was running by the time he hit the street, past the tattoo parlor. Lochlann had said he could use the bathroom at Big Boy to change on his drag nights, which was a godsend—he loved Purgatory, but he hated changing clothes in its bathroom, and forget about trying to paint his face in that terrible lighting.

He crashed into someone coming out of the massage parlor, so hard he staggered.

"Peri?" A hand caught his arm, steadied him. "I mean, Falcon?"

He blinked up at his new boss. "Whichever. Sorry. I didn't mean to—oh, my God."

"What?" At least Lochlann sounded amused rather than irked.

"You told me to call you if I ever saw that cop from last night—he's downstairs. In Purgatory."

Peri wasn't expecting Lochlann's shock. "An undercover cop in Purgatory? Are you sure?"

"Believe me, there's no mistaking this guy for anyone else." Peri hoped his makeup and the darkness concealed his blush. "He's talking to one of the owner's friends."

"Oh, shit."

Lochlann pushed past him and bolted for the club.

Peri watched him go, then shrugged and let himself into Big Boy. Time for the lady to disappear. And time for him to forget about the man who had come so close to making him feel... what? Safe?

If he was that close to forgetting how little safety he actually deserved, maybe it was time for a reminder.

The thought startled him with its intensity. For a second.

Tomorrow night. Yeah. Tomorrow night would be good.

***

The tall blond hot-as-all-fuck Fae rolled his eyes. "I take it you don't believe I'm not who you think I am."

"Short answer—no, I don't. Long answer—hell no, I don't. You're too memorable." Cuinn's voice was as dry as he could make it. Of all the Loremasters who had survived the last battle with the *Marfach* and gone into the Pattern to guard the Realm against the possibility of its return, Brodulein had shown perhaps the least inclination to work and play well with others. Even less than Cuinn himself. If they hadn't needed every magickally gifted soul, and every bit of their bodies' magickal essence, to make the Pattern work and repair the damaged Realm, the majority of the Loremasters would have been perfectly happy to leave Brodulein tending his precious flying horse farm in Glann Súlinach. Probably personally tending to the mares, too. That was just the way he rolled.

"Just my fucking luck." The other Fae shook his

head. "In my defense, I had no idea I was stealing a body."

Over Brodulein's shoulder, Cuinn saw the black doors swinging open to admit, not Conall, whom he was actually willing to admit he *really* wanted to see right now, but Lochlann.

Brodulein froze.

He vanished.

Air rushed in to fill the space where he had been, with a sound like a soft sharp chime.

Chapter Seven

Rian loped back down the stairs into Purgatory, the cool air at the bottom of the stairs closing round him like a blessing and the throbbing bass from the dance floor like a curse, with Conall close on his heels. Cuinn was where he'd left him, more or less, but the sex-with-legs blond he'd called Brodulein was nowhere to be seen. And Lochlann had appeared from somewhere and was looming over Cuinn in a way that made the young Prince Royal feel very possessive. If anyone was to be looming over his consort, it would be himself.

"A Loremaster?" Lochlann's expression as Rian and Conall shouldered their way through the crowd strongly suggested he thought Cuinn had taken leave of several of his senses. "Apart from the fact that that's impossible, Peri was in a panic just now, he said he saw an undercover cop down here talking to you. The male who nearly busted him last night, upstairs at Big Boy."

"Wait, what?" Conall gestured, and a hemisphere appeared around the four Fae, as seemingly insubstantial as a soap bubble but blocking out all sound from the rest of the club. Rian had seen Conall do this channeling before, and knew that the sound barrier worked both ways, and that in addition any non-Fae onlookers would see nothing but images of partiers lifted from elsewhere in the club. Photoshop, Fae style. "Lucien's on the door tonight, he'd never let a cop in—at least, not without buzzing me. And a Loremaster?"

"Yes. A Loremaster." Rian was well acquainted with the frustration he saw on Cuinn's face, though he was more accustomed to being the cause of it, and that under far more pleasant circumstances. "I knew Brodulein for maybe a hundred years, off and on—the off being far more enjoyable than the on—before the Sundering. It was him. Though he claimed it wasn't, and I have to admit, that particular Fae never lost an opportunity to call attention to himself."

"Are you sure he didn't just Fade?" Rian wasn't sure, but he thought Conall was just barely masking amusement. Rian's consort and the supremely powerful mage who looked like the lead singer in a boy band got under one another's skins in a way Rian found highly entertaining.

"Har har." Cuinn swept a booted toe through the spot where the blond had been standing. "Fading doesn't have its own soundtrack." His brow creased in a frown. "I've heard that sound before, too, but fuck me if I remember where or—"

The magickal shield vibrated with the sound of a bell, a chime at once faint and as attention-getting as a thunderclap. And before the echoes had died away, the hot blond was lying on the floor at everyone's feet, wearing nothing but a stunned expression, with acorns and bits of bark clinging to his elbows and what Rian could see of his delectable arse.

Lochlann said it first. "That sound?"

"Exactly that sound."

There was another sound in the air, too, one Rian recognized though again it was out of its usual context, and that was cursing *as'Faein*. And it was coming from the figure on the floor, who had rolled onto his side and was holding his head as if he were either afraid it was about to fall off or wishing it would get on with it.

"What the hell happened to you?" If no one else would ask the question, well, Rian would just ask it himself.

Slowly the blond head swiveled, ice-blue eyes found Rian's. "The motherfornicating *darag* happened to me. And its pet tree savage."

"What the feck are ye on about?"

Fuck me oblivious and suffocate me in my sleep.

Startled, Rian turned to his male, his consort, his love, and found him white as any ghost. *What is it, what's wrong?*

Cuinn stared at the prone Fae, but Rian was of the opinion he was seeing something else altogether. *It's one of the shortcuts we took, setting up the Pattern, coming back to bite me in the ass. Maybe all of us.*

Then a great many things started happening all at the same time. The air shimmered between Lochlann and Cuinn, took on color and form, and became Tiernan Guaire, the owner of Purgatory, in the shredded jeans and grunge rock T-shirt that were his usual working attire. "Is it a party? And no one invited me?"

And lazy tendrils of ley energy boiled out from behind the bar, invisible to all but the assembled Fae toward whom the proto-magickal energy seemed to reach.

And Conall, his apple-green gaze fixed on the advancing ley energy, went nearly as pale as Cuinn.

"GentleFae, whether or not our new arrival is a Loremaster, he's an unShared Fae. And from the look of things, the great nexus is having a lively night. I move we adjourn temporarily, and reconvene in the Royal apartments."

Such as they are.

***

Greenwich Village
New York City

Fiachra had never cared much for turning over control of a Fade to another Fae. However, after re-experiencing the tender mercies of the *darag*, letting the Fae identified for him as Cuinn an Dearmad drag him along to wherever it was he now found himself was a walk in the fucking park.

He was in a small apartment, not much more than a very large bed, a wardrobe, a kitchenette, and a couple of doors going elsewhere. The little space was crowded, occupied by Cuinn, Rian, and two other Fae Fiachra had never seen before.

And one he had, though he hadn't been seen in return. Conall Dary, the mage he'd known by reputation in the Realm and had spent several disembodied decades trying to find, back when he'd still hoped there was a way out of the idiotic predicament he had deliberately put himself in. It was startling to see the mage here in the human world, though he'd heard he'd gone missing, sometime in the year before he himself went through the Pattern. One mystery solved.

Normally, solving a mystery would give Fiachra a warm satisfied feeling. Tonight, not so much. He couldn't quite shake the certainty that his best shot at a genuine warm satisfied feeling was entirely pissed off at him and probably never wanted to lay eyes, hands, or any other body part on him ever again.

"All right, Brodulein." Cuinn's arms were crossed over his chest, his feet planted shoulders'-width apart. "Before we get to the part where you explain what the hell just happened and why your ass is suddenly naked and covered with acorns, I want very much to know how a Loremaster got out of the Pattern. And, more importantly, why."

"Are you out of your fucking mind?" Fiachra couldn't help laughing. "Congratulations, you've come up with something more ridiculous than what just happened to me. The Loremasters are myths, children's stories."

<No, we aren't,> the voice in his head whispered.

"He isn't Brodulein." The dark-haired Fae's aquamarine eyes were slightly unfocused. "I didn't know that particular Loremaster as well as you did, Cuinn, but I met him a few times. And I just caught a glimpse of this Fae's aura... and this isn't Brodulein."

Fiachra would have enjoyed Cuinn's suddenly poleaxed expression quite a bit more if he hadn't suspected his own was very much like it.

"I will be dipped in shit." Cuinn's murmur was barely audible.

Of course, to a Fae from the Demesne of Air, the jade-eyed Fae might as well have shouted. Or sent up a plane and skywritten. Which made Fiachra feel somewhat better. "Does that mean you believe me now?" He did his best to keep the fuck-you-very-much out of his voice, as there was still a good chance he was going to need all the help he could get in fairly short order, and it was hard enough to get help from a Fae who *wasn't* feeling insulted.

"Right now, if someone else tried to convince me I had two testicles, I'd have to count them myself." Cuinn grimaced. "If you aren't Brodulein, or Brodulein's twin brotha from anotha motha, who the hell are you?"

Fiachra took a deep breath. "My name is Fiachra Dubhdara. And my best guess is that I came through the Pattern about five minutes ago, and landed in a pool of living magick at the roots of a *darag*. Which unusually intelligent vegetable I would have considered to be another children's story, were it not for the fact that enough Fae believed in the truth of that particular story to brand my family and my line *adhmacomh* under the assumption that one of my ancestresses had spread her legs for a *darag*'s pet." The epithet *wood-bodied* had lost none of its contemptuous sting for going unheard for the last 17 years of his life.

"But you aren't—"

Fiachra ignored the speaker, another blond Fae, this one with a crystal hand, and plowed on. "It called me a thief, and it was pissed to the wide, but it wouldn't let its pet kill me—it threw me away instead, 17 years back in time, to Central Park in Manhattan. And just now I was lying on the acorn-covered ground under the fucking weed, for that minute or so before it flushed me down the temporal toilet. I think I had to be there—it might have broken the Universe for me to be here and there at the same time."

He looked from one Fae to another, and was secretly pleased to see that most of them looked as confused as he felt, except for Cuinn, who was nearly as pale as the sheets on the great bed. He could work with confused, and with whatever Cuinn was; it was outright hostility he was hoping to avoid.

"That would make sense. More or less." Conall Dary looked more puzzled than the other Fae. But it was a thoughtful puzzlement, an expression far too old for what, on a human, would be the face of a red-blond twink barely out of his teens. Of course, the most powerful Fae mages came into their birthright of magick—and stopped aging—younger than most Fae. "But you aren't *adhmacomh*. Not even a little." *And what else might you be lying about?* the piercing bright-green gaze added silently.

"This isn't my original body." Fiachra had to stop to clear his throat. Fae didn't have issues with theft, as a general rule, at least as an abstract proposition—if one didn't care enough about something to take sufficient precautions to keep it, one had no call to object if someone else took it. However, Fae also hated rules, general or otherwise, and Fiachra suspected stealing a body might be considered a transgression even by Fae inclined to overlook other thefts.

And there was always the possibility that the new voice inside his head was listening. It was important for him to be convincing.

"I was born every inch an *adhmacomh*, and grew up that way. Came into my birthright of magick that way. And once I had my magick, and had learned one end of a sword from the other, I got tired of having blood-debt called on me every time I had to kill

58

someone who insulted my mother or my sister for their dark hair and eyes and skin. So a little over a hundred years ago I decided to Fade permanently. But that was probably the most idiotic thing I could ever have done, and after I'd done everything I could think of to get my body back—including find you, for all the good it did me—I decided to chance the Pattern instead."

A shudder had rippled through Conall's body at Fiachra's mention of a permanently Faded existence, and now he nodded. "I don't blame you. But that doesn't explain how you ended up in someone else's body."

"I'm not sure how it happened myself." *Are you listening, mystery voice? It was a fucking accident.* "When I finally managed to reach the Pattern's tower, I overheard a conversation between a red-haired female—"

"Aine," Cuinn cut in.

"And a male. Older, insubstantial. Not Faded, just… not quite there."

The other Fae exchanged glances, and a few of them shrugged. "Dúlánc, maybe," the dark-haired Fae suggested.

Fiachra cleared his throat again, louder this time. "They were talking about a stretching of the Pattern, and fuck me if I understood them. Said souls were starting to separate from bodies, and that magick was leaking from the Realm into the human world."

"I say again, I will be dipped. In shit."

Fiachra's eyes narrowed as he studied Cuinn. "They mentioned you."

"I'll bet they did. However, I'm not the one in need of character references at the moment. And you still haven't explained how you came to be wearing a body not your own."

Fiachra took a slow deep breath. It wasn't a good idea to let his guard down in a room full of Fae. Even if he did need their help. Or at least an alliance against the voice in his head. "I don't understand that either—and believe me, I've given it some thought over the last 17 years. The two Fae who had been talking disappeared, and I went to look at the Pattern more closely. I remember thinking how beautiful it was, silver threads and blue threads of magick. And while I was looking, a wind came up out of nowhere and tried to force me down into the floor. Only it wasn't a floor any more." Fiachra shivered—he'd stayed carefully away from this specific memory for many years. "I grabbed on to one of the threads, or I tried to. And I don't remember much after that. Only pain."

He opened eyes he didn't remember closing, and was startled to see a most unFae sympathy on the faces around him.

For a second, anyway. "You must have grabbed the thread with Brodulein's body somehow." Cuinn's lips pursed in a silent whistle. "Which means his soul is probably still in the Pattern, and majorly pissed."

"It would appear to be my day to get on the shit lists of mythical creatures."

"Neither the *daragin* nor the *Gille Dubh* are mythical." Cuinn looked as if he would rather be cuckolding a dragon than continuing that line of thought. "Neither, for that matter, are Loremasters. And somehow you incarnated as one."

"Before you open up that particular can of worms, I think I should take my leave." This was the

Fae with the crystal hand. "I'm sure the rest of you are capable of working this out without me, and Purgatory doesn't exactly run itself."

A Fae, running Purgatory... "You're Guaire. Harding mentioned you."

"Tiernan Guaire." The Fae bowed slightly from the waist, and somehow managed to make the bow look sarcastic. "At no one's service but my own, my husband's, and my Prince's, more or less in that order. And now, if you'll excuse me—"

"Wait." The mention of the club was like a bucket of ice water or the magickal shock of a perfect kiss, jerking Fiachra out of old memories and bringing new ones front and center. Suddenly, nothing this group of Fae might want from him was quite as important as finding Peri. "Take me back with you."

"To Purgatory?" The question was Cuinn's. "No chance."

"A'buil gnas le leat a's a'madra dúsigh tu suas leis." It had been a very long time since Fiachra had had reason to tell anyone who could understand him *have forcible sexual congress with you and the dog you woke up with,* and it felt good to do it now. "I've business there."

"You may think you do." Cuinn didn't appear fazed in the slightest. "But you lost half your soul coming through the Pattern, and until you find the human with the other half, join with him, and get it back, you can't be allowed back into Purgatory. Not unless you have a death wish. And feel like taking the Realm out with you when you go."

61

Chapter Eight

Washington, D.C.
Near Union Station

Janek remembered nightmares, from when he was a kid. He'd heard other kids describe their nightmares, usually from whatever horror movie they'd just seen. Chainsaws and starving pigs and aliens that were all teeth. Shit like that never bothered him. His own dreams had been different. He'd always had the same nightmare. He was running, in slow motion. Running for his life. And something was right behind him. He didn't dare turn to see what it was, but he could feel it. And he knew that if he slowed down, even to catch his breath, he was dead. He was worse than dead. And he always woke up sweating and screaming, and usually getting the shit beaten out of him for pissing the bed.

Just like now. Except there wasn't anyone to beat him, and he didn't really need to piss all that much anymore.

And he never dreamed. Being awake and alive was enough of a bitch.

A thin ray of light pierced the boards Janek had nailed up over his basement den's one window, and then tried to pierce his eyeball. He grunted and swiped at the light with one sausage-fingered hand until it went away. *Fucking cars.*

The *Marfach* didn't say anything. It hadn't said anything to him since dickhead Dary had Faded him back here. He didn't dare hope the fucker was dead, though. Not when he could feel its rage, like he'd felt the shadow behind him in all those nightmares, boiling inside what was supposed to be his own head. But none of that rage got through to him, thanks to whatever Lochlann Doran had done to him with his freak-ass sword made of blood. Janek wasn't sure whether he was happy or pissed about that. Sharing the monster's thoughts was a very special hell, but at least when he'd shared them he'd had some way to know what it was thinking and planning.

Now?

Now he slept, most of the time. Or whatever it was he did when he was checked out. Most of the magick that kept him passing for half-alive was gone now, sucked out of him by the dickwad Bryce Newhouse, who would spend a very long time sucking something else if Janek could stay alive after taking Guaire's head. And Doran's sword had made it impossible for the *Marfach* to send him any more of the shit. So being alive took way too much of his energy.

But it had been weeks. Maybe months. And some days he felt stronger. A little. If he could get better—if he could just fucking think straight—he wouldn't need the monster in his head. For anything. Then Guaire would be dead... and it didn't matter much what happened to Janek's body after that.

As usual, it took a long time for him to get up. In his condition, rising from a mattress on the floor was a pain in the ass. And the knees. But he forced himself to get up, because once he'd thought about killing Guaire, he had to go reassure himself that his Fae-killing knife was still where he'd stashed it.

Finally upright, he shambled across the room. He threw a few boards into the metal barrel where he kept a fire going all the time—too fucking much trouble to light it again when it went out, and it wasn't like he noticed heat any more—and crossed to the pile of crates he'd assembled back when it had been easy to stack things on top of each other. Sweeping aside a pile of rags, he grunted in satisfaction at the sight of his small collection. The sound was pretty much the same sound he made when he was pissed off, or hungry, or about to twist someone's head off. Which was as close as he got to happy.

Even in the fire lit gloom of the boarded-up basement, the Fae knife he'd stolen from Kevin Almstead gleamed a keen silver-blue. Pretty. It would look a lot prettier drenched in red Fae blood. Something for him to look forward to.

There were a few other things in the crate, too. He'd lost his everyday knife when he'd shoved it up under Newhouse's ribs and it had gotten stuck in the bone, but it hadn't taken him long to find a new one—even with only half his brain half working, he had a jones for knives. He ran a finger along the blade, smiling.

I wonder if motherfucking Newhouse is dead. His smile faded. There wasn't much he was sure of any more. He'd been sure he'd killed the little pole-dancer whore, Garrett. He'd mostly cut the little shit's curly blond head off after turning him into a bleeding, blistered, broken piece of raw meat, but he'd seen him at Doran's side in Washington Square Park. Right before the hammer fell. Maybe humans who were asshole buddies with Fae didn't stay dead.

There was more in the crate. Things he hadn't paid attention to for a long time. I.D.s he'd taken from some of his victims, back when it was still kind of possible for him to pass as human and he still sometimes gave a shit about what people thought. A pair of huge canvas work gloves that he still used every now and then, when he didn't want to leave bits of skin and body fluids on things he handled. A ring of keys, an old mother-of-pearl compact, a small cardboard box that was heavier than it looked and rattled a little when he poked it with a finger.

There was magick in those things. He remembered being able to see it, back when the *Marfach* had been able to jack his eye and force him to see the way it saw. Ley energy and living magick, mixed together in a way that was supposed to be impossible, thanks to Dary's fucking around with the ley nexus in the basement under Newhouse's apartment in Greenwich Village.

He didn't give a green runny shit about the way magick worked. All he cared about was holding on to enough of the stuff to keep him alive until he killed the Fae who had turned him into a zombie.

Can I use the magic in these?

It took him a few tries to pick up the compact, since his fingers were almost completely numb. It was old, heavy, pretty in a way his grandmother might

65

have liked. Probably had makeup in it. He'd tried using makeup, back when he'd first started to rot. Maybe it worked on old ladies, but it didn't do shit for craters in your face once the muscle started showing through.

The compact popped open with a little click. The bottom was half full of what looked like face powder, and nothing to put it on with. The top half...

Fuck. Janek had forgotten how much he hated mirrors. And he hadn't looked in one since he'd taken over Newhouse's apartment last winter. Newhouse apparently couldn't get enough of his own reflection, but Janek had found and covered every last fucking mirror, because even then the sight of himself had made him want to hurl.

The late summer version of Janek O'Halloran was much, much worse. He'd given up shaving what was left of his head a while ago, because the razor kept taking off skin that didn't grow back properly, so patches of colorless hair alternated with strips of oozing and half-healed scalp. The bottom of the hole where he'd had a gauge in his ear had ripped out a long time ago; his cheek was more crater than skin, and there were a couple of holes that went all the way through his cheek and showed green and broken teeth. White cartilage gleamed on the bridge of his nose and showed a couple of the places where it had been broken. His eye was so shot through with brown blood that it was almost impossible to make out where it had once been blue. And the line where Doran had hacked into his head with his blood-sword was a gouge that went almost down to his eyebrow and was still slowly leaking thick brown blood and grayish brain matter.

That was the good side of his head. Although the crystal side didn't look so bad right now. It was clear, which meant the monster living in it was probably asleep. It looked just like the right side of Janek's head had looked before Guaire put a rod of living crystal through his eye socket and sent him straight to hell. Just like, except for the quarter-sized hole that went through the eye socket and all the way to the back of his head.

The crystal flared a sullen, angry red.

Son of a bitch. It's awake. Janek slammed the compact closed.

Tried to. He couldn't move. Couldn't look away.

His lips moved. He couldn't make them stop.

"How careless of you, Meat." Female laughter came from his throat. *"This is an awkward arrangement, but it will do."*

"Fuck off and die," Janek whispered as soon as he got control of his mouth back.

"Not going to happen." This voice was male, and though the monster wasn't forcing the mental image on him—maybe it couldn't—Janek knew where it was coming from. The filthy, naked man with the matted, insect-filled dreadlocks, long curving yellow fingernails, and erect dick the size of a fucking baseball bat was branded on what remained of his brain. *"You're forgetting, I've changed you. All of you. Everything of you that I've touched, twisted, warped... it's all me. I control it."*

Like fuck you do.

The monster ignored his thoughts. His hatred. *"Look on the bright side. You've been promoted. From meat wagon to meat puppet."*

Chapter Nine

Greenwich Village
New York City

Fiachra suspected he was less impressed than Cuinn wanted him to be. "I've more sense than to go fucking around with the smoke generator behind the bar, if that's what you're afraid of." The question of human insulation from the unknown potential consequences of any such fucking around, and the possible implications of that question for any hypothetical second chance he might have with Peri, he chose to set aside for the present, as being none of the damned business of any of the other Fae in the room.

Cuinn snorted. "That 'smoke generator' is the only known nexus of four mingled elemental magick and ley energy lines in the human world. And I'm not entirely sure it couldn't do some fucking around of its own, under the right circumstances."

Conall cleared his throat. "It's not just the great nexus, it's the Pattern, too. Given that the former feeds directly into the latter now. And assuming our new friend here is telling the truth, he's wearing the stolen body of a Loremaster whose soul is still stuck in the

Pattern, and who might conceivably want said body back."

Oh, shit.

Cuinn didn't turn, but his narrow-eyed gaze cut sideways. "Twinklebritches, have I mentioned recently your amazing gift for making an uncomfortable situation seem truly dire?"

"Bite me hard, Loremaster."

They really aren't going to let me back into the club. "No, really, that's not why I—"

"It isn't?" This was the dark-haired Fae, the aura reader. "Your real reason wouldn't have anything to do with being a fucking Vice detective, now, would it?"

Judging by the glare Tiernan Guaire turned on Fiachra, his occupation might prove to be the deadliest sin of all.

"How does a Fae end up working for D.C. Vice?" Tiernan's voice was like silk. And ice. Ice-cold silk wrapped around Fiachra's sac, and slowly tightening. Gangrene seemed a reasonable possibility.

"It's a long story."

"For that, I have time."

Fiachra shifted his weight uncomfortably, feeling acorns digging into his ass. He was also acutely aware of being stared at. "Look, before we start with the third degree, I don't suppose anyone has a spare pair of jeans? Mine seem to have gone missing."

The blond with the Royal-looking ink, the lost Prince, possibly the only male in the room who had no immediate interest in handing Fiachra his head, laughed softly. "I'd offer you a pair of mine, but I doubt me you could even come close to doing them up." Now *there* was an Irish accent. "Conall, is there aught you can do?"

The mage shrugged and whispered, gesturing, and Fiachra found himself swathed in a silk bathrobe. "Zipper teeth are tricky to get right," the redhead explained with a smirk.

"Your solicitude is appreciated—"

A screaming guitar lick filled the air, its apparent source the young Prince Royal's perfect ass.

it's a long hard night
getting longer, getting harder
can't make it through without some
hair of the dog
hair of the dog—

How Rian managed to make his phone appear in his hand without an awkward period of digging in those tight leathers, Fiachra had no idea. But there it was. "Lasair, what about ye, then?"

Another Fae. Wonderful.

Any Fae's hearing would have been acute enough to let him hear the other end of the Prince's conversation. The senses of a Fae of the Demesne of Air also told Fiachra someone was groaning in the background, and doing his best not to be heard.

"Highness, you asked us to let you know if Bryce sensed anything from the *Marfach*." The voice on the other end was strained, tight. "The dripping dick-tip is apparently awake. And if you want any more details, you're going to have to come to us. Bryce isn't going anywhere for a while."

***

70

#whining# #nosing at newmaster#

i scent newmaster's pain. sickness. i remember this scent. monster, and twisted magick. #whining# newmaster strokes me. #wagging# #falling down# #getting up# newmaster laughs softly.

"Setanta."

#wagging harder#

"Tréan-cú." *firstmaster calls me 'strong hound.' #panting# #barking#*

...someday i will have a real bark...

not-here, then here, many more scents. fae, all of them. i turn around, around, sniffing. i know these males. strongmagick, healingwater, smokescent, wicked smoke's-mate, stonehand.

two new scents. one filled with magick, as much as wicked, almost as much as strongmagick. i am bred to hunt magick. #fangs bared# and one treesoul.

"Here, Setanta. See."

we have practiced this, my masters and i. only two of us can see at once. firstmaster gives me his sight, and turns toward the new scents.

#sitting down hard on my tail# there is only one. magick and tree, in one tall blond fae.

***

Lochlann caught himself holding his breath as the upstairs contingent Faded into the little bedroom of the brownstone's garden apartment, at least until it was apparent that no one had accidentally materialized inside, or partly inside, anyone else. The room was seriously overcrowded, really, considering that of its current nine occupants, all but two—Bryce Newhouse and Setanta, his and Lasair's blind Fade-hound pup, were Fae. There was probably some pithy observation to be made about critical mass, or snark, or a sheer overdose of male beauty.

Whatever that observation was, though, Lochlann wasn't interested in making it. His attention was riveted on the sweating human curled up in a ball of misery on the bed, the bewildered Fade-hound staring at Fiachra, licking his whiskers, and pawing at his nose, and the Fae perched on the edge of the bed beside Bryce. One of Lasair's hands rested lightly on Bryce's hip; the other was clenched in a white-knuckled fist and beat a soft, probably unconscious rhythm on the Fae's thigh.

And Bryce... The sight of the human made Lochlann feel slightly queasy. Not because Bryce had been possibly the most abrasive dickhead in two worlds until he'd Shared with Lasair and received the soul he was supposed to have been born with, but because of what Bryce was carrying around in his gut.

Over a year ago, Janek and the *Marfach* had shoved a shard of the living Stone that housed the *Marfach* into Bryce's abdomen, by way of a stab wound, to make the investment banker amenable to the *Marfach*'s occasional control. And that bit of the monster had rearranged a bit of Bryce to its liking, in a way none of the Fae had been able to figure out how to reverse. Like the *Marfach* itself, it had needed magickal energy to survive, or ley energy when it couldn't get the pure stuff. A fist-sized lump of Bryce's gut, under the skin and out of sight to anyone but a Fae, was deformed—mutated—twisted into a collector for the elusive energy. Kevin had cut the

72

lethal fragment out of Bryce last winter, and the deformity under the skin had been more or less quiet since Conall had force-Faded the monster and its meat wagon.

Now the air crazed and shifted over Bryce's side, in a way Lochlann couldn't look at directly. Every time he tried, he snapped right back to his own personal hell, trying to buy his dying SoulShare's life by feeding magickal energy to the Janek/*Marfach* monstrosity. Trying and failing. The light, the air had twisted around Janek's half-face in just that way as Garrett died. And nothing, not even Garrett's resurrection, was ever going to make Lochlann forget that sight.

No one else could look at Bryce, either. Not even the new guy; the Vice cop was staring at his own feet, looking even paler than usual. And venturing an occasional nervous glance at the Fade-hound. Even a runt like Setanta was enough to strike fear into the heart of any Fae.

"Mother of God." Rian, for his part, looked green rather than pale.

"Thanks, your Royalness." Bryce's voice was barely above a whisper, but for all that it was steadier than Lochlann felt. "Not that I don't appreciate the sentiment, but I'd like to let Lasair see what he can do to make the boogeyman let go of my gut. Mind if I tell you all what happened so he can get on with it?"

"Please." The young Prince had his voice and his face back under control, but it didn't take a mind reader to figure out that his memories of his own encounter with the *Marfach* were fresher than he liked.

Bryce winced, then sighed and relaxed as Lasair

stroked his back. "Really, this isn't so bad, it's nothing compared to what it was like when the fucking zombie was nearby."

Lasair shook his head, sending pale gold curls tumbling around his face. "Quit being brave, *sumiúl.* Tell them what they need to know so they can go away."

Lochlann had never understood Lasair Faol's pillow name for his human SoulShare. *Sumiúl* was a Fae word, hard to translate; it meant someone or something that drew the attention, compelled it. Someone impossible to look away from. And pretty much the whole world had been perfectly happy to look away from Bryce, before the human had met Lasair, because Bryce's picture should have been in the Urban Dictionary opposite "douchecanoe." But Bryce had a soul now, and Lasair was his SoulShare, and it really didn't matter to either of them what Lochlann, or anyone else, thought.

And Bryce *had* saved all their lives, a couple of months ago. Even to a Fae, that counted for something.

Bryce coughed. "This was a hell of a lot of buildup for not much. I'd hoped I was done with this shit, once the motherhumping *Marfach* was out of the picture and Lasair cleaned out the tainted magick I sucked out of—hey, blondie, who let you in here?"

Apparently, Bryce was just noticing the newcomer, whose arm was still clasped in Tiernan's hand of living Stone. Setanta had picked him out a while ago, and was responding to Bryce's ire by baring his tiny fangs in a snarl that would undoubtedly go viral on adorablepuppyvideos.com if it ever got the chance. Lochlann carefully suppressed his snicker, not wanting to wound the pup's feelings. Fade-hounds remembered things like that for a long time. "His name is Fiachra. He's a Fae. And a cop. What else he is, we were in the middle of trying to get him to explain when Lasair called. But one emergency at a time."

"I was perfectly willing to go away and let you deal with this emergency." Fiachra apparently couldn't make up his mind who to look disapprovingly at, so his gaze went to each in turn. "I'm about as useful here as eyeliner on a basilisk."

"Please don't make me laugh, it feels like I'm getting a prostate exam from Nosferatu." Bryce almost smiled. "I didn't really need the entire cavalry anyway. But I figured you'd want to know the fucking *Marfach* is awake. Though I don't think it's close by." He closed his eyes and took a deep breath, letting it out slowly as Lasair ran a hand down his side. "I'd be able to tell. I think."

Lasair reached out to pet Setanta reassuringly, then ran the backs of his fingers along Bryce's jaw. "I wanted to go downstairs and have a look at the lesser nexus. Just to be sure there's no fuckery going on." His gaze never left Bryce as he spoke. "But I'm not leaving him until I draw that tainted magick."

"Good call." Cuinn nodded tightly. "We can take care of that little detail for you. Especially since we have our resident expert in fuckery handy." Color started to drain from his form.

"*Sus do thón,*" Conall muttered, just before he and the others followed.

***

Fiachra was staring at the perfect circle of magick on the floor almost before he and the other Fae had finished taking form wherever the hell it was they'd dragged him off to this time. "I thought living magick was supposed to be rare, this side of the Pattern."

"It is." Conall was apparently over his momentary pique, and sounded almost absent-minded as he studied, not only the circle, but the air around it. Fiachra thought he could make out a faint glistening in the air, like insubstantial blades. "Nothing's touched the ward that shouldn't, by the way."

"What do you mean, you *thought* magick was supposed to be rare?" Cuinn didn't seem any more inclined than he had ever been to take Fiachra's word for anything. "Did something happen to change your mind?"

Not for the first time, Fiachra wondered what Cuinn's history was with the male whose body he was wearing. And he wished Brodulein had been even a little more conversational when they'd been back in Purgatory. Brodulein had known Cuinn and recognized Rian, and Fiachra was under the impression that he'd recognized the rest of the Fae as well. But the farther they were from Purgatory, the less communicative Brodulein was. Assuming the voice in his head was actually Brodulein's.

Fiachra shrugged. "That was what the legends said. The myths." He leaned hard on the last word, mostly for the pleasure of watching Cuinn risk spraining his eyeballs. "A Fae in the human world has only the magick he brings with him."

"Until he finds his SoulShare and can tap into a

ley nexus to recharge without shorting out every line from here to D.C. Right, Twinklebritches?"

"Bite me, leather boy." Conall's tone was bored, but there was a hint of laughter in the corners of his startling green eyes. "And could you try to stay focused for a change? I'm interested in the answer to your question, even if you aren't."

Cuinn grumbled, but said nothing, even when the young Prince dug an elbow into his ribs.

Going through the Pattern does nothing to change Fae nature. Noted and logged. "When I first came through from the Realm, I was under an oak tree." As if to punctuate his statement, an acorn that had been stuck to him somewhere under his new silk bathrobe chose that moment to fall off and clatter to the cement floor. "And there was magick under the tree. Not whatever it was I was seeing back in Purgatory, the smoke machine effect. Living magick, just like this." He scuffed the floor with a bare foot.

Conall went white. "Do you know where you came through originally?"

"No idea."

Cuinn was almost as pale as Conall. "It would have to have been somewhere in Scotland. That's where the *Gille Dubh* and the *daragin* lived. Live."

"'Somewhere in Scotland' isn't much help. But I doubt the *Marfach* will have any better luck finding it than we would if we tried." Conall raked his hand through his red-blond thatch of hair until it stood up like a harridan-bird's nest. "What about Central Park? Was there magick there when you arrived?"

The mage's gaze made Fiachra feel like a bug in a sixth-grader's science project. "No."

"Of course not," Conall muttered, turning that unnerving gaze on the floor. "Seventeen years ago. That would have been long before we broke the Pattern." His head jerked up. "What about now?"

"I don't have a clue."

"Shit. Shit. Shit. Can you find the place where you came through?"

All I want to do is get back to D.C. A cold certainty had been growing in him, ever since he'd watched Peri flee Purgatory, that there was something very wrong. And his success as a Homicide cop was based almost as much on the accuracy of his intuition as on his truthsight.

Still... if this was really the *Marfach*...

"I can take you right to it, if you'll follow me in a Fade."

"Go. We're right behind you."

Closing his eyes, Fiachra reached out, seeking the magick his presence had left behind during multiple visits to the tree over the years, needing both the magick and his memory of the place. Instead of searching near-darkness for an elusive wisp of pseudo-light, though, he found himself staring, blinking, into the equivalent of a spotlight. *Shit indeed.*

"Got it." His voice sounded far away even to himself as he Faded.

The only illumination when he arrived, as it turned out, was the perfect circle of not-quite-light around the base of the oak tree. And as bright as that circle was to his magickal sense, it didn't do much for his retinas, leaving the place the same dark foreboding corner of Central Park it had been 17 years ago. A place that gave up its secrets reluctantly. Almost as reluctantly as a Fae.

One by one, the other Fae took form around him. Conall had barely solidified when Fiachra's skin prickled with the magickal energy of a ward going up. "That'll do till Josh can get here," the mage muttered.

"Let me guess, you Faded without your cell phone again." Cuinn's voice had lost at least a little of its wiseass edge.

Conall's had apparently acquired it. "Show me where you're hiding one in all that leather and I promise not to gag you for a week."

Fiachra could practically hear the dark Fae's eyes rolling as he reached past Cuinn to hand Conall a phone. "Life would be a lot easier if the Royal couple could teach the rest of us how to share thoughts."

Cuinn snorted. "You don't want to spend time in my head any more than I want you in it. Trust me."

Conall gestured impatiently, and a lattice of light and silence appeared around him as he waited for his call to connect.

Slowly the other Fae fanned out. The oak tree at the heart of the magick circle grew just off a footpath, one that didn't appear on any map of Central Park Fiachra had ever seen. The ground rose on the far side of the tree, and at some point the side of the little hill had fallen away, leaving exposed rocks and tree roots.

"This would be a perfect place to hide a body," the Fae with the crystal hand murmured.

"It might have been, if the fucking *darag* hadn't dropped me on top of the recently departed."

Well, that certainly got everyone's attention.

"Congratulations." Cuinn was, not unsurprisingly, the first to recover the power of speech. "I've been keeping an eye on Pattern transits for the better part of

24 centuries, and this is the first time I've heard of an arrival landing on a corpse."

"Don't forget, I had help."

The net of light dropped, and Conall handed back the borrowed phone. "Josh is on his way to the train station, he should be here in—"

The air inside the dome of the ward vibrated with a soft, intense chime.

Cuinn blinked out.

Conall shook his head. "Helpful as ever. Highness, would you mind asking your consort what the hell he's playing at?"

"If I could feel him, I would." Fire flared in the Prince's eyes—Royal Fire, bright enough to see by and hot enough to burn. "I can't sense him, that was never a Fade."

Fiachra shivered as all the short hairs on the back of his neck stood at attention at once. He'd never heard that sound, that brittle chime, but it resonated in his bones. *Fucking instincts*. Be nice if they'd make themselves useful for a change—

"Wait." Rian's Fire went pale, ghostly, and his gaze was fixed on something only he could see. "He says... he says don't come for him. That we're deep in the shit now. And that he has to try to set right what he helped to make wrong."

Chapter Ten

Just outside Drumnadrochit, Scotland

I am thoroughly, epically, and, dare I say it, deservedly fucked. Cuinn stared up into the branches of the ancient oak tree, carefully putting aside thoughts of his bonded mate. Though there were a few others who would be sharing in the reaming out he was anticipating, were the universe a just place.

Of course, a race by which *a'gár'doltas*, vendetta, was considered one of the High Arts tended not to expect much in the way of justice from the universe. Or anyone else.

ASK FOR UNDERSTANDING, SLAIDAR. Cuinn had never expected to hear the leaf-whispering language of the *daragin* and *Gille Dubh* again, not after the Sundering. **YOU WILL RECEIVE AS MUCH AS YOU ONCE GAVE US.**

Fuck me oblivious. "I didn't exactly roll out of bed this morning expecting to defend the details of our 2000-year-old plan to save the Realm, you realize."

The rustling of leaves over his head was about as far from soothing as could be imagined. **YOU DESTROYED TWO RACES, AND NOW YOU**

CANNOT BE BOTHERED TO REMEMBER WHY?

Cuinn grimaced. He'd grown something of a conscience since Sharing with Rian. And ever since the *ceangail* ritual, he'd felt occasional irritating impulses to act in a way he would have called 'mature' in any other Fae. A Fae he was trying to piss off, anyway. "I remember why. I'm just trying to remember why we couldn't compromise."

The laughter from overhead also sounded like wind through the branches, but the sound was touched with moonlight rather than the dawn light actually making its way through the surrounding trees. It also had a keen edge to it. ***Compromise? Was there ever a magick-thief who knew the meaning of the word?*** This, he had already been given to understand, was Coinneach, the *darag*'s *Gille Dubh*, trapped within the ancient oak by the rising sun but wielding words like a grace-blade. The *darag* didn't have a name of its own. Which made sense, you needed two of something before you needed names. Hopefully he wasn't going to have to deal with two *daragin*. One was more than bad enough.

"If there was, he didn't learn the definition from you and yours." So much for maturity. "I seem to recall that you thought you were stronger than the *Marfach*."

NOT STRONGER. SET APART.

Cuinn truly didn't care for the feeling of being loomed over. Still, it could be worse, he supposed. He could have shown up here at night, and be dealing with Coinneach in his Dark Man aspect. Even Loremasters had generally preferred to steer clear of the dark ones, and the availability of the circle of living magick under his feet wasn't a hell of a lot of comfort. "It didn't matter how set apart you thought you were. Before the last battle, the *Marfach* was able to manifest in just about any living magick it fucking well wanted to. It would have snacked on yours just as happily as on any Fae's. Or any gryphon's, basilisk's, Fade-hound's or dragon-fly's. It all had to come into the Realm, and be sealed away on the other side of the Pattern."

It could not have touched our Mothers. Sun and Moon were ever beyond its reach. There was ice in Coinneach's voice. *Given time, our Mothers could have reached out to us, even then. Fed us with their magick, instead of the living sort. But you did not believe in their magick, and you stole our lives without warning.*

"I—"

Fortunately, Cuinn's voice had more sense than he did, and shut down hard.

Fae did not believe in gods. They never had. And in crafting the Pattern and planning the Sundering of the Fae and human worlds, the Loremasters had assumed that when the tree folk spoke of their Mothers, Cradle-mother and Womb-mother, each fostering the other's children, they referred to nonexistent gods. There had been other things to do in those terrible days, other things to think of besides the superstitions of sentient trees. Even trees, and Dark Men, with places among the *Tirr Brai*, the Folk of Life. Magickal beings.

One Loremaster had understood what the *daragin* and the *Gille Dubh* meant, though, in the end. And had said nothing, because he knew that he would never persuade his elders, who were convinced that the *daragin* and the *Gille Dubh* were just overly attached to the things of the human world, and were risking everything in two worlds for the sake of sentiment. And that youngest Loremaster had known that once the last battle was won, he'd need a power source to fuel transitions through the Pattern, one that wouldn't siphon living magick out of the Realm or depend on the Fae elementals who couldn't be allowed to know what was really going on. A third form of magick. A gods'-send, to a race without gods.

So Cuinn had kept his mouth shut. And let two races die.

And he would do it again, if he had to. His compromise had left the Realm just enough living magick to survive until its exiled children had figured out how to send the ley energy home again.

Now all he had to do was figure out some way to get the *darag* and the *Gille Dubh* off that painful subject, in a way that wouldn't get him killed. "We didn't steal your lives. Or if we did, you're the two most talkative dead beings I've ever met." Not quite true—Coinneach was more talkative than Janek O'Halloran, but the zombie was a shade chattier than the *darag*—but close enough for jazz.

The branches of the *darag* tossed, as if in a gust of wind. Cuinn looked up just in time for an empty bird's nest to fall on his face. Mostly empty. *I always thought birds shat over the side.*

MAGICK RETURNS. DESPITE YOU.

If you only knew. "Yes, we've found two other circles like this one."

Two? The branches danced with the *Gille Dubh*'s laughter, pelting Cuinn with acorns. ***There are havens such as this throughout the human world. Here in Alba, the Grove is slowly being reborn, one darag,***

one Gille Dubh at a time. And all over the human world, one pool of magick after another is filled from within. From beneath.

Cuinn tried to keep his face impassive. It wasn't easy. One road opening after another, back to the very gates of the Realm. And only a stretched-thin Pattern guarding those gates to keep the *Marfach* out. *Can you say 'clusterfuck,' boys and girls? Sure you can...* "How many more of you are there?"

WE ARE ALL ONE. Cuinn swore he could hear the tree smirk.

Actually, he just swore. Silently. Then tried again. "Can you tell where the other breakouts are happening?"

Of course. And do you think that is information we would share, slaidar? Fuck, the *Gille Dubh*'s voice was so cold there was practically smoke coming off it. *You will not deceive us again. The havens of magick are ours now. Ours to guard, ours to hide from prying eyes.*

A muscle twitched hard in Cuinn's jaw. *Did I call this a clusterfuck before? My bad...* "Let us sit down and reason together."

SPEAK. BUT DO NOT PRESUME WE ARE INTERESTED IN LISTENING.

***

Somewhere in Central Park
New York City

"So talk to me, Loremaster. Or whatever the feck ye are."

"What?" Fiachra's wandering thoughts snapped back hard enough to sting. Conall and the two other

Fae, whose names he still didn't know, were deep in a consultation that pointedly didn't include him. "Why aren't you part of the focus group over there?"

Heatless flames licked over the young male's skin. "For one, they're trying to work out a way to call the ley energy, once Conall's ready to channel and you're gone. And I'm useless for that."

"If it's myself being gone they need, I'd be happy to—"

The look in the burning topaz eyes the Prince turned on him froze the words in his throat. "No one goes anywhere until we work out how to get my bond-mate back. I may have forgotten to mention, the other reason I'm no' part of their planning is that I'm a fecking fire elemental whose consort's just been kidnapped, and we're all fecking fortunate I haven't burnt down Central Park around us already." Rian raked fingers through his hair, and in a gesture that looked well practiced, grabbed the forelock hanging over his eyes and gave it a wrenching tug, hissing in pain through clenched teeth before letting go.

Fiachra had no clue what to say; everything that came into his head seemed to increase the risk of conflagration unacceptably.

Fortunately, the Prince seemed happy to keep right on talking. "Cuinn told me to stay clear, give him space to work. Space." Rian all but spat the word. "He thinks I can't tell, but I can. Something's shaming him, wherever he is. Something bitter he can't bear for me to see."

For some reason, all Fiachra could see was the hurt in almond eyes, not once but twice. Pain masking a deeper pain.

86

"So I need you to talk to me, Fiachra or Brodulein or whatever the feck yer name is." The voice was that of a street kid, defiant, uncaring. And Rian's body, his leather and ink and piercings, screamed *club kid* and *pain slut*. And *Fae*. But his eyes, his stance, the ferocity of his devotion, left no doubt as to his royalty. "Give me something to think about besides my fear for my bond-mate."

To his own shock, Fiachra understood. Peri wasn't a mate. Wasn't even close. Shit, mating wasn't even a Fae concept, except for the *ceangal* ritual Royals did. Peri couldn't be anything to him. The beautiful masseur's pain was nothing to him.

Except that Peri *was* something.

He wanted to ask the young Royal about this incredibly unFae phenomenon. But if Rian wanted to be distracted from whatever Cuinn was doing wherever Cuinn was, quizzing him about Fae bonding was probably not an optimal way of going about the distracting.

"Were ye truly dropped into Central Park on top of a corpse, then?"

"I was." The thought of finally being able to tell his story to someone who wouldn't assume he was a raving lunatic was oddly refreshing, even under the present peculiar circumstances. "When the fucking shrub threw me away, it was about this time of the night, and I landed right back there." Fiachra gestured in the general direction of the three conversing Fae, between the oak tree and the fall of earth and stone behind it. "And someone had dumped a body there, maybe an hour or two before. A female, badly beaten. NYPD had been tipped off, they were searching, and they found both of us. Lucky for me, however the *darag* got me there, the process left me fucked up enough that the police assumed I was just another victim. And they were chatty enough to let me pick up enough vocabulary to talk with them right out of the gate."

The severe lines of Rian's face and body were softened, at least a little, by curiosity. "You're of the Demesne of Air, then, I take it? So you could understand them?"

Fiachra nodded. "And I could understand the only eyewitness to the murder, as well. The perp thought he'd gotten the girl alone, but he didn't know there was a barred owl in the trees up there on the bank. Which saw the whole thing and was perfectly happy to rat the fucker out."

"Does that have aught to do with how you became a *garda*?"

"It does." His truthsight had played a part in that story, too, along with his talent for manipulating minds, but a Fae had to have some secrets. Especially from other Fae. "And it's also how I learned to say 'He's the one with the owl shit in his hair' in Owlish, if you're ever interested in learning something new."

The Prince's laugh was short and harsh. "I might be, at that—"

A high soft chime filled the air, hung there. And Cuinn stood under the oak tree, red-faced and furious.

The chime left total silence in its wake, long enough for everyone to stare. In the end, it was Rian who broke the silence, the calm tone of his voice like the closed door of a raging furnace. "So tell me, consort mine, who do I have to kill for this?"

Cuinn shook his head.

"Who took you?"

"Where were you?"

Cuinn held up an unsteady hand, cutting off questioning by the other Fae. Slowly he placed a hand over his mouth as if he wasn't sure what might happen when his palm finally made contact with his lips.

Rian went pale. "He says 'The *darag* didn't care to hear what I had to say. So it's made certain that I never speak again."

Chapter Eleven

You can let go of me now, I think.

"Feck that noise."

It wasn't exactly noise.

"Oh, shite."

There were tears on Cuinn's neck. Tears of flame rolling harmlessly over his flesh, to fall and char tiny holes in the sheets of their great bed. Awkwardly he stroked Rian's back, ran fingers through his hair. Months it had been, and he still wasn't used to being gentle with his Royal bond-mate. Rian didn't always need to be hurt, not any more, not since they'd Shared and gone through *ceangail* together. But the younger Fae still craved a rough touch. Which was something Cuinn couldn't give him right now.

Please, dhó-súil. One hand cupped the back of Rian's head, blond hair tickling his palm, holding him close. The other arm went tightly around the Prince's waist. *Please.*

"What are you asking of me?" Rian's voice was muffled in Cuinn's neck and shoulder, and the scent of smoke told Cuinn the tears hadn't stopped yet.

Cuinn looked up, into the mirror over the bed unprotected for the time being by magick. He couldn't see much of himself, only his mate, the swarm of stars that were the Pattern's claiming-mark on a Royal swirling across his back. *Don't cry. Please. Not for me. I earned this.*

"You never did." Cuinn could feel Rian's jaw muscles clench.

Maybe not by myself. But the Loremasters did. And I'm the last one left to pay the price, if you don't count our accidental visitor.

"How can you be so fecking calm about this?"

Someone has to be. And I've had a little more practice at it than you have.

"Sod being calm. A *darag*'s wood like any other tree, it'll burn like any other tree when a Fire elemental tells it to."

I love you. But no.

"If you love me, then don't deny me this." Rian nipped sharply at Cuinn's throat. "Take me to it. I need to watch it burn."

Fuck. Cuinn groaned softly as Rian ground down into him. Rian almost never topped, Cuinn almost never bottomed, but playing at it this way generally drove them both to the brink of madness. Which was a place Cuinn didn't dare go just now. *If a Fae harms a darag, it'll kill any chance that any of them will ever consider giving me my voice back.*

An angry red light flared in Rian's blue topaz eyes. "It had no right to take it from you in the first place."

I'm fucking lucky it was willing to stop with my voice. Cuinn tangled his legs with Rian's and tried to slow the rocking of their bodies. An aroused Fire elemental stopped giving a shit about much of

91

anything except more arousal. And as sexy as Rian could be when the rational side of his brain went switch-off, now was a very bad time for such a thing, given that under the circumstances he might decide he preferred causing pain to receiving it. *The Loremasters basically killed every single darag and Gille Dubh, right before the Sundering.*

Rian's hips stopped moving. Which was a good thing. And it wasn't. Damn. "What? How?"

They refused to come along when we brought everything magickal into the Realm right before the last battle and the Sundering. Cuinn purely hated to tell this story—talking about it made the memories way too vivid for his tastes, and he'd only told his bond-mate parts of the tale. *We knew we were going to banish the Marfach into the human world and set the Pattern to bar its way back—we couldn't afford to leave any magick on the human side, anything for it to inhabit and feed on and twist and turn to pure fucking evil. Most of the Tirr Brai we didn't bother asking for their opinion, we just took them. But we asked a few, including the daragin and the Gille Dubh. And they were the only ones who said no.*

"Why? Did they not understand what was at stake?"

They understood. But they called us presumptuous. Said no one had asked them if they wanted to be defended, and that they didn't need our help. And that they were too deeply rooted in the earth of the human world to move. We were still arguing with them when the Marfach surprised us. Attacked before we thought it was ready. So there wasn't any time left to argue.

"You took the magick."

Yes. Without it, the daragin were just trees. And their Gille Dubh... didn't exist at all.

"Shite." Rian no longer looked ready to set afire anything he looked at, which Cuinn supposed made his excursion into a hellish past worth it. "But you had no choice."

None. Even if he had tried to convince the other Loremasters that there was a third kind of magick accessible to the *daragin* and the *Gille Dubh*, there would have been no time. And he'd needed that magick himself. The Realm had needed it.

Nice try, arsehat.

"I suppose I can see why they hate Fae, then."

That's your human upbringing showing. I seriously doubt any Fae other than the two of us will sympathize.

"I'm not sympathizing." The Fire was back, smoldering now rather than blazing. "I'll still be well pleased to see them burn. But I suppose I can wait until you no longer have need of their aid to get back what they stole."

Cuinn chuckled—that, at least, he could still do. *You're as diplomatic as any Fae Prince ever.* Maybe a little distraction was called for after all. *Twinklebritches is going to come by after he and Josh take care of the situation in Central Park, see if there's anything he can do for me.* And there would be time enough tomorrow to start worrying about the probability of a host of unguarded wells of living magick opening up at random all over the human world. And about a rogue Loremaster who might or might not have plans for the Pattern. Shit. *Care to give me something else to think about for an hour or two?*

93

Chapter Twelve

Garrett's key stuck in the studio door, the way it always did. He didn't worry too much about it, just jiggled the key and worked it until it finally deigned to turn and slide the deadbolt. He and Terry were probably going to have to replace the whole door before they opened anyway.

The afternoon sun slanted in through the soap-frosted windows. The light didn't quite make it halfway to the back of the mostly empty space—the former club-wear boutique was a lot deeper than it looked from the outside. Garrett stood, hands on hips, and peered back into the dimness to the rear. Piles of boards showed where flimsy interior walls had been knocked down; the tiny dressing rooms that had been here when he and Terry signed the lease on the space had probably been great for quick and dirty blowjobs, but there wasn't much they'd be good for in the dance and exercise studio he and his business partner envisioned.

Going legit was a scary thought, the good-scary kind. Not that he was ever going to give up dancing at Purgatory, not while he could work his own kind of magick on a crowd—but Terry's business proposal had set him free to start down a whole new path he'd never let himself consider before.

The door clicked open behind him. "Hey, Ishkhan, you're early." Ishkhan Minassian was a Purgatory regular—and a licensed carpenter and general contractor. And in exchange for the promise of a free spot in the studio's first class of pole dancers, he was contributing the lion's share of the labor for the renovations and calling in favors for the stuff he wasn't licensed to do himself. It was a slow process, but at least they knew it was being done right.

Arms slid around Garrett's waist from behind, and he was enveloped by a familiar scent. "And your second guess would be...?"

Garrett grinned as an insistent mouth sought, and finally found, his ear through his curly blond hair. "I wish we had the mirrors up, you're so fucking sexy when you do that."

Lochlann laughed and drew him closer. "Patience, *grafain*."

"That's not the first thing you make me think of." Garrett crossed his arms, and closed his eyes as Lochlann stroked his forearm. Fae had a hard time keeping their hands off their SoulShares, for which Garrett tried to remember to give thanks at every opportunity. "Patience, I mean. Wild love tends to be on my mind a lot when you're around." *Grafain*, 'wild love,' was the pillow name Lochlann had given him not long after they met. He liked it. A lot.

He could feel Lochlann's lips curve in a smile against his ear. But the smile was followed by the warm breath of a sigh. "I just got back from Greenwich Village. I was hoping I'd find you here."

Garrett turned in Lochlann's arms. "You went back?" His own night last night had been an early one. He'd gotten home from Purgatory a little after two; Lochlann hadn't made it back to their shared suite at the Colchester for another couple of hours after that, and they'd both been up until just after dawn as his Fae lover shared the story of how he'd spent the night.

Lochlann nodded. "I wanted to see if there was anything I could do. As a healer."

"For Cuinn, you mean?"

"Bryce, too, actually. But mostly Cuinn."

"*Bryce?*"

"You didn't see how fucked up he was when the *Marfach* woke up." Lochlann sounded as if he didn't quite believe his own words. No wonder. Six months into his impossible relationship with Lochlann, Garrett was still working out what made Fae tick, largely by watching the way they interacted with each other, with their SoulShares, and with other humans. And he'd come to realize that compassion wasn't something that occurred to a Fae, except when it came to the human whose soul that Fae shared. Even Lochlann, a master healer among the Fae, used his gifts more out of a sense of duty than any innate empathy, except where Garrett himself was concerned.

Fae aren't human, he reminded himself. And expecting them to be was a sure way to get hurt. Though SoulSharing did something to them. "Fucked up or not, Bryce is still, um, challenging."

"You're telling me." Lochlann buried his nose in Garrett's hair and breathed deeply, then drew back just far enough to look into his eyes. "There wasn't anything I could do for either one of them."

"Do you need to tap directly into the ley energy?" Pure ley energy was dangerous even to a SoulShared Fae acting without his human partner—even Lochlann, who could call the energy to himself and didn't have to be in physical contact with a ley line, needed to take precautions. And by "taking precautions," a Fae would mean having his channeling ability enhanced by means of sexytimes with his human partner. "I'm not dancing tonight, I could take the train up to New York as soon as Ish gets here."

Lochlann's smile started a sweet familiar heaviness in Garrett's groin. "Thank you for the offer, *grafain*. But there's nothing I could do for either Bryce or Cuinn even with your help. They were both injured by magick."

Garrett frowned. "That makes a difference?"

"A big difference." Soft lips gently brushed Garrett's forehead. "There are a lot of different kinds of Fae healing magick. There's—look, I don't want to lecture you."

"Lecture me." Garrett tiptoed and kissed Lochlann's throat. His partner didn't often talk about his fellow Fae, or life in the Realm—he called it 'ancient history', and in Lochlann's case it kind of was, since Lochlann, at a few decades older than Cuinn, the last of the Loremasters, was the oldest living Fae, somewhere in the neighborhood of two thousand five hundred years old. "Please."

What started as a soft groan turned into a chuckle. "If you insist. There are Fae healers from every Demesne, but only healers from the Demesne of Water, like me, can heal without causing more pain than they're healing. And even Water healers tend to

97

specialize. It's an inborn thing, not something we can control. Some of us can only cure illness, some only burns or blunt force trauma or wounds that break skin."

"I've seen you cure all those. At the same time." It wasn't a memory Garrett liked to revisit, and he couldn't help the shiver that came along with it. But after Janek and the *Marfach* tortured him, Lochlann had healed too many burns to count, a crushed kneecap, gashes from razor wire, and oh yeah, Garrett's slit throat. Not to mention his AIDS.

His Fae lover gathered him even closer. "I'm old school. A generalist. They don't make them like me any more." Garrett could feel Lochlann's cheek brushing his curls. Being short was a wonderful thing sometimes. "But there's still one thing I can't touch. Enchanted injury."

"Injury by magick."

"Exactly." He felt Lochlann sigh. "In Bryce's case, part of him has been changed, warped by the piece of the *Marfach* he carried around for so long, and now that part resonates to the monster. Like a tuning fork or something. Lasair can draw out the ill effects, but I can't do a fucking thing about the underlying problem. And then there's Cuinn."

"Were you able to figure out what the *darag* did to him?"

He was instantly sorry he'd asked, as Lochlann stiffened. "No. The magick of the *daragin* is completely different from Fae magick. And the result isn't like any channeling I've ever seen or heard of. Cuinn can make any sound he likes, as long as it isn't an attempt to communicate. He can't whisper. Hell, he can't even move his lips for someone to read. If he didn't have the *ceangail* bond with Rian, he wouldn't be able to communicate at all."

Garrett pulled back far enough to let him look up at his partner. Lochlann had always had the power to make him forget to breathe, just with a look, and aquamarine eyes and wild dark hair backlit by the afternoon sun made his knees threaten to go wobbly on him. Still, he framed his lover's face in his hands and did his best to look stern. "You said your skills are inborn, and so are your limitations. Which means you don't get to beat yourself up about not being able to do anything. You'll figure something out. Or one of the others will."

The anger lingered in Lochlann's eyes and the set of his mouth, just long enough that Garrett was ready to chide him again. But then Lochlann shrugged, and it was gone. "Maybe the new kid on the block will have some ideas."

"The Vice cop?" Garrett blinked, trying to keep up with the change of subject. "With the stolen body?" At least, that's what he'd thought Lochlann had said, in the wee small hours of the morning. Right before Garrett's *okay, this is getting too weird even for the resurrected mate of a Fae* filter had kicked in.

"Yes. He told us his line was shunned for being what we call *adhmacomh*—it means 'wood-bodied,' it implies that a Fae looks like he has *Gille Dubh* blood. Black hair, tanned skin, dark eyes, like the spirits that live in the *daragin*." Lochlann grimaced. "It was an insult even when I lived in the Realm, but it apparently got a lot worse after the Sundering."

Garrett said nothing, but his fingers strayed into

Lochlann's midnight-dark hair. The Fae chuckled and took one of Garrett's hands in his. "Just the dark hair alone isn't enough to earn the insult. And maybe if there's truth to the old stories, Fiachra might have some insight into how the *daragin* magick works."

"I hope so. I can't imagine Cuinn of all people not being able to speak."

"I think quite a few Fae would consider the present situation an answer to prayer, if Fae believed in gods." Lochlann's tone was dry. "But Cuinn would—"

The door swung open. "Uh oh, sorry!"

"Ish!" Garrett laughed as Lochlann released him and they both turned toward the door. The stocky, greying contractor had obviously come ready to work, with a tool belt Garrett could see turning Batman green with envy. "Don't worry, we're on our way out."

"We're on our way next door," Lochlann corrected gently. "I want to work on that adductor strain you mentioned last night."

The day I turn down your offer to work on a strained groin, bury me, 'cause I'll already be dead. "Lead on, I follow."

Chapter Thirteen

They told me not to do this. They all did.

Fiachra suspected this wasn't the strongest possible argument against his own inner urge to descend the steps in front of him. For one thing, the compulsion of the Summoning wasn't going to let go of him until he got to its source, no matter what his fellow Fae might have to say on the subject. And for another, if his inner urge was actually the voice of another Fae, reminding it that other Fae opposed what it wanted was maybe the worst idea imaginable, the equivalent of waving a red cape in front of an already pissed-off bull. Why Fae had never came up with that form of entertainment, he wasn't sure.

And for yet another, if he didn't haul ass down those stairs pretty damned soon, he was liable to find himself going into Big Boy Massage and looking for Peri. Which he wanted to do more than he wanted to venture into Purgatory, actually, and he thought he was finally starting to understand why.

A human would never mock him as *adhmacomh.* Beyond a doubt, Peri didn't give a flying duck fuck about Fiachra's dusky skin, black hair, dark eyes.

For the first time in 17 years—maybe the first

time in his life—Fiachra wanted someone to see him as he really was. He wanted his own face back, his own body. He wanted to see Peri with his own eyes.

Would the voice in his head like that idea? Or hate it? And what was it capable of doing about its preferences, either way?

And what would Peri think, if Fiachra tried to tell him the truth?

Hell with it. The ley energy wasn't boiling out from under the black glass doors, and no one was coming or going through them, either. Fiachra descended the stairs and slipped quietly through the doors.

No bouncer on duty this time, which was a relief. Fiachra had no problem with using his own magick on humans, but the kind of manipulation he'd performed on the guy last night wasn't his, and he tried to save it for special occasions.

Everything looked different. The house lights were up, except for the lights in the pit full of black leather furniture but presently empty of writhing bodies. There were a few men at the bar, and more sitting or standing at the high-tops just off the dance floor. There was music, but it was barely audible and sounded like a warm-up or rehearsal track for a red-haired dancer working one of the poles on the unlit dance floor. Even without the mood lighting and the sweaty sexed-up crowd, though, it was impossible to mistake Purgatory for anything other than what it was, the raunchiest gay club in D.C.

And Fiachra was still being drawn. Toward the bar.

<Closer.>

Fiachra stiffened at the sound of the voice that wasn't, yet was, his own.

"You apparently have issues with following directions."

Fiachra turned on his heel to face the source of the sardonic voice. Tiernan Guaire stood at the edge of the pit, hands on hips, wearing a glove on his crystal hand, a faded T-shirt proclaiming him the property of the College of William and Mary wrestling team, and a smirk that Fiachra was beginning to suspect was permanent. "Tell me you didn't expect anything different."

"I was hoping for just a trace amount of common sense. Call me a Pollyanna." Tiernan gestured toward a door Fiachra hadn't seen before, light spilling out from a crack in the black wall behind the pit. Ordinary light. "Step into my office, will you? There's a little talk I've been wanting to have with you."

***

"Sit down, will you? Being loomed over is annoying as fuck, and you're made of loom."

The chair opposite Tiernan's desk wasn't quite big enough to accommodate Fiachra's long frame. It amused Tiernan to watch the other Fae lower himself into it and try to rearrange himself to fit.

His amusement wasn't lost on the big blond cop. "*Blas mo thón.*"

Tiernan grinned, but the grin didn't make it all the way to his eyes. "I'm a married male, I don't taste other males' asses even when they ask nicely."

Fiachra shrugged. "I usually don't have to ask at all."

103

"Which is something of a liability in your line of work, I would think." The smile faded from Tiernan's face; slowly he leaned forward in his chair, resting his elbows on the desk, fixing Fiachra with a stare. "If a guy just drops to his knees and starts giving you a rim job, he could always claim in court that it was consensual."

Fiachra's face went an interesting shade of red. "I'm not doing that kind of bust any more. I told Harding I wanted off that rotation."

Which brought up all kinds of interesting questions Tiernan had been saving up for the last couple of days, having to do with how the hell a Fae became an undercover Vice cop. But those questions were going to have to wait their turn behind a few others, more pertinent to his main concern. Namely, keeping Purgatory open and unmolested by D.C. Vice. "Good for you. Now would you mind telling me why the bleeding fuck you won't stay away from here? Are you under orders?"

"Yes. Harding thinks I'm going to help him shut you down. Has it all planned out, in fact. I heard the whole megillah when I checked in at end of shift, after I got back from Central Park." Fiachra waved a casual hand. But his body language was anything but casual. "Now ask me if I give a downwind fart about his plans."

Tiernan's pierced eyebrow arched. "You make no sense, even for a Fae. And keep in mind that the Fae offering that assessment is personally acquainted with both Rian Aodán and Cuinn an Dearmad, poster children for total incomprehensibility."

Fiachra shifted in his too-small chair. "How do I not make sense?"

"By your own account, you've spent 17 years building a human career in the human world. Maybe the human gods know why, I sure as shit don't. And fresh from your perch atop that 17-year pile of makes-no-fucking-sense, you expect me to believe you're flipping all of it the double-barreled ird. Why?"

Fiachra rubbed the back of his neck, like a Fae who had a pain in it. Going by his expression, he probably did. "Actually, it all made sense until about ten seconds ago. Thanks all to hell."

"I live to wreak havoc on your world view." Tiernan leaned back in his chair, arms crossed behind his head. "But since I appear to be on a roll, maybe you wouldn't mind telling me how you ended up a member of D.C.'s finest. A Fae in Vice, no less. As a race, we generally devote ourselves to the propagation of vice, rather than its eradication." Marriage to a lawyer hadn't done anything to curb his innate sarcasm, but it had certainly improved his vocabulary.

"Har har." Fiachra's body language was getting more uncomfortable by the second. "You seem to be under the impression that I owe you an explanation."

Cop doesn't like getting grilled? "If you expect me to let you into my establishment, against the advice of the Royal mage and my own better judgment—"

"*Royal* mage? I remember when the Prince Royal of Fire was stolen, and I believe your Rian is that baby—"

"Big of you."

Fiachra ignored him. "But there's a new Princess Royal in the Demesne of Fire, and she rules from the creche with her doting daddy the King, as it's ever been. So how is her big brother a Royal in the human world?"

Tiernan's eyes narrowed. "He's the Prince Royal of the Demesne of Purgatory, and don't fucking forget it." What had started as a joke, the collection of a band of exiles into an exile Realm, had somehow become reality of a sort, when that Realm acquired a Prince of its own. "And nice try at changing the subject, but let's find our way back, shall we?"

"No problem. You were about to tell me why I should tell you anything."

Tiernan drew in a deep breath and held it to the count of ten. Kevin kept telling him it was a good calming exercise. Maybe someday it would work. "This place is under my protection. For a reason. If you, an unShared Fae, should accidentally make contact with the energy that lives under this floor, you will almost certainly die, and in the process damage or destroy the only thing keeping the *Marfach* from getting back into the Realm. And possibly fuck up the only conduit allowing ley energy back into the Realm to become living magick and keep the whole Realm from dying." This deep breath worked a little better. "So you refusing to take no for an answer is a big fucking pain in my ass."

"Maybe you should have thought of that before you had someone channel a boss-level Summoning from somewhere in here."

Tiernan froze. *Did we—shit, yes. We did.* "That was before we kicked the nexus in the nuts. It's a lot...livelier, now. And we didn't think we were going to reel in a Loremaster."

"I told you, I'm not a fucking Loremaster."

"I'd imagine you are as far as the nexus is concerned. All that stored magick and channeling ability? You're going to be like 6'5" of catnip if you get anywhere near it. And we *still* haven't gotten to the part where you tell me why you're working for Vice."

"It isn't that big a mystery. I told you the *darag* dropped me into the middle of an active murder investigation in New York. I was the only one who could understand the only eyewitness, and once they caught the son of a bitch, I was able to tell them his alibi was full of shit."

"You're a truthseer?"

Fiachra winced—*he probably didn't mean to let that slip.* But one thing about truthseers, they tended to be terrible liars. "Yeah. And since coming through the Pattern, I've acquired a knack for getting people to change their minds. Which all came together to make me a damned good Homicide detective. Which is what I was, until I finally couldn't stand the Summoning any more, and had to either transfer to D.C. or go completely ratfuck crazy." He shrugged, the roll of muscles something of a distraction in his tight T-shirt. "No openings in Homicide here, so I took what I could get. Vice."

"Makes sense. Except that it still doesn't make sense."

"*Se an'agean flua, a'deir n'abhann.*"

'The ocean is wet,' says the river. The equivalent, *as'Faein*, of the pot calling the kettle black. Tiernan elaborately scratched an eyebrow with his middle finger. Which made him feel better than any number of deep breaths. *I gotta be me...* "So your special set of skills was helpful to the humans. Since when did a Fae ever give a non-aerodynamic flying fuck about helping a gaggle of strange humans?"

"I..."

Tiernan enjoyed the way the other Fae's expression resembled that of a deer staring into the headlights of an oncoming car. "And you needed to come to D.C. That I can believe, and we may want Conall to do something to modify the damned Summoning. But why go through all the transfer shit, just for the privilege of continuing to take orders from humans?" He himself had occasionally worked, over the 150 years or so he'd wandered the human world before his husband had given him Purgatory as a wedding present, but only for his own amusement, to indulge a whim—a Fae in the human world always had exactly as much money as he might need, just for the asking, and generally had no inclination whatsoever to do as humans told him.

"I... think I hate you."

"You seriously never thought about any of this? In 17 years?"

"No." The word was gritted out from between clenched teeth. "Which, now that you've brought it to my attention, irritates the shit out of me."

Tiernan was no truthseer—even if that particular talent weren't strictly a gift of the Demesne of Air, he'd spent enough of his life avoiding various hard truths to invalidate any claim he might otherwise have had of being on a first-name basis with the concept—but there was something about Fiachra's frustration that corroborated the other Fae's version of events. "Just thinking out loud here... if you've gone 17 years without seeing something that incredibly obvious, you're either stupid as a stump, or there's some other factor at work here."

108

"It's been a while, so memory may be deceiving me, but I believe I killed the last score or so of males who compared me to anything made of wood."

One corner of Tiernan's mouth quirked up. "Been a while for me, too, but I'm still a *scian-damsai*, and you'd better believe I'm never out of arm's reach of a blade." Which was the plain truth, and he had more use for the skills of a blade-dancer than he liked of late. Let the other Fae wonder where he was hiding his knife. "And to drag this discussion kicking and screaming back on track yet again, your chosen employment and your obsessive interest in Purgatory have the side effect of bringing a Loremaster—or his body, at least—closer to the Pattern. Total coincidence, I'm sure."

A soft knock on the office door interrupted total silence from the Fae cop. The knock was immediately followed by a soft click, and the door opening just wide enough to admit Conall's head. There were dark circles under the mage's peridot eyes, and while he still looked like he'd need to use a fake I.D. to get served at the bar, there was something about his expression that gave away every minute of his 300-plus years.

"What the bedazzled fuck are *you* doing in here?" Conall blurted, glaring at Fiachra, before Tiernan could so much as open his mouth. "I *knew* I should have drawn you a picture last night."

"He was just leaving." When Conall started cursing, prudent Fae knew to make themselves scarce. Not that there were all that many prudent Fae. Tiernan doubted Fiachra was one of them.

"No, I wasn't."

109

Sometimes I hate being right.

"Yes, you were." Conall gestured, and Fiachra was yanked out of his chair. He hung in the air by the collar of his T-shirt, his toes barely off the floor and his head nearly brushing the ceiling.

Tiernan tilted his head, admiring Conall's handiwork. "Did Lasair finally give in and teach you that channeling?"

"No, with him it's a special gift. This is as close as I could get—"

Conall was yanked into the office by an invisible hand and slammed back into the wall as Fiachra landed in a crouch on the floor. Oddly enough, going strictly by facial expressions, the cop looked like he was in a total panic, even as he calmly straightened to face Josh, who was charging in like thunder with murder in his eyes.

Conall shot out a hand and grabbed Josh, holding him back. "*Anái crua, adhmacomh,*" he snarled. And Fiachra choked on air gone solid in his lungs, going an alarming shade of dusky blue. But the cop must have said something, somehow, despite his obstructed airway, because suddenly Tiernan's office was host to a small tornado, slamming the door shut, sending computer monitors crashing to the floor and rocking Conall back again, hard enough that Tiernan heard his head hit the wall.

Tiernan clung to the edge of his desk, white-knuckled. Elemental earth magick quickly anchored him and the desk to the floor and freed him to concentrate on other things. Such as how to keep one pissy mage and one pissy Loremaster-equivalent from completely trashing his office. And each other. His

110

Noble magicks were no match for Conall's sheer firepower or the magickal potential stored up in the body of a Loremaster. But, then, all he really had to do was get their attention. He hoped.

Generating blades of living Stone from the crystal of his hand was easy. Throwing them left-handed was less so. Making sure they flew straight through a gale was a pain in the ass. But it was all worth it to see Conall and Fiachra both standing like statues, blades quivering in the wall bracketing each of their heads, tufts of blond and red hair drifting down through the suddenly still air. "I have fucking had enough of both of you."

Fiachra cleared his throat. "That wasn't me."

Conall blinked slowly, as if he were remembering how to do it. "I believe you. Which means we have more than one problem."

Josh wrapped his heavily-inked arms protectively around Conall, glaring indiscriminately at both Tiernan and Fiachra. "Conall needs to use the nexus chamber. He was drained after last night. And this didn't help."

"Next time don't pick my office to play Vincent Price and Boris Karloff."

"If we do, I get to be Vincent Price." Conall's voice was muffled by Josh's chest, but Tiernan got the impression the mercurial mage was grinning.

"I thought Boris Karloff was Dracula." Fiachra stepped away from the blades, rubbing the side of his head where a lock of hair had been sliced away.

Tiernan shook his head. "You really need to get the hell out of here. Once Conall starts replenishing his magick, an unShared Fae isn't going to be safe anywhere below ground until he's done. Plus, you've

111

just begged to be schooled in classic movies, and ain't no one got time for that right now."

"I'll go. But it isn't going to be easy."

"Oh, right." Tiernan waited for Conall to look up. "At your leisure, o mighty one, do you think you could make your Summoning a little less irresistible? No way to tell how many more Loremasters we might end up having to chase out of our basement."

Conall tried to speak, cleared his throat, and tried again. "That's a good point. I might not be up to reworking the channeling right now, but I'll figure something out."

"That isn't quite what I meant." Fiachra drew a deep breath, blew it out slowly. "I think there's someone else who doesn't want me to leave."

"*Scamallach siladh pol'bod.*" Yeah, that piece of news rated an 'infected dripping dick tip.' Tiernan stalked out from behind the desk and crossed to Conall and Fiachra, yanking the crystal knives out of the wall and channeling to reabsorb them into his hand. If only he'd worked that trick out sooner, like a year and a half ago, he could probably have killed Janek O'Halloran without letting the *Marfach* escape from the ley lines that had been its prison for millennia.

Water under the mother-fornicating bridge.

Conall's smile was only a memory; the redhead leaned on Josh as he turned to Fiachra. "I think we need to talk. You, me, our Loremaster, maybe Lochlann, he's at least met Brodulein. But I have to replenish first, and rest, and you need to get your preternaturally well-rounded ass away from here. Can you find Cuinn and Rian's apartment again, and meet me there at, say, 2;00?"

"This morning? Yes, I don't have to report for duty until tomorrow afternoon—and you can keep your comments to yourself, m'lord Guaire, Harding's said enough to me about his plans for this place that I want to keep an eye on him just to make sure he doesn't order up a fucking raid."

"Did I say anything?" He'd been about to, of course. "Although I'll be happy to even out that trim I just gave you if you call me 'My Lord' again. Now get the hell out of here, all of you. Josh, I need to go upstairs and borrow your computer to order some new monitors, thanks to the Dueling Wizards…"

Chapter Fourteen

"I think you may need to shackle me this time."

Conall could feel the rumble of Josh's chuckle behind him as he pressed his thumb to the little truesilver panel set into the wall beside the door to the nexus chamber. "You know how I hate that."

Conall reached within and teased out a tendril of living magick, "*Scathán*," he whispered, *wings,* and channeled the power into the silver. The power and his key dropped the channeling binding the door, and he glanced back over his shoulder with a tired grin as he stepped through. "One of the many things I love about you—you're always willing to go the extra mile."

As usual, Conall could see perfectly well by the not-quite-light of the ley energy billowing up from the floor. Tiernan had mentioned once that he'd first found the great nexus under Purgatory's sub-basement mostly on a hunch; he hadn't been able to see the lines of energy at all without working one of the Noble magicks of Earth on the floor, turning it to transparent crystal.

Things had changed, to put it mildly. Ever since the SoulShared Fae of Purgatory had started tapping into the nexus, the nexus had responded, growing more and more active. Bringing in a bona fide Fae Royal and installing him in an upstairs apartment had only made things worse—though moving the young Royal and his consort into Tiernan's empty New York apartment had taken some of that pressure off. And punching a hole through the Pattern to create a conduit for the ley energy to pour into the Realm? Conall had never been to Niagara Falls, but he'd seen pictures, and the thick whorls of mist and foam at the bottom of the falls looked awfully familiar.

Of course, his SoulShare was breathtaking by leylight, daylight, or in utter darkness, explored by fingertips while blindfolded. Maybe especially then. *Easy, Conall. He's already agreed to chain you. Save something for later.*

Behind him, Josh switched the lights on; his human could see by leylight if he had to, as a result of their flawed SoulShare, but it was hard on him. The chamber didn't look any neater with the lights on than it had when they were off, either. The black leather chaise lounge in the middle of the room was where it was supposed to be—not an exceptional surprise, as it was bolted to the concrete floor—but whoever had been the last to use the chamber had left toys scattered all around.

"Must have been Rian and Cuinn." Josh ran the soft leather strips of a flogger through his fingers before dropping it in the drawer of the table at the end of the chaise.

Conall did his best to keep his face expressionless as he bent and picked up a Wartenberg wheel from the chaise. He didn't fool his partner, though. Not that he'd really thought he could.

"You're pissed." Josh took the sensation toy from him, set it on the table, and rested his hands gently, possessively on Conall's shoulders. *Scathácru*, the dragon tattooed on Josh's left forearm, was blinking lazily at the brightness of the chamber lights, tasting the air with his glittering tongue. The chain tattooed on Josh's right wrist gleamed the silver-blue of truesilver, ready to take on form when magick was channeled. His human was the most beautiful male Conall had ever seen. "Because of what happened to Cuinn."

Conall nodded, sighing deeply as Josh took him into his arms. "I thought maybe I was just angry because I can't do anything against the *darag*'s magick. Wounded professional pride. But when he…" He swallowed hard.

"I saw." Josh kissed Conall's unruly red-blond hair. "I promise, I won't tell him."

Unable to reply, Conall just nodded. His embarrassment would be acute, if it ever got back to Cuinn that he, Conall, had had to blink back tears when the insufferable Loremaster tried and failed to call him Twinklebritches. Tiernan had noticed, he was sure—the Noble had never referred to him as 'o mighty one' before.

Conall hated it.

"Let's get your magick replenished." Gently, Josh guided Conall to sit on the chaise, then urged him to lie back and raise his arms over his head. "We'll clear your head, you'll be able to think better. You're exhausted."

"What you do to me doesn't exactly clear my head, you know," Conall mumbled. But he did as he was told. Only a total idiot would say no when Josh

116

LaFontaine was offering to restrain him and tease him to the point of reality-warping orgasm. All for the sake of allowing him to draw sufficient ley energy from the great nexus to restore the living magick he'd spent erecting a *Marfach*-proof ward around the oak in Central Park and trying in vain to reverse whatever the *darag* had done to Cuinn.

Conall closed his eyes with an unsteady sigh as Josh covered his face with gentle kisses. With Josh, sessions in the chamber were never just about the magick. Or, rather, they were about more than one kind of magick. Fae magick, the kind Conall channeled. And a purely human magick, one Fae had lost long ago. If they'd ever had it to start with. Love.

He felt Josh push his shirt up over his head, and then he was being kissed again, thoroughly enough that he hardly noticed the leather-padded cuffs closing around his wrists. He could get out of them with a thought and a word, of course, but he wouldn't. Not unless Josh said he might. Still, he tested the chains. He always did. He needed to feel them.

Josh wasn't his Dom, not exactly. More like his safety. His trust. In the Realm, his channeling power had been so overwhelming that it sucked magick, and life, out of everything around him. The greatest power since the Loremasters, and he'd hardly dared to use it. But when Josh bound him, everything was safe.

Josh moved to kneel over him, and Conall finally opened his eyes again. He couldn't help returning his partner's smile, any more than he could help trying to arch up into the body held just out of his reach. *If I'm ever too tired to respond to that smile, don't bother calling the healer, there's no hope for me.*

"Tell me what you need, baby."

Yet another delight, the way Josh treated him as something precious. He wasn't going to get tired of being nuzzled any time soon... warm breath in his ear and the rasp of a couple of days' growth of beard against his cheek was almost as good for what ailed him as drawing on the nexus.

Almost. "Take it slow, *dar'cion*. If I draw too fast when I'm this depleted, I'm going to end up with a headache that would stop and drop a charging bull elephant."

"Take it slow, with you looking at me like that? You don't ask much, do you?"

"Like what?"

"You know perfectly well like what." Josh's low chuckle was practically edible. "You're wearing your very best 'I want to be so deep in your throat when I come you won't even have to swallow' smile."

"And here I thought I was exhausted." Actually, he could feel the siren call of the ley energy, growing stronger as he became more aroused.

Josh's immediate answer was a kiss that would have knocked Conall on his ass if he hadn't already been lying on it. "You really have no idea how intensely sexy you are, do you?"

"Apparently not. Give me a minute, will you, while I try to make both of my eyes track in the same direction?"

More laughter. Conall was pretty sure Josh knew just how much he loved the sound, and was doing it on purpose. Delicious. "Sorry about that."

"No you aren't."

"Guilty." Josh rolled his hips, making Conall see

118

white sparkles and forget about contradicting him for a few seconds. "What was it you called Fiachra? Right before you nearly asphyxiated him? I was wondering if I was going to have to stop you from ripping his head off."

"Air magick doesn't do that kind of thing—it's almost impossible to make wind shear decapitate someone. Although..."

"Maybe I shouldn't be encouraging you to talk shop." Josh bent and nipped at Conall's lower lip, then stroked with his tongue. "What did you call him? *Adma*-something? I'd thought I was getting better with the Fae language, but I've never heard you use that word before."

"I've never had reason to. It's an insult that only applies to a few select Fae." Conall tried to reach for Josh, but subsided when the chains clanked. "Fae who bear a resemblance to a race of tree people." He could sense the ley energy, closer with each of his heartbeats, and worked his body against Josh's as best he could. Seeking more arousal.

And continuing to talk, because trying to concentrate on a Fae history lesson was about the only thing that was going to keep his arousal from going completely off the rails and earning him a massive headache. "A lot of Fae think the *Gille Dubh*—the ones that look more Fae, or more human, I suppose—and the *daragin*, the trees—are mythical. Mages know history better than most Fae, but even we thought all the tree people died during the Sundering."

Josh said nothing, just watched, running his hands open-palmed over Conall's chest and teasing his nipples with his fingernails. Conall's breath caught

119

hard as the ley energy made contact, and the light around him seemed to brighten as his pupils dilated. The energy was called by arousal, and it also enhanced it.

Keep talking, Casanova. "We don't know much, but we know the tree people refused to come into the Realm—the Fae lost the advantage of surprise over the *Marfach*, waiting, hoping they'd change their minds. But they decided they'd rather die than join us in the Realm."

"And for that, what they were—what they are— has become a curse." Josh's expression was as unreadable as his hands were eloquent.

"That's part of it." Conall was having trouble getting his breath. He could feel the ley energy flowing into him and being transmuted into living magick, the way it seemed he could feel cold water down his parched throat on a scorching summer day, his body drawing off what it needed even as he drank. "To a lot of Fae, though, it's enough of an insult to suggest that someone's mother or grandmother or honored ancestress had reproductive sexual congress with a tree."

Josh tried very hard not to laugh. It didn't work. "You also have an incredibly sexy vocabulary."

"I'm lucky you're sapiosexual." Conall started to smile, but gasped instead, as Josh reached down and gripped his groin. "You told me your grandfather taught you all kinds of *voyageur* curses. Teach me."

"Some other time. I like you frustrated."

"You must really love me now."

Josh laughed. Again. *So* damned sexy. "Fiachra doesn't look that different from most of the other Fae.

120

Other than being tall, if that's what you mean by *adhmacomh*."

"It isn't." Conall wrapped his hands around the chains that bound him to the chaise, straining against them as Josh teased at the waistband of his jeans. "What you saw upstairs isn't his real body—that's Brodulein, one of the original Loremasters."

Maybe it was the knowledge that the Pattern itself was here, under the chaise, just one world over, that sent a sensation of pure cold rippling down Conall's spine. Brodulein, or his body, had been so close...

To what?

"How did a Loremaster end up on this side of the Pattern?" Josh must have felt the shiver, because he lowered himself to cover Conall, sliding his forearms under him, cradling him, the heat of his body even more welcome than the rising swirling tide of ley energy from beneath.

Thank you, dar'cion. "Fiachra did on purpose what I did by accident right after I met you. He Faded his physicality." Conall couldn't help shuddering. He would give almost anything to forget the moment when his human had looked straight at the mirror in which his disembodied essence had been trapped, and hadn't seen a thing, but that moment of despair was embedded in his soul. "He told us that before he Faded, he had dark hair, tanned skin, brown eyes like smoky quartz. Classic *adhmacomh*. But when he went through the Pattern, he somehow ended up with Brodulein's body. And I can't believe the Pattern doesn't have a reason for wanting him here."

Josh frowned. "Do you trust me? To tell you what to do?"

Conall blinked. "Of course I do." His relationship with Josh wasn't that of a sub with his Dom, but there were times Conall found a bliss he'd never known how to imagine in being able to let go. To let someone else take charge, someone he trusted with his life.

"Then you need to stop talking about Fiachra, and Brodulein, and the Pattern, and Fading. Right now. And let me give you something else to think about." Josh smiled, but his beautiful eyes were stern. "You're shaking, and you look like you haven't slept in a week, and I'm not sure you even notice the ley energy rising, and I don't like it."

Josh's hand smoothed down Conall's side, soothing and arousing at the same time, and Conall's back arched into the touch. Conall let out a long slow sigh...and as he breathed back in, he could feel the ley energy, the stuff of magick, rising around him and filling him. Washing over him, a wave, a tide. Called by desire, arousal.

Josh, touching him. Kissing him. Loving him. Opening him.

Mine.

Chapter Fifteen

"So why the guyliner? It's not like you need it."

Peri sighed. "I wasn't supposed to work tonight. I was getting ready to go out when the boss called." The masseur who had been scheduled to share the slow Sunday night shift with the wiry redhead occupying the chair on the other side of the lobby had apparently had an ugly breakup with his boyfriend. Either the fourth breakup or his fourth boyfriend, Peri wasn't sure. He didn't think Lochlann had been sure either. But whichever, Peri's plans for the evening were fucked, halfway through his eyeshadow.

Probably just as well. Or so he'd think if he were being reasonable. He'd had no intention of being reasonable tonight, though.

"I would kill for a look like yours, if I only knew who."

"And I'd kill to just look normal." The words came out with more of an edge than he'd meant. Usually he'd apologize for that, too. Not tonight.

I don't even know who I am. Starting with the ridiculous name his mother had given him. He could still remember her murmuring it to him, and that was okay, but no one else called him by his full name.

Ever. So his name was a mask, he supposed. His first one.

His bleached blond hair was a disguise. Falcon, with her padding and her tucking and her five-inch heels, was a disguise. If he could get even further away from the man he'd been that night outside the Guard House with Yukio and the others, he would. As long as he left himself a way back, on the nights when the guilt got to be too much.

Tonight was supposed to be one of those nights. But it wasn't going to be now.

The heavily frosted glass of the door flared a brief, muted red as a sirenless police car sped by. Peri ground his teeth. Fiachra had seen through his disguises. A fucking cop.

He didn't just let men see through his masks. It was dangerous. The man behind the masks was the man who was supposed to have died instead of Yukio.

He hadn't let Fiachra in. But Fiachra had gotten in anyhow.

"Hey, you all right?"

Peri waved the redhead off. "Don't worry, I'm fine."

The door opened, letting in a wave of humid night air along with a customer.

Okay, so I'm not fine.

"Peri. Please. I just want to talk."

"Like hell you do, Officer."

"Detective, actually. But off duty."

Slowly, Peri got to his feet. His 5'9" was never going to intimidate the blond god's 6'5", but at least he'd hold on to his dignity. "On duty, off duty, it doesn't matter, you can still arrest me."

"If I'd wanted to arrest you, I would have done it on Friday night."

Off on the periphery of Peri's vision, the redhead was watching, slack-jawed, as Fiachra walked up to Peri and took his hand. Peri didn't care about the ginger. He *did* care about the way his heart rate kicked up into the danger zone when the cop touched him. And that strange energy was back. In spades.

And those eyes.

Fiachra nodded toward the door to the massage room the two of them had used on Friday night. "Please."

***

Peri shook himself as the door closed behind them, looking around as if he wasn't quite sure where he was or how he'd gotten there. Fiachra snarled—not at the gorgeous masseur, but a silent snarl, directed at himself. Sort of. *If you're fucking with Peri's head, you Loremaster son of a bitch...*

There was no answer. Fiachra thought that was a good thing.

"What the hell are you doing back here?" Peri was looking at the wall, not at him, and his voice was unsteady.

"I'm not sure." He'd been trying to come up with the answer to that question since he'd left Tiernan's office. Since he'd known he was going to end up here before the come-to-Jesus meeting in New York. And *I'm not sure* was the best he could do? "I'm not an idiot. Not exactly. And I'd have to be an idiot, not to know you don't want me here. But I couldn't stay

125

away." He laughed, a short harsh sound. "Shit, does that ever sound like stalker material."

"Yeah." To his astonishment, Peri was smiling. Just a little. "But I don't think that's your gig. You don't need to stalk."

"True enough."

"So let's try again. Why did you come back here?"

Because there's a possibility you might have half my soul. Yeah, that would work beautifully. The trouble was that given what he'd learned from the other Fae he'd encountered last night, it made sense. Almost as much sense as the possibility that he'd gone stark staring mad.

But without the explanation he couldn't give, and only half believed himself, what was he left with? Madness, basically. Fae didn't love. Fae didn't have grand passions. Life was too long, and Fae nature too fickle, for any thought of a serious attachment to any one Fae—or any number of Fae—to make any sense. And if he was incapable of so much as considering an attachment to a Fae, how much less so to a human?

Yet here he stood, thinking about it. Unable to think about much else. Even the high drama of last night had only been a distraction. And he hadn't told Tiernan, or Conall, or Josh about this particular reason for needing to be around Purgatory. It was none of their fucking business.

And Peri was staring at him, waiting for him to yank his thumb out of his ass and answer a simple question.

He couldn't. Instead, he took a step closer and rested his hands lightly on Peri's shoulders, gently caressing with open palms. *Let's see what we can find together.*

Peri jerked away, stepping back, nearly running into the wall. "Don't."

"Why not?"

The human's laugh was strangled. "Are you serious? How am I supposed to trust you?"

There was more to it than that. A truthseer could tell. But if he pushed, he had a feeling Brodulein would take the pushing as an invitation to pull the kind of mindfuckery he'd usually reserved for murder suspects under interrogation. The way he'd bulldozed the bouncer last night. And Fiachra would manscape with a cheese grater before he'd give the bastard an opening to do that to Peri.

"What if I can persuade you?"

Sure enough, *<I can do that for you,>* the voice in his head whispered, softer than soft.

Fuck with him and I swear by any human god who will listen that I will end you. Even if it means ending us both.

Silence. Good.

"I don't see how you can do that." Peri's foot started edging toward that damned kick switch under the massage table.

Gently but firmly, Fiachra moved him away from the table. "I've been thinking about that. Will you at least hear me out, before you try to get me thrown out again?"

Peri flushed. It didn't make him any less gorgeous. "I suppose it's your quarter. Even if you aren't on the meter."

"That was my idea, more or less." Of course, now

that he was trying to put into words the only halfway logical idea that had come into his head in the last day and a half, it sounded idiotic. "It's just as illegal in D.C. to pay for sex as it is to take money for it. Which means that once I actually pay you, I'm as much a criminal as you are."

Peri pulled away again, but not to kick the switch, only to lean against the wall, cross his arms in front of him like a wall, and slant a skeptical look up at Fiachra. "You don't look thrilled at the prospect of paying me."

Shit, how to explain this to a human? Without giving everything away? "I'm not, exactly. But not for the reason you probably think. Where I'm from... offering someone money for sex is the ultimate insult."

"Why?" Peri frowned. His eyes, his beautiful dark eyes... Fiachra's own were almost as dark, or had been once. "I mean, that's kind of weird. Pointing out that someone takes money for sex, calling them a whore, sure, that's a putdown to some people. But how is it an insult to pay someone when you're the one doing the paying?"

At least he's interested. He's talking. "Sex is supposed to be about mutual pleasure. And if I offer you money instead, it means I have no intention of giving you anything else. I expect to be serviced. I'm buying you... as if you're an object that only matters to me for the amount of pleasure I can wring out of you."

Peri was staring at the floor, somewhere between Fiachra's feet. "Well, when you put it that way, I suppose I can see the insult. But it's what I am, so don't worry about it." He shrugged, a tight movement of his shoulders that hurt to look at.

128

"*No.*" He nearly took Peri by the arms again, but the human's slight flinch warned him off as clearly as any words. "You are *not*. I wouldn't treat you that way. I don't think I could." This time when he reached out, Peri didn't pull away. "I only want you to trust me."

"I still don't get it."

Fiachra felt Peri shiver, and just for an instant he felt as if his hands were cupped around the body of a hawk or a falcon, a small fierce bird that wanted nothing more than to fly away.

And if it did, there would be a hole in Fiachra's life, his soul, that he might never understand. And would never fill.

"Just say yes."

Peri swallowed hard. "What do you want to do?"

***

Why the fuck did I just say that?

Fiachra's smile changed his whole face. It was still intense, like nothing Peri had ever seen, but the other man's smile supercharged the insane electric butterfly action going on in his stomach. He was holding the live wire again.

I ought to let go.

"How much for full service?"

Jesus. Everything I thought I wanted, on Friday night. "House cut is 50."

"And what's your add-on?" Fiachra's hands wouldn't stay still; they caressed his arms, his shoulders, fingertips brushed his neck.

He shook his head. "Don't pay me. Not after what you told me it means to you."

Peri wished he could read the cop's expression properly. There was no reason in the world for the hope he thought he saw in those glacier-blue eyes.

"Fifty it is, then."

Fiachra dug in the front pocket of his shorts and came up with a crumpled bill; he smoothed it out, gazed at the face of Ulysses S. Grant for a few seconds, and tucked it into Peri's hand with an air of finality. "There."

"I don't think you're actually a criminal until you get what you paid for." Peri worked the bill into his own back pocket. Now that he was committed, he figured he could enjoy the way his heart was racing and his hands trembled. He was going to get his wish, the one he'd made Friday night when he'd first laid eyes on the insanely tall blond. And then it would be over. He could quit obsessing.

And if he didn't get interrupted again, and finally managed to get himself killed tomorrow night? No regrets.

Chapter Sixteen

"Maybe you should sit." Peri's smile as he urged Fiachra back toward the padded table was all the wake-me-up his cock needed.

Fiachra obeyed—Peri's slender fingers and luscious smile could have persuaded him to do damned near anything—and groaned, low and heartfelt, as those fingers reached under his T-shirt and raked slowly down his abs.

"You are so fucking ripped. But then I knew you would be." Peri teased around the waistband of Fiachra's shorts, slowing as his fingertips encountered Fiachra's moist tip, already shoving its way out and determined to get in on whatever action was going down.

Peri knelt, and then leaned in; his tongue curled out and danced over the swollen, darkened head, darted down the sides of his shaft, teased soft blond hair. His cock responded as eagerly as it could under the circumstances, straining at the denim.

"Oh, shit," Fiachra whispered, catching his lower lip between his teeth almost before the words had escaped. *If it feels this good already...*

The petit blond human sat back on his heels,

frowning slightly. "I should have asked, do you need a condom?"

"No." Not for the reasons Peri probably thought—Fae couldn't catch human diseases, couldn't carry them. But there was no need or way to explain that. But he also didn't want Peri to think he was into the thrill of barebacking with strangers and didn't give a shit about his partner's health. As strange as it felt, Fiachra wanted this human to think he was better than he actually was. "I have to get tested monthly, it's part of my job."

Which had the advantage of being true—even when he'd been working Homicide, a detective never knew when he might get into it with a suspect and blood might fly. Though he always messed with the lab tech's head, had her stick her own finger instead of his and forget she'd done it. He didn't want to think about what a laboratory would make of a sample of Fae blood.

Peri's smile was the most sensual thing Fiachra had ever seen. And he'd just seen those same lips teasing the head of his cock. Skillfully, Peri undid the button of his shorts and reached inside just long enough to save Fiachra's boys from a painful pinching as he slid the zipper down.

Fiachra imagined he could hear his cock groaning with relief as it sprang free.

Oh no, wait, someone *was* groaning. Him.

"Tell me when I need to stop." One cool palm weighed Fiachra's balls; the other wrapped around the base of his shaft. "Though I'll probably be able to figure it out for myself."

Fiachra rocked his hips into Peri's hand. And bit

his lip again when the human responded, working his uncut length with a grip just tight enough. "I may surprise both of us," he croaked.

"Don't do that." Peri placed a light kiss on the smooth skin of Fiachra's head, the gentle touch of his tongue a perfect contrast with the firmness of his grip. "Let me play a while." Fiachra wasn't sure when he'd started gripping the sides of the table, but he must have at some point, because he could hear wood creaking.

And he could hear whispering. Skin on skin, as Peri released his balls and gently traced fingers up the insides of his thighs. The catching of breath, almost subliminal groans.

Why do I need this so much? The words murmured themselves in Fiachra's mind, the way the owl's had. *Need you so much? Damn you.*

The whispers were a language, the language of Peri. Like the language of the *darag*. But where leaf on leaf had whispered disdain and anger and old pain, the human's touch whispered...

No. No. He was imagining it. He had to be.

Peri silently urged him to raise up, and slid his shorts down his legs, slipped off his trainers, shoved everything away and slid in closer, rubbing a smooth cheek up the inside of Fiachra's thigh, tonguing a ball into his mouth. *So much better than I deserve. Even once.*

So much emotion in that wordless whisper. And it made no sense. Peri was doing what he did for a living. The human didn't know how he'd moved into Fiachra's head, had no idea his name had been moaned into a Fae's pillow. Where was all the feeling coming from?

133

...the same place mine is...

No. Not just no, hell no, that beautiful borrowed human word the Fae hadn't forgotten in two millennia. Hells to the no, he was not falling in love. He couldn't be. Fae didn't. Didn't know how. And even humans didn't fall that fast except in their own wish-fulfillment stories.

And wishes don't come true.

Except that a wish he'd never dared to make was kneeling at his feet and giving his erect cock the sweetest tongue-bath it had ever known. Lapping at his taint. Like a cat. But that smile, no cat ever smiled like that. Pure sex.

"Can you hold out a little longer?" Peri's smile was almost shy. "I mean, if you want to fuck me, that's all right, I'm down with that...but you taste really good." Yes, he was blushing. "If you wouldn't mind..."

Fiachra let go of the table with one hand and buried his fingers in Peri's soft blond hair. "I'll manage somehow." His voice came out husky, maybe half an octave lower than he was used to. "Take your time." His whole body was alive with magickal energy; a Fae channeled most strongly, most easily, when he was aroused. *There are going to be fireworks in a few minutes...*

Peri nibbled lightly on Fiachra's wrist, kissed his palm, before scraping his teeth lightly up the slightly curved shaft bobbing in front of him. *How long can I make you last?*

If this was a language, and not just his fevered imagination, his gift would let him repeat anything he'd heard. He traced his thumb around the curve of

Peri's ear, let golden silk slip between his fingers. And gasped as Peri's warm velvet mouth sealed around the head of his cock, his lips eased down the shaft. *I need to make you—*

He wasn't sure what the gasp added. Whatever it was, though, Peri reacted with a groan Fiachra felt all the way to his taint and slid his arms around Fiachra's hips, taking his cock until he felt the head nudge the back of Peri's throat.

And then Peri swallowed, and Fiachra saw stars. Whole fucking constellations he hadn't seen since his last night in the Realm. More than that, he couldn't get his breath. Not when his whole body was shivering like a bell, struck by a hammer forged from the same ore, in the same fire.

SoulShare.

Peri laughed. Sexily, sensually, joyfully.

The joy was what did Fiachra in.

"Stop." Maybe the hardest word he'd ever spoken, and it was possible only because of what came after. "I need to have you. Now." He tugged at Peri's hair, pulled him off his cock, and urged him to stand up.

Peri obliged, a little too fast, swayed and staggered and fell into Fiachra's arms.

Fiachra kissed him. Held him, wore him like a second skin. Like it was the most natural thing he'd ever done. Instead of the most unnatural.

And Peri held him. Slowly, almost reluctantly, and Fiachra found himself holding his breath until it was done... but Peri held him.

Hands ran lightly up and down his back. *Why am I letting you hold me?* One hand dipped down, felt briefly along Fiachra's waist. Where he'd stashed the cuffs on Friday night. *I shouldn't. I shouldn't trust you. But fuck that. Hold me. Please.*

It had been centuries since Fiachra's eyes had stung with unshed tears. Watching his mother and his sister endure the taunts it had fallen to him to avenge. Now there was no one for him to avenge. Now there was only this slight, stunning human male, and a need Fiachra couldn't control and didn't understand.

He didn't want to let go, not even long enough to make Peri ready. He settled for keeping one arm wrapped around the human while he slid Peri's red nylon running shorts down his legs with the other.

"I, um, need to turn around. Or straddle you. Or something." Peri's blush was back. Fiachra liked it.

"In a minute." Peri's smile was irresistible. For a second, Fiachra wondered what it would look like rimmed with the deep plum lipstick Peri had worn last night. What it would feel like, taste like, to kiss him that way.

Another time.

This time he returned the smile, then kissed Peri one more time and slid down from the table. Taking Peri by the hips, he turned them both so he pinned the shorter male against the table. "Lube? Oil?" He whispered them into Peri's ear like endearments. Which they were, kind of.

"There's a drawer at the end of the table."

Fiachra didn't want to step back, any more than he'd wanted to let go—for one thing, he was thoroughly enjoying the heat of the erection pressed against his thighs—but he had to, for Peri's sake. The Fae whose body he'd stolen was hung like a Royalsforest stag. Yes, he still wanted his old body

136

back. But it would be nice to be able to keep at least a few parts of this one.

The human was still in the way, though, so Fiachra picked him up and sat him down on the table.

"Hey!" Peri laughed, spreading his legs to let Fiachra slide the drawer open between them.

Fiachra stroked Peri's cock as he rummaged through the drawer, pushing aside crumpled tubes of lube in favor of a small glass bottle. Peri's endowments were about average in size for a human, but like the rest of him, his shaft was so perfect it left Fiachra damn near breathless. The humanscaping only added to the allure as far as Fiachra was concerned; he caressed the silken skin with one hand while he flipped the top off the bottle with the other.

"Oh, sweet Jesus," Peri whispered.

Fiachra understood the sentiment, if not the deity. When he touched Peri this way, he could feel echoes of Peri's response in his own body, his own soul.

"Mind the oil." Peri waited until Fiachra's hand closed around the little bottle, then reached around behind him and hauled his T-shirt off over his head, stroking Fiachra's shoulders and chest as soon as they were bare. *Why does being close to you make me want to laugh? And why is laughing with you the fucking sexiest thing I've ever done?*

Fiachra was no longer sure if Peri's touch-speak was a thing of sounds, or something else. He also no longer cared. He needed to be inside the exquisite male. Inside his skin would be ideal, but he was willing to settle for being buried so deep in the human that the effervescent seed of a male Air Fae would tickle his nose from the inside.

He shook oil into his palm and stroked his cock. Again. A musky scent teased at him, something animal. He poured a thin stream of oil at the base of Peri's cock, letting it run into his dark puckered hole, smiling at the human's faint unsteady moan. He re-capped the bottle and slipped it back into the drawer, then took Peri's ankles and hooked the human's legs over his own broad shoulders.

"Oh, fuck..." Peri's words were barely audible, even to an Air Fac.

"In a minute." Fiachra circled the pad of his thumb over Peri's taint, and slipped two fingers gently into him, stretching him. He could feel the faint sweet burn in his own ass; his cock lengthened and twitched in anticipation. Magick surged in him, wanting its own unnatural confinement to be over. And his skin shivered, as if it barely contained some great delight, a joy that might burst free at any moment.

Fiachra suspected he knew what that moment might be. "Are you ready, *állacht*? Ready for me?" *Beauty*, yes, he was that.

"Jesus, of all the stupid..."

Peri's breathless voice, his smile, forced Fiachra to grip the base of his own cock with his free hand, tight as any steel ring, to keep from shooting all over that perfectly shaved groin. Even as he groaned, though, he laughed. He couldn't help it. "Do I need to wait?"

"Fuck you." Peri was laughing too.

The human's laughter was completely unFae.

And it made everything perfect.

But then it faded. "Let me turn around." Peri's gaze dropped.

138

"Why do you—"

"Please." He slid his legs off Fiachra's shoulders, easing up onto his elbows. "Don't treat me like something I'm not."

Fiachra's eyes narrowed. "Am I not allowed to treat you like a male whose smile I would give my left nut to see just because money changed hands?"

Peri stared.

"We agreed I'm not renting you, right? So I'll do everything I can to make you pass out from pleasure if I fucking well feel like it." Fiachra could feel his face flushing. *Where is all of this coming from?* Fae didn't act like this. Didn't feel like this.

Then he remembered Conall, looking at Josh. Cuinn and Rian, both of them Fae to the core, every breath either one took all wrapped up in the other.

Peri's my SoulShare. Or I'm insane. And I don't think I'm insane.

Peri's lower lip was caught between his teeth. Fiachra wanted to tease it out with his tongue so he could bite it himself.

"Lie down, *állacht.*" Fiachra leaned in and kissed Peri. Hard. Just to make sure he did as he was told.

Peri obeyed. Very slowly. "What does that mean? What you just called me?"

"It means 'beauty,'" Fiachra growled. The friction of skin against skin was delicious, but it apparently wasn't getting him any closer to the skin inside skin he needed. "But I'm thinking *sallacht* would suit you just as well."

"And that means…?"

"Mind-blowingly stubborn."

Peri's reluctance vanished, with a startled laugh.

139

Fiachra's first few oiled inches slipped inside Peri before the human thought to tighten around him. Or maybe it was deliberate—when Peri gripped his cock with his tight ring of muscle, Fiachra had to grab the sides of the table to keep his knees from buckling.

Peri smiled knowingly up at him—*hell, yes, that was deliberate*—and wrapped his legs tightly around Fiachra's waist, urging the Fae deeper even as he made him work for every inch.

Fiachra was sweating by the time he felt that tight ring around the base of his cock. He was also about a heartbeat and a half from losing it. Already. Peri fit him perfectly, and the slightest movement by either one of them was enough to make his sac tighten.

"If you don't ease up a little, this is all going to be over a lot faster than either one of us wants." Fiachra lowered himself over Peri, running the tip of his tongue around the human's lips. Wondering, again, what it would be like to hold Falcon. To kiss her. Would Peri like that? Or was Falcon no more than a mask?

At least he only wears his mask when he wants to.

"Over?" There was still laughter in Peri's voice, but it was breathless now. His fingers dug into Fiachra's sides, and his heels into Fiachra's thighs. "Give me some credit, will you?" Muscles rippled along Fiachra's length; Peri's hips moved in a tight circle. "I'm just getting started—"

If there was more, Fiachra didn't hear it. His cock curved, tried to kick in the tight confines of Peri's hold. He dropped to cover the human, shouting with the fierce pleasure of his release.

Pleasure, power, and joy. The pleasure damned

near broke him. The magick was an explosion, barely contained. The joy was what held him together.

SoulShare.

He could feel Peri shivering under him as the pleasure let go of him. Slowly, carefully, he worked his forearms under the human. He'd never felt the need to do anything like that before.

"Holy shit." Peri's reverent whisper was warm against Fiachra's collarbone. "Don't make me move for a while, okay?" Gentle hands spoke in whispers of their own, all up and down the Fae's back. *No one's ever made me feel like this before. Never in my life.*

"Take your time, I could use a minute myself—"

<Take his mind. Now. I will help you.>

Fiachra froze. The voice was clearer, stronger than he'd ever heard it. *What do you mean?*

The voice's laughter was his own. Yet it wasn't. The sound creeped Fiachra the fuck out. <He must take you the same way you took him. Then the SoulShare will be complete. And you can safely bring me back to Purgatory, and the nexus, and the Pattern.>

Fiachra could feel the ancient Loremaster's eagerness as if it were his own. Which it most definitely wasn't. Not for the things Brodulein wanted, anyway.

<You have scruples? Here, let me do what needs to be done.>

"What did you say?"

Fiachra didn't realize until Peri spoke that he was whispering. He didn't recognize the words, other than to know the sounds were from an older version of the Fae language than any he knew. And he could feel Brodulein drawing on his inner magick, preparing a channeling. A Loremaster-class channeling.

141

He's going to force Peri's mind.
Fuck no.

"I'm out."

Fiachra didn't look at Peri as he dressed. He didn't dare. Eye contact was an essential part of any mind-control channeling. But he didn't need to look. He could hear the faint hitches in the human's rapid breathing. He could smell the salt of tears.

I can't explain. There's no way. But I can't let Brodulein have him.

Fiachra stepped into his shoes. "Close your eyes."

"What the fuck?" Peri's voice was tightly controlled, but a truthseer knew the truth of every spoken word.

Anger. Heartbreak. A lowering darkness.

"Just do it. Please."

Silence.

Fiachra turned, not daring to breathe. Peri lay back on the massage table, his legs dangling over the end. One hand covered his softened cock; the other covered his eyes. Not well enough to hide the tracks of tears, though.

He'd curse later, when he was alone with the *bodlag* in his head. For now, he bent and kissed Peri's perfect mouth. Stole a kiss, really. He knew better than to think the human was in any mood to give him one.

"This isn't over. I promise. I'll be back when I can."

"*Anata o fakku.*"

Quietly, Fiachra let himself out of the massage room and hurried out into the humid August night.

'Fuck you' in Japanese was a fitting shot across Brodulein's bow.

Chapter Seventeen

Bored with me already, your ladyship?

The female sniffed audibly. An odd sensation for each member of the troika, being able to hear one another, see one another, instead of outmaneuvering one another to gain access to the single vantage point in their shared sensorium. *I would not say 'bored', no.*

Let me know if things start getting tedious for you. I'm sure I can think of something to do. The male grinned and glanced pointedly down at the dirty, long-nailed hand fondling a hard-on the length and thickness of his forearm.

The female was decidedly unimpressed. *Are you that eager to follow our meat wagon's instructions?*

What?—oh. The male snorted with laughter as he got the joke. "Go fuck yourself." It wasn't a bad impression of Meat, really, all one had to do was pretend one's tongue and lips were slabs of decaying liver. *I think I'll pass, actually. I saw you threaten Kevin Almstead with that lovely vagina dentata of yours.*

The female smiled, preening slightly at the compliment. *Of all the imaginings of the Fae, I think I like that one best.*

A soft cold clacking sound from a dark corner of their crystal-bound awareness reminded them all of the ultimate cruelty of Fae imagination. The *Marfach* had been bodiless at the time of the Sundering, impossible to kill and free to inhabit any creature imbued with magick. And after its banishment, for as long as it lived in the ley lines, the Pattern had been its dark impassable window, all the Realm represented in its intricacies, all visible to it. It had heard the stories Fae told of their supposedly vanquished foe, and had heard the stories grow to legends and the legends to myths. Some of the myths it liked, and took for its own. The slender cold lethal female. The filthy dreadlocked priapic male. And the abomination, pale chitin, razor teeth, startlingly beautiful opal eyes, its whip like tail formed of tiny iterations of itself, each imbued with the gnawing hunger of the whole. The *Marfach* needed to be none of these, but it took great pleasure in seeing itself as each. Becoming each, if only in its own mind. It was freedom, of a sort.

After a year and a half trapped in living Stone encased in the rotting body of an extremely unlucky petty criminal, though, it was no longer accustomed to being all three entities at the same time. However, it had little choice in the matter. Since Lochlann Doran's blood-blade had all but severed its connection with its meat wagon, it took all three of its personalities to control its increasingly putrid host.

Your thoughts are evident. The female's voice was like cold liquid metal. It made the male horny. Which was news to no one, really. *Something must be done about poor Meat.*

I'm guessing you don't mean find him a nice

144

girlfriend or boyfriend and set them up in a little house in the suburbs. Of the three of them, the male had embraced the language and idiom of the human world with the most enthusiasm.

His usefulness is nearly at an end. The magick he received from the Fae is all but depleted. The female's lip curled in a delicate sneer. *We need to...*

Trade in our ride? The male's laugh would have waked the dead. Janek just kept snoring. ***You're right, your ladyship. The only thing that keeps Meat, here, going is his delusion that we'll give him Guaire to play with someday. And even that isn't going to be enough for much longer.***

The female nodded slowly. *We need a new host. However, the accident that created our home of living Stone is unlikely to be repeated.*

Accident, my ass. The male scratched the referenced portion of his anatomy, vigorously and with a great deal of evident pleasure, before resuming his stroking. ***Guaire killed Meat. Mostly. And that isn't going to happen again—you can't kill what's already dead.***

Poor Meat. The female laughed, a sound like icicles shattering. *Where shall we get a fresher body? From the new Fae?*

Not fucking likely. The male dug through his matted dreadlocks with two fingers until he found one of the tiny scorpions nesting there, then cracked its chitin between his fingers and flicked it away. ***Meat would need luck and a five-minute head start to be able to catch a paraplegic with one crutch. And the new Fae is a fucking Loremaster besides.*** Seeing Brodulein—one of the Fae who had assembled the final watery trap for the bodiless *Marfach*, and thus directly assisted in its banishment at the Sundering—walking down the street in Washington, D.C. had been a major kick in the balls.

If we could only channel the magick trapped in this wretched Stone, we could subdue any Loremaster without need of Meat's pathetic assistance. And Conall Dary would be nothing but a memory of blood-soaked earth. The female smiled, flashing just a hint of serrated fangs.

I love it when you talk dirty. But you know as well as I do that no Loremaster could have come through the Pattern. They're all inside it. The male stroked his erection almost absently, playing with a fingertip in the sticky trickle flowing from the tip. ***Which means Brodulein Mare-fucker had to have come*** out ***of it somehow.***

The female's smile widened; the tip of her tongue flicked over the points of her fangs. *Do you think the Pattern is unraveling, then?*

It's a possibility. The male went from grinning to frowning. ***But before we can get at it, we have to get through the ward Dary put up.***

The female turned even paler than she had been, which took work. *That level of pain...is not survivable.*

The male nodded, grimacing, his fondling hand stilled for once. ***I'll give up my third share of the Realm's magick to whoever will hold Dary down for me so I can fuck him till he bleeds out through his asshole***.

YOU ARE BOTH FOOLS.

The clacking hiss shaped itself into words, a sound mortals described as the grating of burning bones, or compound fractures dragged across broken stones. Even the male and the female fell silent as the monstrosity dragged itself into what passed for light in their crystal prison.

It looked from one to the other, its opal gaze fouling what it touched. *I FEED ON PAIN. YOURS WILL FEED ME AS WELL AS ANY OTHER.* Hand-sized scorpions dropped from the creature's tail to skitter around the floor. *WE WILL FORCE THE DEAD THING THROUGH THE WARD. HIS PAIN... AND YOURS... WILL BE HORRIFIC.*

More clattering, a sound that might have been laughter.

DELICIOUS. AND I WILL BECOME STRONG. STRONG ENOUGH TO SHATTER THE WARD AND DRIVE THE DEAD THING TO THE NEXUS. EVEN IF IT IS DEAD IN TRUTH BY THEN. A second set of jaws darted out of its mouth and devoured a scorpion. *NOTHING WILL STAND BETWEEN US AND THE REALM.*

The male and the female looked at one another, avoiding the abomination's hot gaze, uncertain in a way they had never been.

TRUST ME WITH YOUR AGONY. AND WE SHALL ALL FEAST.

Chapter Eighteen

August 12, 2013
1:57 a.m.
Greenwich Village, New York City

Fiachra's feet dragged as he climbed the cement stairs leading to the door of the brownstone. He'd been wandering around Greenwich Village for hours. With all the shit going on, he should have been planning, and he knew it. But mostly he'd been trying to forget what had happened at Big Boy Massage.

No. Not quite true. Yes, he'd been visiting his old New York haunts. Including the old oak up in Central Park, to stare at the glistening lethal soap bubble Conall had built around it—lethal to the *Marfach*, anyway—and at the magick welling up from the earth, already creating a tiny sliver of the Realm. And he'd been reminding himself that he *ought* to try to forget about Big Boy, *scair'ain'e*, Peri. That was the best way, maybe the only way, to keep Peri safe from both Brodulein's designs and the *Marfach*.

For his part, walking around with an unfinished SoulShare made him feel like an amputee. But if that was the price of Peri's safety, he'd pay it.

He looked up at the door, with its pebbled-glass front, its carved wood frame and wrought-iron street number. There were Fae on the other side of it, and a whole shitload of problems. And he didn't want to deal with any of them. He wanted to go back to D.C., and find Peri, and try to make right what he'd made so horribly wrong.

Instead, he glanced around to be sure no one was looking and Faded up to the third-floor studio Rian and Cuinn called home.

He was the last one to the party, as he'd suspected he would be. The Royal couple stood in the apartment's kitchenette, Cuinn looking over Rian's shoulder as the Prince measured coffee into a contraption that would have looked at home on a spaceship. Conall was looking out the window, down into the Village. And Lochlann was staring right at Fiachra as he took form, dark brows knit together in concentration.

Fiachra glared back. Something about the Fae healer had irritated him from their first meeting, and he thought he'd figured it out. Lochlann's hair was as dark as his own had once been. Darker, even. But his skin was fair and his eyes were a precious shade of aquamarine. Lochlann, he was sure, had never been called out as a tree-spawn. Never heard his sister publicly mocked by a lover for having sap between her thighs. Lochlann's darkness was just fine with everyone. While he'd had to run away from his own.

No. He hadn't had to run. But he'd done it.

Now… he wanted his darkness back.

Lochlann shook his head. "Damn. I still can't get a solid read on your aura, Detective. But you definitely have two. Though the one tied to your physical body is actually fainter than the other."

Everyone was looking at him now. Fiachra shrugged. "Probably because we're so far from Purgatory. It's a different story back in D.C., I suspect. Brodulein was getting ready to do a channeling a few hours ago in the massage parlor."

"He was what?"

"Son of a *bitch*—"

"What in the second circle of Dante Alighieri's Hell do you mean, 'a few hours ago in the massage parlor'?" Conall's tone was clipped, his green eyes gleaming dangerously. The twink was suddenly every inch the master mage.

"Which circle of Hell was that?" The voice was Rian's, but the drawl was all Cuinn. "You're being awfully erudite tonight, Twinklebritches."

A muscle twitched in Conall's jaw. "Don't call me that again until you can do it with your own voice. And it's the circle of Lust. Seemed fitting." The mage's peridot gaze had never really left Fiachra. He got the impression Conall would be very happy to nail him to the wall with it. And probably could. "Unless you have another candidate for favorite sin."

"No, lust works as well as anything." Fiachra was vaguely familiar with the work of human literature Conall was referring to, but 17 years was nowhere near long enough for him to have read the entire body of human fiction, even if he'd seen a point to the exercise. "I'm not sure what it's supposed to feel like when you find your SoulShare, but I think I've found mine."

"*Magarl lobadh*," Lochlann muttered. "It's Peri, right?"

150

Fiachra stiffened. *Fuck off,* he wanted to say. He was having a hard enough time working through feelings impossible for a Fae, toward someone no Fae would ever admit to having any feelings for. Asking him to proclaim said potential feelings to every Fae within earshot was just too damned much.

But if something wasn't done about Brodulein, he didn't dare get close to Peri again. And he sure as hell wasn't in any position to do anything about Brodulein on his own. Never mind the *Marfach*. "Yes. It's Peri. But I walked out on him. Brodulein is pushing me to finish the SoulShare, and I'm sure he has his own reasons for it."

"Brodulein, or the Pattern?" Conall frowned. "Not that there's necessarily any difference between the two, for this purpose."

"Cuinn, God damn it, slow down. I can't keep up!"

Startled, Fiachra—along with everyone else— turned to Rian, and to Cuinn behind him. Cuinn looked ready to stroke out; Rian was nodding, hands on Cuinn's shoulders, obviously trying to calm him down. But the flames flickering up and down the Prince's hands and arms didn't look calming.

Cuinn closed his eyes and drew a deep breath. Rian did the same. Another, in perfect unison. Both sighed. "Cuinn says, 'I'm fucking sick of the Pattern dicking with SoulShares.'" Rian looked down at his hand, as Cuinn clasped it, white-knuckled. "We were working blind, we didn't know then what we created. But they know now, or they fucking well ought to."

Fiachra couldn't help arching a brow. "Wait a minute. You're telling me you're upset because

Brodulein, or the whole Pattern, is trying to fuck me and Peri over?"

"This is an issue why?" Rian was the one who spoke, but Cuinn was the one who smirked.

Fiachra shrugged. "Altruism is a word I never heard until I came to the human world. And I never thought I'd hear the notion coming from a Fae."

"It isn't altruism." Conall gestured at Cuinn and Rian, an 'I've-got-this' wave of the hand. "Not when they could still be fucking with any of us. The Loremasters originally wanted us to think the SoulShare process was completely random—no way to know where a Fae would end up, or who his soul would end up being incarnated in. They even lied to Cuinn about that."

Cuinn nodded grimly, his expression suggesting that if he were capable of speech, he would have a few choice words on the subject. And Rian's smile as he overheard what was going through his consort's mind had no good humor in it at all that Fiachra could see.

Conall cleared his throat. "They can control some elements of what happens. Not all. And for every aspect of a transition they control, something else gets FUBAR." The slender mage wrapped his arms around himself, as if he felt cold despite the heat of the summer night. "They wanted me to hook up with Josh immediately, and they managed it—I literally landed right at his feet—but in exchange for that kind of precision in the delivery, they lost control over what happened to my ability to channel magick, and it ended up in Josh, who couldn't use it."

"So you think there's something deliberate about the pairing of me and Peri." It wasn't a question.

Lochlann laughed, with the same kind of not-humor Rian was still exhibiting. "We'd be surprised as hell if there wasn't. Thanks to you and Lasair, we know there's magick bleeding through from the Realm into the human world. Which is probably related to the somewhat unsubtle way we rammed a conduit for the ley energy through the nexus and the Pattern. And for all we know, the Loremasters have a plan to fix the Pattern from this side. Whatever their idea of fixing it is. Hence you arriving in a Loremaster's body, with a SoulShare who happens to hang out a lot at Purgatory and just started working upstairs from it."

Conall appeared to have gotten over his momentary chill. "And let's not forget your unusual degree of devotion to a job that would eventually get you into Purgatory even if you didn't Share with Peri. Although that notion is so dangerous my blood pressure threatens to spray out my ears just thinking about it."

"What I do and how I do it is my choice. Not theirs."

From the way heads shook all around the room, Fiachra guessed he was in a minority of one when it came to that particular belief. Cuinn and Rian exchanged glances, and Rian's voice answered. "Again, we don't know for sure how far their reach extends, when it comes to a Fae or human SoulShare. But if they could give Lochlann's human SoulShare drug-impervious AIDS, I'm pretty sure they could fuck with your head and turn you into a conscientious ask-no-questions cop."

Breech-birth of a septic feral sow.

Fiachra had seen a cartoon once, on a lazy

Saturday morning many years ago, starring a coyote with what looked like OCD and a bird whose attitude was pure smart-assed Fae. Every few minutes, it seemed, the coyote would run, or drive, or be pushed off a cliff. And for a while he'd hang in mid-air, defying gravity. Until he looked down.

Fiachra had just looked down.

Seventeen years, he'd been played. By beings who had been playing their game for thousands of years.

"Why are you telling me all this?"

Rian answered him. "Because like it or no, you're one of us now." Every inch of him, and every word, proclaimed the young male Prince Royal. "Part of the Demesne of Purgatory."

"*Sasann muid le chéle*," Lochlann added. *We stand together.*

Allies. As strange a concept as that was for a Fae.

The Prince wasn't finished. "And we need your aid. To put a stop to whatever it is the Loremasters have sent one of their own here to accomplish."

"If you want my help, then give me yours." It was almost time for him to check in with Harding—not out of any sense of duty, not any more, but to make sure the son of a bitch didn't have any plans that might get him killed. Fiachra started to Fade, leaving his last words hanging in the air.

"Help me get my true self back from the bastards in the Pattern."

If he was going to fall, he was fucking well going to fall as himself.

Chapter Nineteen

Washington, D.C.
August 12, 2013
3:25 a.m.

Peri leaned against the tiled wall of the shower and fumbled with the shower valve, wincing as the cold spray hit him and turning the valve as far left as it would go. Even when it warmed up all the way, the water in his apartment was barely tepid, which was a pity.

Hauling himself upright, he filled his palms with coconut-scented soap and started to gently clean his shoulders and upper arms. The bruises were nothing to worry about, they'd fade, but he'd need to be careful with the bites. And no strapless gowns for Falcon for a while.

He laughed, surprised by how normal he sounded. He'd show his marks off with pride tomorrow night. Tonight. Whatever. And then, with any luck, they wouldn't matter any more.

Once he'd taken care of the ragged marks on his shoulders, he grabbed the shampoo and lathered his hair. He hissed, as much in startlement as in pain, as he ran his palm over the back of his head. Probing the lump with his fingertips made him queasy; he backed into the stream of water from overhead, and stared at the red swirling around his feet.

Lochlann's going to be pissed. The boss was fine if any of his boys wanted to cater to a rougher trade, but it had to be consensual. He'd been adamant, when he'd hired Peri: he wouldn't let Big Boy get a reputation as the kind of place where a client could get his rocks off with violence.

"Because then I'd have to deal with them, and I hate the paperwork when I kill a client," Lochlann had explained. Peri was sure he'd been kidding.

Pretty sure.

Yeah, he should have put a stop to it when his last customer decided to "take the fight out of" him by throwing him against the wall. He could have.

But he hadn't wanted to. He'd needed it. Or so he'd thought.

What the hell is going on with me? He splayed out a hand on the pristine white wall to steady himself, just in case that jelly-kneed feeling came back unexpectedly. *I'm not a pain slut.*

No. He just had a good old-fashioned case of survivor guilt. Which he usually dealt with just fine, except when he didn't. But when he didn't, when he couldn't deal, he didn't ask a client to rough him up, he went out and made yet another sad half-assed attempt to write the ending to his story that it should have had five years ago. Then he cried, and slept not quite like the dead, and woke up and got his ass back to work.

What had changed?

That was easy. Fiachra.

The water was pink now, rather than red. Peri supposed that was better.

The big blond cop was every fantasy he'd ever had, only six inches taller and maybe one or two longer. With eyes like nothing he'd ever seen before and hands so gentle they made him want to melt like a cat in a sunbeam.

So naturally, he walks into my life and I go completely off the deep end. Makes total sense.

Actually, it did, in a way. He sighed and started to rinse the shampoo out of his hair. He'd been living on borrowed time ever since that night outside the Guard House. Corny as hell, but 100 percent true. He'd been living in time his best friend was never going to have. Yukio was never going to be kissed like magic by a prince straight out of the *yaoi* manga they'd whispered over together as kids. He wouldn't have a fantasy protector.

Yukio had had a real one. But the real one let him down.

That was the problem. Fiachra reminded Peri of everything he didn't deserve, and everything he'd failed at. All wrapped up in one impossibly gorgeous package. So to speak.

Oh, and the cop had also pulled out, zipped up, and left Peri lying in the wet spot. Hadn't even been able to bring himself to look Peri in the eyes when he kissed him good-bye.

Why did he even bother to kiss me?

He hated how gullible he'd been. He hated the way he'd let himself be suckered. *"I only want you to trust me."* Fuck that.

157

Most of all, he hated that he could still taste that last kiss.

Peri twisted the valve with one hand to shut off the water, and yanked down the towel he'd draped over the door to the shower stall with the other. He padded out of the bathroom, leaving a trail of wet footprints past the clothes he'd discarded on his way to the shower, toweling his hair dry as he walked. His breath hissed through clenched teeth as the rough towel rasped over whatever he had going on on the back of his head.

Maybe I shouldn't be sleeping. He'd read somewhere that sleeping with a concussion was a bad idea.

Fuck that too. He tossed the towel aside as he gracelessly face-planted into the mattress. He'd sleep. And if he woke up, then he'd start making plans.

Chapter Twenty

"Sorry to have kept you waiting." Harding lowered himself into the chair behind his desk with the sigh of a male grateful to be in familiar surroundings. "A couple of local boys dealing heroin over on Fulton Street ran for it when the uniforms showed up and decided to try for fucking political asylum at the Azerbaijani Embassy." The senior detective started leaning back in his chair, slowly and carefully, as if he expected the ancient contraption to dump him on his ass on the floor. "I thought I was never going to get out of there."

Harding's office—the entire building—could not have contained all the fucks Fiachra did not give about his boss' comfort level. "Kind of the same way I felt here." He carefully avoided looking at the clock on the wall. Two and a half hours he'd sat here, fighting every minute not to storm out and Fade back to Big Boy. Or as close as he could get to the apartment address Lochlann had texted him. Even though there was no way to explain things to Peri, and no reason for Peri to listen if he tried.

Harding put up a slow brow. Fiachra could see where he might be intimidated if he were human;

despite the detective's dimples and easy smile, he was capable of going from zero to don't-fuck-with-me in about a second and a half. "Did you have someplace else you needed to be, Darkwood?"

Fiachra, of course, was not human. And he finally understood how the Loremasters had harped the tune for his own personal *rinc'lú*, his little dance, for 17 years. They had made a fool of him for that long. But he danced for no human. Not that way. Never again.

Still, Purgatory was a Fae place as well as a den of sweetest iniquity, and Harding and Vice had to be kept out. And he was the only Fae in a position to take care of that particular piece of business. So it was probably best if he tried to be civil. "Home in bed might have been nice, given that it's my night off and it's nearly sunrise."

"Yes. Your night off." Harding reached into a desk drawer and pulled out a creased manila folder stuffed with what Fiachra recognized as surveillance logs, receipts, newspaper clippings. It was Harding's Purgatory file, and where any rational detective in this day and age would keep the whole thing on a computer, probably on his phone, Harding apparently needed to be able to run his hands over it every once in a while.

He dropped the folder on the desk, then fixed Fiachra with a level stare. "There's a conspicuous lack of anything with your name on it in here. Despite the fact that I sent you out of here after your Friday night shift with instructions to start scoping the place out."

Fiachra entertained a brief fantasy that involved telling Harding precisely how much water his 'instructions' carried. "I haven't—"

Harding held up a hand. "If you're going to tell me you haven't been back there, let me save you a little trouble. You're aware there's an ATM across the street from the tattoo parlor?"

"Yes…"

"It has a security camera." Fortunately for Harding's continued longevity, he didn't look smug. "You went into Purgatory early Saturday evening, and you must have come out behind someone even taller than you are, though I'm not sure that's even possible." The sandy-haired detective's smile was mostly free of anything resembling good cheer. "Then you went back to the club on Sunday early in the afternoon, and visited Big Boy Massage again around 8:30."

"And who went through all that footage, to be learning all that?" Fiachra thought he could feel Brodulein trying to set up a channeling. He couldn't tell exactly what the Loremaster had in mind, but he couldn't imagine it being anything he'd have a problem with. The motherfucking *nascód ar más'cranách*, boil on a sow's ass, was *spying* on him.

"Calm down, Darkwood."

"I am calm."

"If you say so." Harding shrugged. "There was a break-in on Saturday night at the check-cashing place two storefronts down from the ATM. They didn't discover it until Sunday night when they were locking up, and I was the only one free to review the security cam footage. And you're hard to miss."

Fiachra's truthsight saved Harding from having to reach down his own throat to recover his nose. "All right. I was there. What's the issue?"

161

Harding tapped the folder with two fingers. "The *issue* is that there's nothing in here. You've been in Purgatory twice in the last two days, and didn't get thrown out either time. You've been in there longer than any other undercover officer has ever managed." He leaned forward, resting his elbows on the desk to either side of the folder. "I need what you know, Darkwood."

"And you'll get it. When I write up my report." Fiachra tried to shrug, but his shoulders were too stiff.

"Your report's late."

Fiachra kneaded the bridge of his nose. Not to fight off a headache, though that was rapidly becoming an issue, but as an outward sign of his effort to stop the rush of magick to the spot just between and over his brows. As a Fae of the Demesne of Air, his own magick was channeled through his voice, his breath; this tingle was something different. The gift he'd used in so many interrogations over the years wasn't his gift at all, it was Brodulein's. And it would probably be better not to let the Loremaster do anything to Harding that he, Fiachra, wasn't sure how to undo. For now. "Things came up."

"Was that the reason for your return trip to Big Boy?"

Slowly, Fiachra lowered his hand, not clenching it into a fist until it was out of Harding's sight. "I beg your pardon?"

"I suppose I could have phrased that better." Harding didn't sound apologetic. Not at all. "But if you're compromising our investigation of Purgatory over a prostitute, I don't need to tell you there will be consequences."

162

You bet your pert ass I'm compromising our investigation. Still, appearances had to be maintained. For a while. "I trust this isn't some half-assed way of calling my professionalism into question." The *Faen* word for "diplomat" came from an ancient root, and literally translated as "the one leaving the fewest bodies on the floor." Fiachra was slightly surprised he was capable of diplomacy at the moment.

"Kindly demonstrate your professionalism and file your report."

"You will have my report when I am entirely fucking ready to give it to you."

Finally, a few beads of sweat appeared on Harding's forehead. "By tomorrow night, Darkwood. And I trust I'm not going to be treated to a chronicle of your personal life in lieu of a surveillance report."

Fiachra pushed back his chair and unfolded himself to his full height, glaring down at Harding. "You are the last person in the world to whom I would submit a report on any aspect of my personal life. *Sir.*" The last word had edges even a human ought to have been able to sense, and hung in the air as he stalked out of Harding's cubbyhole of an office.

There was no way in any human hell Fiachra was going to let Brodulein make the senior detective forget a single word he'd just said. There was no point to making someone pay for words he didn't remember uttering.

Chapter Twenty-One

Peri stared at the brimming shot glass on the bar in front of him. His third. He thought. Might be his fourth. Really, he shouldn't be doing it this way. Big fruity drinks would get him the kind of attention he was fishing for, in a place like Bobwire. Nobody noticed shots of Southern Comfort. But the bartender had just rolled his eyes when he'd asked for a mojito. And besides, he didn't want to wait that long to get shit-faced.

At least he'd picked the right place this time. He was sure of that. His encounter with Officer Tall-Blond-and-Studly had prompted him to check the online police reports, something he hadn't thought to try before. And this place would have gotten a gold star if D.C.'s finest gave gold stars to establishments Most Likely to Require Riot Gear for Pacification. But really, the thrash metal forcing its way out of inadequate speakers and twisting his guts was all the confirmation he needed. Sooner or later, someone in here was going to kill somebody.

He just had to make sure it happened tonight. And that the somebody was him.

Peri picked up the shot, and glanced from side to

side. No one to toast at the moment. So he raised his glass to his own reflection, in the mirror behind the bar. His bruises had purpled up nicely, and the bite marks on his shoulders were appropriately ghastly. But damn, he was still pretty. He'd been mistaken for a girl twice already tonight, but not by anyone drunk enough to take offense upon discovering his error.

Soon.

He slammed down the shot and set the glass back down on the bar, fighting a wave of dizziness. *Already? Son of a bitch.* He never had a problem holding his liquor, despite being short and slender. But he was having trouble focusing, and he suspected that if he let go of the bar, he just might find himself on the floor.

Bathroom might be a good idea...

Making his way through the crowded bar and into the men's room was a challenge, given the unpredictable way the floor kept tilting and the industrial-gray walls kept changing configuration. But getting up and moving seemed to help; by the time he made it to the men's room, he didn't feel nearly so ready to drive the porcelain bus. He did, however, need to piss like a fire hose. And having a bit of a lean with one arm against the wall over the urinal while he yanked down his running shorts struck him as an excellent idea.

Once he'd emptied himself enough that he could notice things other than his own discomfort, he became aware of laughter. Right next to him.

"Dude, you are seriously fucked up."

Still leaning on his forearm, Peri turned his head just enough to see watery blue eyes, a nose that had been broken at least once, a slack-jawed grin, closely-shorn brown hair receding in front, and a head that somehow went straight to torso with nothing like a neck in between.

"*Seriously* fucked up." The guy shook off, laughing.

Might as well get started. Though the thought made him feel queasy all over again. He stared at Buzzcut's junk, just long enough to make it perfectly obvious that that was what he was doing, then let his slightly unfocused gaze travel up to the man's rapidly reddening face.

"Not yet." He forced a smirk. "But was that an offer?"

"You little *shit*—"

Peri didn't stick around for the rest of the barrage of profanity that followed, just hauled his shorts up and bolted, diving back into the crowd like a cliff diver hitting the water.

Buzzcut wasn't enough, couldn't give him what he was looking for.

Hopefully, Buzzcut had friends.

***

"It's his night off. So fuck off."

Fiachra stared at the lean hard-muscled African-American masseur. He remembered the male's easy smile from his first visit to Big Boy, but that smile was nowhere in evidence at the moment. In fact, with his furrowed brow and crossed arms, he looked ready to put Fiachra's head through a wall.

And if he could be sure Peri would be on the

other side of that wall, Fiachra would be inclined to let him. Trouble was, Fiachra's truthsight left no room to doubt the male's declaration. Which meant he had no way to dispel the sense of dread wrapping around him like... well, like a body bag.

"If he comes in, tell him I'm looking for him."

"He don't need no cops on his ass. Get out."

For an instant, Fiachra was tempted to change the male's mind in a very permanent way. But that risked waking up Brodulein, and he wasn't going to do that. Not this close to the nexus, and not when there was a chance the Loremaster or his motherfornicating friends in the Pattern could yank the chains of human SoulShares at a distance... *they could give Lochlann's human SoulShare drug-impervious AIDS...* He could wait for his own vengeance for what the Loremasters had done to him, fucking with his head. But if anything happened to Peri, and they were responsible...

The doorframe rattled as Fiachra slammed the door to Big Boy Massage behind himself. No one seemed to notice; all the passers-by appeared to be intent on the open, beckoning doors at the top of the stairs to Purgatory. Or on the window display at Raging Art-On. On anything, really, but a disturbance at the massage parlor.

Now what? Peri might be down in Purgatory, but going down there after him also risked waking Brodulein—it was sheer luck that his other forays hadn't done so, and Fiachra didn't feel like tempting fate just now.

Wait. Wait just a damned minute.

Just past the cheery, well-lit display window of

167

Raging Art-On, a recessed entryway opened onto the tattoo parlor's entrance, the door to a shop front under construction, and a locked and magickally warded door. Warded, but for announcement, not to disable or kill—those particular wards were around the building as a whole, and weren't meant for him—so Fiachra had no qualms about Fading to the far side of the door and taking the stairs two at a time.

There were two doors opening off the landing at the top of the stairs. Fiachra raised a fist to hammer on the one to his right—

—and found himself frozen, unable to so much as blink.

Should have expected that—

The door swung open. Conall glared up at him, and if Fiachra could have stepped back a pace to avoid the fury in the mage's green-fire gaze, he would have. "What part of 'get your ass away from here' escaped your comprehension?"

Ordinarily, an Air Fae would consider that an insult requiring the letting of blood. Fiachra was willing to settle for considerably less, and waited impatiently for his lungs to start working. Conall cocked a brow and crooked a finger, apparently noting his predicament, and sweet air rushed in.

"Wasn't there a 'preternaturally well-rounded' prefixing your original description?" Fiachra croaked.

Conall's eyes rolled. "Get in here where I can at least ward you properly."

Fiachra obeyed, but he didn't wait for the mage to finish the new inner ward before clearing his throat. "I need your help. Right now." His voice was tight—not surprising, given the way his jaw tried to clench around the words. *Never admit to another Fae that he has something you need. As well put the noose around your neck and hand him the rope.*

Fuck that noise.

"It's Peri, isn't it?"

Fiachra blinked, as much at the gentleness of the voice as the astuteness of the question. "Are you a mind-reader?"

"No. But you just rolled over and showed me your throat." Conall shook his head wonderingly. "The only thing that will make a Fae that crazy is his SoulShare."

No point in arguing, then. "Something's wrong with him, he's in trouble. I've felt something going on since I met him, but it's worse now. Much worse." There wasn't much room for a male Fiachra's size to pace in Conall and Josh's small apartment, but he made the best use he could of the space. "I suspect the Pattern's fucking with him. And I don't know where he is."

"You want me to do a Finding?"

"If you can."

"Oh, I can. A couple of different ways." Conall frowned, his intense expression at odds with his tousled hair, tight shorts, and sleeveless Washington Mystics T-shirt. "Do you have anything of Peri's? It doesn't have to belong to him—something he's touched would probably be enough."

"He's touched me." *I can still blush. Who knew?*

Conall didn't look much more comfortable than Fiachra felt. "It would be nice if that worked, but unfortunately it doesn't." He cleared his throat. "Well, that was the easy way."

169

"Then let's do it the hard way."

Conall laughed. He didn't sound amused. "This channeling is Loremaster-caliber shit. Cuinn taught it to me after he had to use it to bring Lochlann and Garrett back from the dead. He figured it would be better if more than one of us knew how to do it."

"You are bullshitting me."

"I bullshit you not, truthseer." Absently, Conall chafed his right wrist with his left hand. "I've never done it, I'm not sure I can, and I'm going to have to literally be inside your head to even attempt it."

Fiachra took an involuntary step back. "How do you propose to do that?"

"Considering I can't actually read your mind, I'm going to do the next best thing. I'm going to Fade my physicality, share your body, ride your feelings for Peri, and try to figure out where he is once I get there."

It's going to get fucking crowded with three of us in here. And there were at least a dozen other good reasons not to do this. But the terror he'd felt upon awakening at sunset, the cold sweat, and the grim certainty that Peri needed him left all other considerations in the dust. "Do it. Before I realize how little I want a strange Fae leaving his grubby fingerprints all over emotions I'm not supposed to be able to have."

"Believe me, fingerprints are nowhere in my plans." Fiachra wasn't sure, but he thought he saw Conall shudder. "I don't normally do this with anyone other than my *scair-anam.*"

"Do I need to do anything?" Fiachra wiped suddenly sweaty palms on his jeans.

"Just hold very still. And when I tell you to do something, do it."

170

"But how—"

Color and substance drained from Conall's form before Fiachra could finish his question, leaving the blond Fae with nothing to do but try not to move and wonder what the hell he was supposed to be waiting for.

Think of Peri.

The voice sounded like his own. Almost.

Feel. The voice was strained, tight. *I need the connection. Your connection.*

For the space of a heartbeat, Fiachra resisted. Turning his emotions over to the mage, giving them over to be the substrate of a channeling, felt... final. Irrevocable.

And it felt like a violation. Maybe he didn't understand his feelings for the stunning blond human. No 'maybe' about it, actually. But the feelings were *his*. If anyone was entitled to share in them, it was Peri. Not Conall.

But if he didn't allow the violation, he was never going to have a chance to try to make his case with Peri. Because Peri was going to die. He was sure of that.

So he closed his eyes, and he remembered. The way his heart had raced when he first saw Peri, in the lobby at Big Boy Massage. How he'd struggled to calm his breathing, keep his voice even, as he disappeared into the tiny massage room that first time. A light, quicksilver tingle of joy, following the touch of Peri's hands, first hint of the supernatural at work. The taste of a first kiss—

Holy. Fucking. Shit.

The cool precision of Conall's voice might have been funny, if Fiachra hadn't also been able to sense the mage's wide-eyed alarm. "What is it? Where is he?"

171

No place I'm ever likely to go, that's for damned sure. He could almost feel Conall's gaze darting from side to side. *Maybe you know it, I'm sure it gets more than its share of police attention.*

"Where?" Fiachra gritted his teeth to keep from shouting. It didn't work well.

It's a bar. Looks like concrete walls, industrial paint job. Music that tries to punch you in the kidneys, I can't hear it but I can feel it. Not nearly enough light for humans.

"Could be a couple of places I can think of." Fiachra frowned. "Low ceiling or high?"

Low. There's a big Confederate flag hanging on one wall, sagging. Naked blonde blowup doll hanging over the bar.

Fiachra knew the place. Bobwire. He'd been there last week, ruining a meth dealer's night in the men's room. What the festering fuck was Peri doing there?

Three—no, four—pool tables in back... Conall's voice trailed off to silence.

"What is it?" Fiachra wasn't sure he was going to be able to hear the answer over the pounding of his heart.

Peri's being held down on one of them. And a couple of skinheads just broke a pool cue in half.

"*Tá'siad marh.*" Dead they certainly were. They just didn't know it yet.

Shit, let me get out of you before you start Fading—

As the apartment vanished, Fiachra hoped the mage had made it out.

Dealing with the inconvenient human witnesses was going to be hard enough without an irritated passenger getting in his way.

172

Chapter Twenty-Two

Peri stared up at the ceiling, at the filthy wide-bladed fan that wouldn't stay in focus no matter how hard he tried. Watched it go around. Around. He heard yelling. Shouts of encouragement, mostly. The skinhead hunk who'd gotten hard when Peri tripped and fell against him was screaming at the two who were trying to break a pool cue. Trying to make them hurry. Because he needed something to sodomize the sick fuck on the pool table.

Which was him.

I wanted this.

He winced as his left arm was wrenched.

About fucking time.

His stomach didn't seem to realize he was being held down. It wanted to roll over. Or was that the table tilting? Only three drinks... four?

Sleepy. How could he be sleepy when the music was like a hammer and the lights were blades cutting into his eyes?

I don't know. Just want to sleep. Yukio would be there waiting for him, if he could only fall asleep. For real, this time.

I can tell him I'm sorry.

Will he forgive me?

A loud snap, like a bone. Cheers. Laughter.

The crack was like cold water dashed in Peri's face. Just for a second, anyway, as Hunky Skinhead loomed over him, clutching the jagged piece of wood.

I don't really want to die. Not like this. God, my head...

Hands yanked at his shorts.

Fiachra...

He wanted to apologize to the dead, sure. But he was going to have a chance to do that soon.

When it came to the living, he wasn't even going to get to say goodbye.

***

The stall in which Fiachra had cuffed his perp was empty. Probably because the toilet was plugged, overflowing, and foul. Not that he cared. He was reaching for the door almost before he had finished forming.

Strained to reach, unable to move.

Son of a bitch.

<I've been called worse.>

Not his own voice. Not Conall's. Which left one other possibility.

Fuck. Conall woke you up.

<You have no time to argue. And you have to trust me. Now.>

Don't make me laugh. Fiachra wasn't sure which was more overwhelming, the stench in the stall, the jet-engine roar of the music, or his own urge to throttle the motherfornicating Loremaster in his head.

<I wouldn't dream of it. Now shut up and listen.>

To his own astonishment, Fiachra did as he was told. Not that he had many other options.

174

<Good. You have time to stop those folathóin *or rescue your* scair-anam*, not both.>*

The voice was not what Fiachra had expected. Calm, decisive. *What do you propose?*

< I can handle them magickally while you rescue your Peri. It will be my pleasure. But you have to let go and trust me to do it.>

It seems to be my night for letting strange Fae take over my—

Even over the pounding music, Fiachra heard a scream. High, shrill, raw.

Let me go, damn you!

Fiachra slammed into the stall door, smashing it closed and then off its hinges. It didn't even slow him down. Neither did the four men between him and the men's room door.

<Just get him and run. I'll take care of the rest.>

***

Pain. Sweet Jesus God.

Peri didn't care any more about his throbbing head. Or how drunk he was. He wanted to die. But not like this. He fought, he twisted like some rabid animal. He'd felt the sharp wooden shard drive into the muscle of his ass, felt something break off. Jagged. Burning.

"Hold fucking still, you little faggot shit!" Someone punched him in the side of his head.

And all of a sudden everything felt underwater again. Far away. Almost peaceful. Better.

Was this how you felt, Yukio? Peri hoped it had been like this. Floating. Not the agony of nearly having a shattered pool cue rammed up his ass.

175

"Hold him, Kurt, goddamnit!" Hunky Skinhead was snarling at the guy holding Peri's left leg, angrily shaking the butt end of the pool cue, blood flying off the polished wood and splattering around. "I'm going to give the little shit what he wants."

No. Not like this.

Peri blinked. The hunk was rising up into the air. And his face was turning a dark, ugly shade of red.

"Peri!"

Not possible. He was dreaming. Or stone drunk. Fiachra couldn't be there. Couldn't be snarling at the men holding him. Like a wolf. Sexy as fuck. Gathering him up. *Yeah, this is a dream.*

"I've got you, *m'állacht.* Hold on. If you can.*"

Fiachra was cradling him. So good. Except he really needed to hurl.

Something shook the skinhead. Like a dog shaking a chew toy. The skinhead choked, gurgled. Struggled. Peri turned his head to watch as Fiachra carried him toward the door. He thought he heard a sound, over the music. A snap, but not like the pool cue. Wet. Muffled. Hunky Skinhead went limp. Fell to the floor, off to one side of the table, as if someone had tossed him there. Garbage.

"I would have let him suffer more," he heard Fiachra mutter as he kicked the door open. "But it wasn't bad for improv."

Fiachra started off running. Then skidded to a stop, which made Peri's stomach lurch. And shifted his grip, which drove the fucking splinter deeper into Peri's skin and muscle.

He didn't even notice he was crying until he felt Fiachra's shirt soaking up his tears.

"Look at me, *m'állacht.* Look at me."

Fiachra was bending over him, surrounding him somehow. Making him feel safe.

I'm not supposed to feel safe. Peri swallowed hard and turned away, burying his face in Fiachra's damp shirt.

"Fuck. I don't want to do this."

Before Peri could ask what Fiachra didn't want to do, the cop whispered something Peri didn't understand. And just like that, Peri looked up at him. Like he'd never wanted to turn away. Which he hadn't. Not really.

Fiachra's eyes were amazing. So beautiful. Like jewels.

I am so fucking drunk.

Fiachra was whispering more things Peri didn't understand. But he was pretty sure the blond god was swearing.

"What is it?" The words didn't come out right.

Fiachra didn't answer, just slid one hand up the back of Peri's head. And swore again as tears ran down Peri's cheeks.

"You're concussed." Fiachra almost spat the word. "I have to get you home."

"No." Peri tried to shake his head, but that hurt too much. "Just put me down." Cradled in Fiachra's arms like this, he wasn't quite sure he wanted to die. But he wasn't supposed to be warm and safe, either.

"Like hell." The words were harsh, but the kiss on his forehead wasn't. "Tell me where you live."

Again, Peri wasn't being given a choice. He was pretty sure he got his address out before his eyes closed and he checked out.

***

"I hope you did something to fuck with the heads of the witnesses." Fortunately, the address Peri had whispered before blacking out was only a little over four blocks from Bobwire, and even with a human in his arms, Fiachra could run faster than any human conveyance.

<I have had 17 years to learn how to manage a crime scene.> Brodulein's inner voice was dry. *<I daresay there will be no trouble from the humans. Especially the dead one.>*

A normal Fae would be bitching about Brodulein stealing his vengeance on the waste of organic molecules presently lying dead on the floor of the bar. Fiachra was no longer a normal Fae. There was no room in him for thoughts of his own vengeance. Not when he burned, he thirsted for Peri's. Yes, he understood why Brodulein had had to be the one to kill. But he had been far too quick. There was not enough capacity for pain in that human's body or soul to pay for what he had done to Peri.

<Your rage feeds your haste and spends magick like water.>

Fiachra almost failed to hear Brodulein's murmur. "Let it," he snarled.

<If you spend it all, you cannot heal him.>

Peri shifted in his arms, murmured wordlessly without opening his eyes. His soft blond hair tickled Fiachra's nose.

The Fae's jaw clenched tightly. He slowed. He breathed deep, trying to focus on the scent of Peri and ignore the blood scent. Forget what he'd seen on the pool table, center himself on the male in his arms.

And like cobwebs binding a gale, his *scair-anam*'s presence bound his anger in a fragile peace.

Damn Brodulein. Damn him twice, for being right.

He started to run again, this time at a normal, more nearly human pace.

"Almost there, *m'állacht*," he whispered into Peri's ear. "Stay with me."

<Is this the number? Your human's dwelling?>

Fiachra didn't want to look up. A Fae who failed to heal from an injury for as long as Peri had been wounded was dying; Fae healed swiftly from any wound not mortal. And 17 years as a homicide detective, learning all the ways humans could be made to die, had not turned Fiachra into an optimist. Looking up was too much like a farewell.

But he had to. "This is it." A weathered brick building, three cement steps leading up to a glass door veined with cracks. "How are you with locks?"

Fiachra thought he heard laughter. *<Allow me.>*

There was a loud click, and the door swung open. Peri lived on the second floor; Fiachra had to turn sideways to negotiate the dark, narrow stairwell with the human in his arms. A hallway at the top was lined with more doors; before he could open his mouth, every lock clicked.

<I have occasionally been called impatient.>

"You tempt me to like you." Fiachra stopped outside Peri's door. "One more time?"

The door opened; a soft magickal glow caught, kindled, brightened. Peri's apartment was small, and would probably have been as shabby as the building as a whole, if not for the human's eccentric—and baffling—decorating choices. The walls were covered with old movie posters and prints of antique Japanese art; the furniture was plain, but draped with fabrics as lavish as an Arabian Nights wet dream. Had he been able, Fiachra would have smiled.

Brodulein, too, was apparently studying the walls. *<Who or what is Xanadu?>*

There was no time to explain Olivia Newton-John on roller skates to a Fae Loremaster. "Later."

Fiachra eased Peri down onto the sofa, falling to his knees on the threadbare carpet. Now that they weren't out in the arguably fresh air of the humid D.C. night, the reek of alcohol was unmistakable. But so was the scent of blood. Carefully, he rolled the slender male onto his side, to get a better look at his injuries.

"Holy shit," he whispered, staring at the jagged six-inch piece of wood protruding from Peri's buttock.

<I concur.> The disembodied mage's tone was edged with frost. *<If that stick had found its intended target, your male would be dead.>*

Fiachra had to close his eyes. He couldn't look. Looking invited the rage back.

<His head wants healing as well.>

"Shit." Now he *had* to look again. There was dried blood in Peri's hair, on the back of his head, and a mostly-hidden lump almost the size of an egg. "I don't suppose you have true healing magick."

<No. My gifts are elsewhere.>

Fiachra eased Peri onto his back once more, his hands unsteady. He needed to see his human's face. His human. Yes. "There is some healing skill in my bloodline, or so my mother said. Though no one in my House was ever asked to heal. Not that I remember."

<Because you were adhmacomh.*>*

180

Fiachra's jaw clenched tightly. "Yes." No Fae, no matter how dire the need, would have asked for help from any Fae of his House.

<If there is truth to the gossip about your lineage, it works in your favor, and your human's. The daragin *were able to heal, if persuaded.>*

Strangely, the old taunt lacked its usual bite. Probably because he had much better things to be angry about. Not to mention one very good reason to try to stay calm.

"Any healing I can do won't be painless." No healing gift ever was, unless the healer was of the Demesne of Water. "In fact, it could be worse than what's already happened to him."

<That would be difficult.>

"Thanks ever so fucking much."

He thought he felt Brodulein shrug. *<I do have one channeling which might be helpful. I lack a Water Fae's healing gift, but I can use running water to carry his pain away swiftly.>*

Which beat hell out of letting the pain of regeneration burn its way out along every nerve, the way it did when any Fae not of Water tried to heal. "Will the shower do?"

<Perfect.>

He slid his arms under Peri and lifted. The human was so slight... yet Fiachra remembered the strength of the legs once wrapped around him, the force that had met his thrusts. Slight could be strong.

<He is strong. He will live.>

Fiachra could feel himself turning red, and stumbled slightly on his way to the bathroom. "Eavesdrop much?"

181

<It is difficult to avoid, since the mage woke me so thoroughly.>

Again Fiachra gritted his teeth... breathed in deeply of Peri's scent, to clear his head. Or whatever it was Peri's scent did to his head. "After I heal him... and after you've done what you need to do.... I need you out of my head. When he wakes up." The thought of a stranger—the stranger who had so casually suggested forcing Peri's mind, back at the massage parlor—overhearing what was going to pass between him and Peri was fucking unbearable. "Go back to sleep. Or whatever."

The bathroom door stood ajar; Fiachra found the light switch with an elbow. No bathtub, just a shower. Good, easier to manage. He eased Peri down, holding him awkwardly upright with one arm as he opened the shower door and reached in to turn on the cold tap.

<About what happened at the parlor...>

"That case is closed." No, it wasn't, but the Loremaster would answer for his fuckery later. "All that matters to me right now is that you do what you say you're going to do and then leave the two of us the fuck alone."

<I will likely have little choice but to sleep, at least until you return to Purgatory. After the events of the last few days, it is likely that what we are about to do will deplete most of your remaining magick.>

"You're just one bright ray of sunshine after another." Fiachra waved his hand under the stream of water. It wasn't as cold as he wanted, but it would have to do.

Fiachra thought he heard a sigh. *<I will end our interference with your male. And I will leave you alone with him. As long as I can.>*

"So you admit you were interfering."

No answer. Which was an answer.

"Why the change of heart?" He held Peri close, as close as he could. Body contact would help him channel, and give him something to think about besides his very real desire to go nuclear on a Loremaster's ass.

<I rode your thoughts. And his.>

Peri stirred, groaned.

"Let's do this. Now."

***

Jesus fucking Christ leavemealone quitfucking MOVINGme

It was dark. Warm. Quiet. Not really quiet, someone was talking, but Peri couldn't understand the words. Didn't matter. He didn't care. Dark and warm and almost quiet was good. But somebody kept moving him. And moving made him need to puke.

Water. Cold water. Peri yelled.

Every nerve in his body was stripped bare. Flayed. And he remembered. Remembered everything, through a haze of pain and alcohol.

He sucked in a breath to scream. Breathed in water.

"*'Nois, tú lobadh tón-grabrog!*"

No need to scream. Sweet relief was flowing down, from the top of his head all the way to the cold water pooling in his sneakers.

"Are you gone?"

Fiachra's voice. Making no sense.

"No, I'm not gone. I'm here." The words came

183

out indistinct, falling over one another. *Shit, I am so drunk...*

But he'd been something else, too, just a minute ago. Something worse than drunk.

Hadn't he?

"Peri?" The arms around him tightened. Kisses on the top of his head. "Peri!"

"Peregrine," he slurred.

"What?"

"Peregrine. Took. Katsura." Peri raised his voice, to be heard over the rush of the reallyfuckingcold water, and enunciated as carefully as he could. He wasn't sure why it was suddenly so important for Fiachra to know his real name. Except that Fiachra had carried him out of hell. Maybe that was enough.

He wasn't sure, but he thought Fiachra was laughing. Not making fun of him. Just... laughing. He could hear joy. A joy he'd heard, or felt, somewhere before. Maybe he'd be able to remember where once he sobered up.

"Peregrine Took? Really?" More kisses. And more laughter. Though it sounded like the tall blond god didn't really know how to laugh. Maybe he didn't do much of it.

I could fix that. "Blame my mother." He tilted his head back and looked up. He wanted to see the laughter. But everything spun, and he staggered into Fiachra, his sneakers squeaking against the wet tile floor.

The cop caught him easily, held him close. "Fool of a Took." Peri could feel the warmth of Fiachra's breath against his lips. They were almost kissing.

Almost, but not quite. Peri was tired of 'almost'. He closed his eyes, waiting for the kiss he knew was coming.

Bad idea. Everything spun again, and his knees

184

went weak. Fiachra caught him again, with one arm, and he must have used the other to turn off the water, because suddenly everything was really quiet.

"Fool of a Took," Fiachra repeated, even more softly. "Why did you do it?"

No need to explain to him what 'it' was. Tears trickled down Peri's cheeks. He was a weepy drunk. He hated it.

But having his tears kissed away helped.

"Can I lie down?" His voice wavered, no matter how hard he tried to keep it steady. "I'll tell you. I promise. But I don't feel good."

"*T'mé amad'n.*"

"What does that mean?"

"I'm an idiot." Fiachra picked Peri up like he weighed nothing at all. More kisses brushed his cheeks. And before he quite knew what was happening, he was in his bedroom. In his bed. And dry.

How?

And Fiachra was wrapped around him. Warming him. Holding him. God, the man smelled amazing. Like wind. Like rain. No, mist. Surrounding him, making a little world for them to be alone in.

"Can you tell me now, *m'állacht?*" Lips brushed the back of his head. So gently. And the back of his neck.

A shudder rippled through Peri's body. The last few hours—the last few days—were like a bad dream. In some ways. Most of the parts with Fiachra were beautiful. But the rest felt unreal. Like the kind of dream where there's something important you have to do, but you don't know what, or where, or when. Only that it's important, and you'll never make it in time, and you're going to fuck it up.

185

And every dream has a little kernel of reality.

It's three in the morning, but it's not really dark. New York City is never really dark. And it's never quiet, either. Especially not in this part of Alphabet City, with club kids spilling out of every door, or trying to push their way in, all night long. He's not sure why they went to the Guard House, maybe it's Niko and Roger's kind of place, but it isn't his, and it sure as hell isn't Yukio's. Wasn't. They're all laughing their asses off as they stagger out, though.

Yukio is beautiful, in his boa and his five-inch heels and his short shorts and his bleached blond hair and his perfect plum lips. His best friend since forever, since they both realized that girls were never going to be interesting and that they both had a killer crush on Mr. Levesque, their seventh grade science teacher. And now he's visiting, and maybe he'll stay, and Niko and Roger are helping to show Yukio what a good time is like in New York.

Only he's craving a cigarette, and Yukio's allergic. It's why they had to leave the Guard House, Yukio couldn't breathe with all the smoke. So he drops back a little and leans against the wall of a building, digging in a pocket for the cancer sticks. Yukio looks back and whistles for him to catch up, but he waves his friend on. He'll catch up.

He fumbles a cigarette out of the pack, and the lighter. It's windy, and it takes him a minute to light up, curling one hand around the tip of the cigarette to catch the tiny flame, but finally he's leaning back against the wall, drawing in smoke, blowing it out and watching the wind snatch it away.

It takes him another minute to notice the shouting up the street. The ugly sound of it.

Faggot, *he hears. And* fucking queer. *And* break your fucking ass.

He drops the cigarette and starts to run. There's a crowd. Some are quiet. Some are shouting.

Some are cheering.

He can't see over them. And he's afraid to push through them. Terrified. But he tries.

They don't let him through until it's over. Niko's face has been slashed, Roger's doubled over and retching, one eye swollen shut.

And Yukio...

"You thought it should have been you."

Peri was sobbing too hard to speak. All he could do was nod. He let Fiachra roll him over, and buried his face in the cop's broad chest. For years, he'd thought he needed to die, to make things right.

But he'd been wrong. What he needed.... was exactly this. To be held. To cry out the heartbreak, and the guilt, and the anger, and the pain of being left behind. To weep until his eyes burned and his breath caught in tiny hiccups. While strong hands stroked his back, whispering in a language he could almost understand, and soft kisses fell on his hair and his cheeks.

And a muscular leg wrapped around both of his, gathering him in.

"Sleep, *m'anam-sciar*," Fiachra murmured. "I'll be here when you wake."

Chapter Twenty-Three

Lucien suspected that the Urban Dictionary's definition of "dead" was a picture of Purgatory at 7:00 on a summer Tuesday evening. The boss wasn't in the house yet, no one was on the poles, and the only two guys in the cock pit were both checking something on their phones. Grindr, probably. Damn things ought to be lighting up like the Fourth of July. Or they would be if the place weren't so quiet.

He waved at Mac until the bartender looked up from his side work. Didn't take long—it had been a running joke between the two of them, since 1979 or so, that between the two of them they had one functioning head. Mac grinned at him; Lucien felt himself flushing, like he nearly always did, but grinned back, then pointed at his watch, and at the door. *Better take my break now, before it turns into insanity as usual around here.*

Waiting for Mac's nod, he turned and pushed open the thick black glass doors. They looked like they ought to be too heavy to open, but the way they were mounted, they opened as easy as Daisy Chaine after three gin and tonics on drag night. Though Lucien knew how to lock the great doors down in just under three seconds—handy knowledge to have.

The matching set of doors at street level stood wide open. Not much light was coming in, though; Lucien frowned as he climbed the stairs to street level, at least until he realized what the issue was. Black clouds were rolling across what he could see of the sky, dark enough that the street-lights had come on early. And he thought he could smell rain. *Maybe this fucking heat is finally going to break.*

He didn't really have anywhere in mind to go—the last time he'd hit the coffee shop across the street this late, he'd been up until sunrise the next day, and had kept Mac awake with him. No good. And his only other nearby options were the tattoo parlor and Big Boy Massage, neither of which were an option for a 15-minute break. Or appealed to him all that much, frankly. Though one of these Christmases he was going to get his back shaved and surprise Mac with that tiger tattoo Mac had always wanted to see on him.

He didn't need to go anywhere, though. It felt good just to stand there in the first breeze he'd felt in a week, and watch the sky and look for rain.

"Lucien de Winter. Just the man I was looking for."

Lucien didn't have to turn around. Not when all the hair prickled on the back of his neck, the way it always did when a cop came nosing around Purgatory. Plus, he knew the voice. "Good evening, Detective Harding."

Slowly he wheeled around to face the Vice detective. Any other man would have been intimidated—Lucien wasn't tall, but he was broad, and what Mac laughingly called 'ridiculously well-muscled' when he wasn't busy moaning from all the things those muscles could do to him. And bald, with curly grey-and-black hair sticking out from under the neck and sleeves of his stretched-tight Purgatory T-shirt like it was trying to escape. Most troublemakers never even tried to put up a fight.

Detective Russ Harding, unfortunately, was one of the few men who never seemed impressed by the show. "Do you have time to answer a few questions?"

Lucien sighed. "We've done this dance before, Detective. So if you're planning to ask me questions you know I can't answer, you might as well get the handcuffs out now."

Harding shook his head. "We both know your boss' husband would have you sprung before I could even get you back to the station. Besides, I didn't bring my size XXL cuffs." One corner of the cop's mouth quirked up in a smile that could probably get half the club's patrons volunteering to bottom for him in two seconds flat.

Not Lucien, though. Bear he might be, but he was no daddy. He preferred men his own age, even for window-shopping, and of course he had Mac to go home with at the end of the night. "So we're done, then?"

"Not necessarily. My questions have nothing to do with any investigation of your boss. Or the club." The smile was still there, but it wasn't as friendly. "This is something different. I need to know what time one of your patrons left the club on Saturday night. I don't give a shit what he did while he was in there, just when he left."

Lucien crossed his arms over his chest, an act which flexed his biceps just enough to stretch the stitching on the sleeves to capacity. "I don't ask for names."

"You couldn't have missed this guy. About 6'5", hair so blond it's almost white—"

"Lucien?"

Mac's strained voice behind him trumped anything Detective Harding might have wanted out of him. He turned his back on the cop and caught Mac's hand in time to help him up the last step. "Your leg?"

Mac grimaced and nodded. "I'm not sure Kick-Ass' socket is a good fit."

Lucien swore under his breath. His partner had been waiting for his new C-leg for months. And he'd been through a couple of extended sessions with his prosthesis specialist just last week to make sure the new leg's socket didn't aggravate his residual limb pain. "How long till Doc Jaime gets back from his vacation?"

"Another week yet." Mac tried to smile, but Lucien could see the deep lines around his eyes that only came out when he was hurting like a motherfucker. "It might just be the same old story, damned neuromas, it's too early yet to tell. But I'm done for the night, whatever it is."

"You need me to run you home?" Lucien's Harley was parked in the alley behind the club.

"Nah, I'll just flag down a cab." Mac's grin widened. "And on the bright side, I'll be able to ride in with you tomorrow—I'm coming in early to make up the time."

"Tiernan's making you make up your shift?" Lucien couldn't have kept the growl out of his voice if he'd wanted to. Which he didn't.

191

The growl earned him a laugh. "No, I asked for the extra hours. Someone has a birthday coming up, remember?"

"How can I forget? I've gotten three birthday cards so far from AARP." Lucien rolled his eyes. Which made Mac laugh again. Which was all good.

"Get used to it." Mac's gray military-style brush cut was the only thing about him that hinted he was almost ten years older than Lucien. "Fifty-five's barely freeway legal."

Lucien didn't bother answering—an empty cab was cruising down the street, and he stuck out an arm. His arms were hard to ignore, given that they were the size of some guys' legs, and the cabbie obligingly pulled up to the curb. Lucien opened the door and ushered Mac in, growling again at Mac's wince as his right ass cheek hit the seat.

"Get home, get the damned leg off, oil up and take your meds. I'll be home by two."

"You are the by-God homeliest mother hen I've ever seen." Their joke, coupled with another one of Mac's smiles and a quick kiss, left Lucien grinning like an idiot as the cab pulled away.

"Is he all right?"

Lucien had managed to forget Harding was there, and his grin quickly faded. Still, the man was at least trying to be polite, and pissing off the cops for the hell of it wasn't good business. "He'll be fine. He's breaking in a new leg."

Harding turned to watch the cab disappear around the corner. "How did he lose the original, if you don't mind my asking?"

Lucien did mind, kind of, but what the hell. Mac

didn't mind talking about what had happened to him, and it was something to talk about besides the private business of Purgatory's clientele. "He lost it in Vietnam. Back in '72."

"Bullshit."

Lucien's eyes narrowed in a way that would have had most men backpedaling like maniacs. But Harding wasn't intimidated. In fact, he was grinning, and Lucien started to relax. A little. "Yeah, he still has his boyish figure. Unlike some of us."

That got a chuckle, and then a cleared throat. "Look, I have to meet someone in a few minutes. So what can you tell me about the guy I'm looking for?"

The professional bouncer's wall came back down with a slam that should have been audible all up and down the street. "Nothing. I didn't see him come out of the club. I must have been busy with something else."

Harding slowly put up a brow. Lucien slowly didn't give a shit. He'd let his guard down for a minute, when he shouldn't have, but that minute was all Harding was going to get.

And Lucien definitely wasn't going to let the cop know that there was something about his questions that was genuinely irritating him. He remembered seeing the big blond in Purgatory on Saturday night. He remembered watching him come down the stairs to Purgatory. He remembered deciding not to let him in.

And he remembered being told that he remembered no such thing.

Chapter Twenty-Four

Fiachra's head jerked up well before the peal of thunder that woke him had finished rolling around the room. Peri apparently hadn't moved a muscle, not in however long the two of them had slept. And neither had the Fae; he was still wrapped around the human like a second skin, like armor. Rain rattled against the window beside the bed, and almost no light made it through the sheer curtains. Barely enough to see by, even with the enhanced senses of a Fae.

Fortunately, the only thing Fiachra wanted to see was right in front of him. He buried his nose in Peri's soft blond hair, breathing deep. He could still smell tears. All Peri's, of course. The tears of an Air Fae were ephemeral, wisps that vanished as they rolled down a cheek.

Peri's breathing was soft, even. Fiachra was the one who trembled, now. He'd slept for hours—maybe even a day and a night around—yet he still felt exhausted.

Brodulein warned me. Said most of my magick was going to be used up by the healing. Which was fine with him. Although it would have been nice to hold on to enough to wipe out Peri's memories of what had happened to him at Bobwire. The thought of Brodulein fucking with Peri's head was intolerable... but Fiachra would give anything he had, anything he was or had ever been or would ever be, to erase those minutes of terror and pain his *scair-anam* had suffered. As un-Fae as such a thought was, as alien as it made him to himself.

.Slowly, gently, he stroked Peri's arm, watching his own pale unsteady hand glide over perfect porcelain skin. *That's not my hand, it's Brodulein's.* He closed his eyes and took another deep breath, this time fighting an irrational anger. *I need to touch him, and I can't. Not as myself.*

The touch he craved went beyond the demands of the SoulShare. Fae in their natural habitat weren't exactly experts on emotion, and it had taken him a long time even to put a name to what he was experiencing. Something different from the magickal call of soul to soul. Compassion. He'd seen it in humans—he was on a first-name basis with brutality, given his job description, but close contact with violent death also meant bearing witness to the thousand sacrifices, great and small, humans made when they tried to take on some share of the burdens of others. Time after time he'd watched it happen, but he'd never known it himself, never understood it or even imagined it.

But his heart had broken when Peri wept in his arms.

And now... now he felt someone else's wounds as deeply as any of his own.

Someone else who had every reason to despise him, whatever face and body he wore.

195

Peri, oblivious to Fiachra's turmoil, murmured in his sleep and curled in more tightly on himself. Fiachra inched closer—

—his back pocket vibrated.

Fuck me, if it's Harding… But no, the vibration was wrong. And besides Harding, he'd only given his number to a select few people. Who weren't really people. Grimacing, he eased his phone out of his pocket and checked the display. Conall.

"What do you want?" The faintest of whispers was enough to make him heard to another Fae of the Demesne of Air, as he quickly channeled down the phone's brightness—easier than making the damned touch-screen do what he wanted.

"Well, I really wouldn't mind hearing how your expedition went last night. But since there wasn't anything on the news last night about an unexplained pocket-nuke-sized detonation around 25th and R, I worked out for myself that things must have gone all right. Not to mention the fact that the only reported fatality at Bobwire last night involved a skinhead who was said to have jumped off a pool table and broken his neck, and no one who saw it happen found his actions particularly remarkable. That kind of had 'Fae' written all over it."

"Brilliant. Hopefully you also deduced that I had other things to do besides call you to report in." Fiachra's reply was unusually mild. There was only so much sarcasm a whisper could carry, after all. "And I repeat, what do you want?"

Fiachra thought he heard a sigh. "I need you to get your—" Conall paused, interrupted by thunder; a second later, the same crash made the window in

Peri's bedroom rattle in its frame. "Holy shit. I need you to get your ass back here so we can talk about Brodulein. As soon as you've done what it takes to make it safe for you to get this close to the nexus."

"M-hm." Fiachra wasn't paying much attention; he was too intent on making sure the thunder hadn't wakened Peri.

"Hey, you could at least pretend to be impressed. That was a Fae using a euphemism to refer to sex."

"If you're not feeling well, I fail to see where that's my fault."

"Funny male." Conall didn't sound amused. "The nexus and the Pattern haven't been quite right since we rammed the new ley line through both of them, and I think all the activity of late—especially your little time-hop in Purgatory—has destabilized at least one of them even more. Possibly both of them. Brodulein is an additional complication we can't afford."

"I don't think Brodulein is a complication. Necessarily." Fiachra was only slightly startled by his own words. His opinion of the Loremaster whose body he'd stolen had been changing since the moment the male had killed Peri's attacker. "I'm not sure what he wants, but I don't think he's here to fuck you over."

"Hopefully those thoughts are your idea and not his."

"*Scílim g'fua lom tú.*"

Conall laughed, his mirth the kind only another Fae would understand. "I can live with that for now. Call me when you've Shared. I have a plan. If you're still interested in getting your body back, that is."

The phone went silent and dark.

197

***

No one will ever hurt you again.
Not even me.

So strange. No one was speaking. Peri was sure of that. He wasn't alone, God no. There was a body curled around his, a hand as gentle as a sigh running up and down his arm, whispering softly against his skin, and every breath he took was filled with a scent he was never going to forget. And there was sound, sure, rain driving against the window like nails, which made sense given the thunder he thought he'd heard and the occasional flicker of lightning he could sense even through closed eyelids. Yet he heard words.

Please let me in. Let me help.
Let me...

He remembered Fiachra settling him in his own bed, wrapping himself around him. Before that, in the shower... he remembered some of that. The memories of Yukio's death, as vivid and horrible as on the night it happened. Sobbing in strong arms, something he'd never been able to do before. Letting the weight of the story break his heart open, and then fall away from him.

And before that... No. No. He couldn't remember that. He wouldn't.

Except for the part where Fiachra rescued him. He'd remember that.

Maybe.

Why did he come for me? The last time he'd seen the detective before the nightmare was in Big Boy, and the humiliation around that particular memory still stung. He'd welcomed the dark cloud, after that. He'd wondered why the darkness was so much deeper than it had ever been before, yes. But Jesus God, how it had hurt. To feel that incredible, mind-shattering bliss, and then to have the man who'd given it to him pull his dick out and walk away, almost without a word.

Almost.

Hadn't he promised to come back?

Yes. And he had.

But why did he leave?

Did that really matter, in the end? Fiachra had wanted to earn his trust, had put his job at risk by paying Peri for sex. For... well, a hell of a lot more than just sex. And whatever had gone wrong at the end of it, he'd promised to come back. And he'd come back. He'd found Peri in the middle of a hell of his own making, and he'd saved him from it.

He felt a kiss on the back of his neck, brushing against the short hairs there. It made him shiver.

"Peri?" Warm breath, stirring the same spot.

"Yeah." He cleared his throat. "I mean, I'm awake." *Lame*.

The hand that had been stroking him urged him to roll over. And he found himself looking into the most amazing blue eyes he'd ever seen. Even in near-darkness, somehow he could see the exact shade of blue looking back at him. "What an incredible sight to wake up to."

"What?"

Fiachra really seemed confused. Which confused Peri. "Your eyes. They're amazing."

The blond immediately closed his eyes. *What the merry hell?*

"They aren't mine. I stole them. Along with the rest of this body."

Peri was surprised by how calm he felt. *I'm still concussed. Must be.* "Keep talking, I'm pretty sure I'll wake up eventually."

Fiachra laughed, but he didn't sound amused. "You're awake, *m'állacht*. And I have a hell of a lot of explaining to do, and I don't think that was the best way to start." A flash of lightning showed him the faintest of smiles touching Fiachra's lips.

Peri really, really wanted to kiss those lips. He wondered if Fiachra would mind. "Feel free to start over, if you think it would help."

"Thanks for the offer, but I don't think there *is* a good way to start." The blue of Fiachra's eyes brightened somehow—reflecting lightning? Peri didn't think so. "Most Fae would probably settle for skipping the explanation and melting your neural circuitry with incandescent sex."

"I don't think I'd mind—wait, most what?"

"Fae." He could feel Fiachra take a deep breath. "I'm a Fae."

Eyes. Beautiful blue eyes like he'd never seen before. And yeah, the sex *had* been incandescent. "Tell me more."

"Really?"

"Really." Peri rested a hand on Fiachra's arm, and once he'd done that, he couldn't help caressing it. *Maybe he's crazy. Maybe we both are. But right now, I don't feel like arguing about it.*

"Neither one of us is crazy, *m'állacht*."

"Did you just—"

"Read your mind? Not quite." Soft lips touched Peri's forehead. "Some Fae, like me, can understand any language they can hear. And your touch.... it's very eloquent."

200

Peri felt himself turning what was probably a spectacular shade of red. His hand stilled, until he saw how disappointed Fiachra looked and started stroking again. "Go on." And, when the cop hesitated, "Where did you come from?" Not exactly the first thing on his mind, but a legitimate question. And it sounded at least a little more intelligent than *what the fuck do you want with someone like me?*

Fiachra's eyes narrowed, and Peri remembered too late about the touch thing. *Shit.*

Another gentle kiss. "I came from the Realm... we don't have a fancy name for it, any more than you humans do for your world." Soft laughter ghosted over Peri's skin. "I came over from the Realm... oh, hell, call it 17 years ago, it might as well have been."

A finger touched Peri's chin, tilted his face up. "And just for the record, I don't want a damned thing with 'someone like you.' Only with you."

Peri's eyes burned; tears slipped sideways, down his temple and onto the pillow. No one had ever talked to him this way before. "This can't be real," he whispered.

"I'm real, *m'állacht—*"

"I know you are. I didn't carry myself home from Bobwire, and I sure as hell didn't blow my own mind on the table at Big Boy." A little of Falcon's steel and sass helped his voice stop shaking. But he didn't want to hide behind Falcon. "What doesn't feel real is you wanting me." What it felt like was something out of a story.

Stories can be rewritten...

"You apparently have no idea how wantable you are." Fingertips ran lightly along Peri's cheekbone as

201

thunder rolled through the room. "There's so much I need to explain to you, but talking is such a huge fucking waste of time right now for both of us."

"What else do you want to be doing?" Peri knew the answer, or at least he thought he did. He just wanted to hear Fiachra say it.

Instead of words, he got a kiss. A kiss that straight up owned him. And asked to be owned back. Tongue searching his mouth, hands roaming his body, and all the while inviting him to do exactly the same thing.

Just for a minute, Peri forgot that he didn't, couldn't, believe what was happening to him. Because it was happening. No denying it. Fiachra rolled onto his back and took Peri with him, hands gliding down Peri's back, gripping his ass, holding him close, and that white-hot mouth never stopping.

"If I told you..." Fiachra's lips moved against Peri's, and Peri had to fight to keep from biting at those lips. "... told you that when I came to your world, my soul was torn in half and you got half of it... just how crazy would you think I was?"

It was weird, how little Peri had to think to answer that question. "Not so much. Because it almost makes sense. Except for the part where you walked out on me." *Fuck. I didn't actually want to* say *that.* "Why would you do that, if I have half your soul?"

Fiachra tensed, Peri could feel it. But he didn't pull away, and Peri breathed a sigh of relief.

"I thought the Fae this body belongs to was about to try to take it back. And if he *had* tried, it would have involved forcing your mind. And there was no fucking way I was going to let him do that."

It all makes perfect sense. As long as I go along with it. "Is he going to try again—the other Fae?"

"No. He took care of the asswipe who attacked you in Bobwire, and that tired him out."

"Took care of?"

Fiachra smiled. If wolves smiled, Peri thought they probably looked like that when they did it. "He's dead. The asswipe. Though if it had been me handling the job, I would have taken longer about his death and enjoyed it more."

The words, the tone went perfectly with the smile. "I thought you were a cop."

"I'm a Fae." Fiachra said it as if it explained everything.

Maybe it did.

Or maybe he, Peri, had gone from a bad case of survivor guilt to full-blown insanity. Stranger things had happened.

Now Fiachra was kissing him again. Small, tentative kisses, up and down the line of his jaw. Sexy as fuck. Still made no sense, but maybe that was part of what was so sexy about it.

Sexy and scary. Because there was something behind the sexy, something deeper and stronger and maybe unstoppable. Peri wasn't sure how he knew this. Maybe the hands running up and down his back were telling him. Or maybe it was the kisses. Or the serious hard-on nudging at his pelvis. One thing was certain, though. Whatever it was, he wasn't ready to have it end again, the way it had the last time.

"Are you going to leave again?" His voice was muffled in Fiachra's shoulder.

"Hells to the no."

***

Hells to the no, I'm not leaving. Not when I have my arms around the other half of my own soul.

Why did that thought make him so fucking nervous? A human would give anything, everything he had, to be as sure as Fiachra was that he had the completion of his soul, his bosom companion, in his arms.

It would probably help if I were human.

Instead of being psyched up for his happily-ever-after, he was on the brink of losing control. Nervous as a cat. Or a Fae.

Maybe compassion was just too alien.

Or it took more courage than any Fae had.

Peri was watching him, dark almond eyes wide. And Fiachra didn't think it was just the SoulShare that made him want to lose himself in those eyes.

He understood the SoulShare, or at least he thought he did. Two halves of one soul, coming together, like two magnets. Like gravity. He could cope with that. There was no helping magnetism, or gravity.

But a magnet's breath didn't catch in its chest when another magnet looked at it. Gravity's heart didn't race at the touch of a male's hand.

Neither did a Fae's.

I want to finish the SoulShare. That's instinct, nothing more.

Then what was this other longing?

I want to get my own body back.

Again, true. As far as it went. Conall's cryptic words had been as much taunt as promise. Which made perfect sense, since Conall, too, was Fae. *Being in someone else's body has become one level of alien too many.*

He curled a hand around the back of Peri's neck, groaning at the feather-soft brush of hair along finger and thumb. *And...I want to see my own hands hold Peri, watch him look into my real eyes.*

But what if Peri didn't feel anything when he looked into eyes of smoky topaz instead of blue, ran his gifted fingers over tanned skin and through coarse dark hair?

Why did the answer to that question matter so fucking much? If they were drawn together by instinct, and completing the SoulShare was the only way for Fiachra to get his body back? What did the beautiful human's reaction to his true form...to *him*...matter to a Fae?

I want what I want. If Fae had a racial coat of arms, that would be the motto picked out in gold under the crest.

Once Peri discovered that a host of Fae Loremasters had fucked with his head, nearly driven him to suicide, for the sake of a 2000-year-old game...was it going to matter a damn what Fiachra wanted?

Peri shifted his weight on top of him, rocking his pelvis just a little. Just enough.

Fiachra suspected even a SoulShare might not be enough to win and hold his human.

One chance.

***

Peri sucked in a breath through clenched teeth as Fiachra's fingers sunk deep into the muscles of his ass and kneaded firmly. *I'll give you exactly eight hours to stop that.*

"You have a deal. Though I may want to renegotiate in a few hours.'

Peri felt heat rising to his face. "Did I say that out loud?"

"You certainly did."

"Look, I don't..."

Peri's voice trailed off as he looked down into gorgeous ice-crystal blue eyes. Faceted eyes, he could see now, like jewels. Inhuman eyes, somehow anything but icy. Slowly large hands slid down to his thighs, pulled them apart to let pelvis grind against pelvis in a sweet hot rhythm.

Why am I fighting this? Peri ducked his head, closed his eyes, swallowed hard. *I'm trying to make myself believe I don't believe him.*

Just one problem with that. He *did* believe.

He'd grown up on one kind of fairy tale. The kind he'd heard from his mother, who had named him after a hobbit and filled his childhood with as many happily-ever-afters as she could get her hands on, especially after his father died. But he'd discovered another kind of fairy tale as he got older. Stories where the fey folk weren't the kindly companions of those fondly-remembered books and movies. They were inhuman, incomprehensible. Sometimes they meant well. Sometimes they didn't.

Sometimes those stories ended badly, for careless humans.

But sometimes they were doors onto wonder.

And a Fae was holding him. Right now. Wanting him.

"What do you want from me?" He whispered the words, so close to Fiachra's lips that they touched.

Fiachra trailed a finger down Peri's spine. "Just you—"

"What do you *really* want?" Peri smiled, just a curve of the lips. Fiachra wasn't a Fae out of any story he'd ever heard, old or new, but most of the stories agreed on a few things. It was difficult to make any of the fey folk give you a straight answer...but once they did, they were bound by their word.

Not that he wanted to bind Fiachra. Not really. He just wanted to know where he stood.

He could feel Fiachra's fingers interlacing behind his head. Thumbs caressed his cheekbones. And it seemed to him that the soft touch whispered *everything*.

"If you'll complete the SoulShare bond with me, it'll be safe for me to try to get my own body back. And then..."

Lightning flashed, and almost at the same instant thunder shook the walls. Peri was looking into crystal eyes, and barely noticed.

"Then what?" he whispered after the thunder died away.

"Then we'll see if you still want me."

Fiachra still smiled, but there was a touch of sadness in the gemlike eyes, and Peri caught his breath. "How could I not?"

"Don't ask questions you don't want the answers to."

How do you know I don't? But he didn't ask that. "Then how do I complete this bond with you?"

The sadness was gone. Peri wasn't even sure he'd

seen it. "Remember what I did for you, back at Big Boy?—what we did for one another?" Thumbs played with his earlobes, and somehow that was the sexiest thing ever.

"You don't seriously think I could forget?"

"Humans have been known to forget sex with Fae. You have stories about it." One hand smoothed down Peri's back. "But I'm glad you didn't." This smile was different. More human. Maybe. "Just do unto me as I did unto you."

He wants me to top him? Peri hoped he didn't look as incredulous as he felt. "And then what happens?"

"I'm not sure." Fiachra raised his head and caught Peri's lower lip briefly between his teeth. "Shall we find out?"

Peri kissed Fiachra. Hard. The kiss gave him a few seconds to think of something intelligent to say. Except, how the hell was he supposed to think of anything when he was kissing a Fae? "You're going to have to tell me what you like," he managed at last. "I'm not used to topping."

He didn't realize his cheeks had gone hot until he felt cool palms pressed against them. "Do whatever you want." *Jesus, those eyes...* "Remember how you felt my pleasure?" The tip of Fiachra's tongue traced around Peri's lips. "I suspect whatever you feel is going to drive me completely insane. And I've been wanting to know what you'd feel like in me since I first laid eyes on you."

Peri's cock had had just about enough conversation. His hips rose, fell, ground down against the man—the Fae—under him, rubbed his cock along the length of Fiachra's. Left them both breathless. "You're going to want me to use lube?" He hadn't intended for it to come out a question—of all the fucking times to be self-conscious about his size!

Fiachra's laughter was low and smoky and made Peri's toes curl. "I think you're going to want to. I plan to make you see stars, *m'állacht*."

"You're going to have to reach it, then, it's on your side of the bed."

"What—oh." Fiachra stretched, slid the drawer of the bedside table open, and felt around until his fingers closed around a crumpled blue and purple tube. This he set on the bed beside him with a satisfied chuckle and the barest hint of a wink.

Oh, God. His lower lip held firmly between his teeth, Peri eased back until he knelt between Fiachra's spread thighs. The Fae's legs went on to the ends of the world, hard-muscled and as perfect as the rest of him. Peri slid his hands under Fiachra's thighs and lifted. Fiachra didn't need much urging. He lifted his legs and hooked them over Peri's shoulders with a gleam in his eyes that was enough all by itself to make Peri's cock kick.

Another flare of lightning left Peri blinking. He didn't bother waiting for the afterimages to fade, though—he sucked hard on two fingers and slid them deep into Fiachra's ass, just as another crash of thunder shook the room.

Fiachra responded with a groan low enough to do some shaking all by itself, and a grip on Peri's fingers that demonstrated exactly why Peri was going to need lube. Peri wrapped his free hand around the base of Fiachra's cock and bent almost double, letting himself enjoy the musky scent for a second before taking the head into his mouth.

"Peri, damn it—"

Peri laughed. He couldn't help himself, even if it did mean letting Fiachra's cock slip out of his mouth. Maybe there really was some kind of Fae magic in the air, a wind blowing away a darkness he'd lived in but had never noticed. He'd spent the last five years, give or take a little, giving pleasure to strangers. And he'd been glad—mostly—not to feel much of anything himself when he did it.

Giving Fiachra pleasure... felt amazing. He could almost feel pure delight tickling his skin. *Is this really all it took? Letting him in? Believing him?*

"I'm glad one of us finds this funny." Fiachra's voice was a low grumble, but there was pure wicked laughter in his incredible blue eyes. And the tip of one long finger played around Peri's lips, teasing. "But do you think I could trouble you to—oh, *fuck…*"

Looks like I found his sweet spot. Peri stroked again, and shivered as Fiachra's eyes unfocused and his head fell back. "Trouble me to what?" The words were thick and unsteady.

Peri didn't understand Fiachra's reply, but he knew cursing when he heard it. He took Fiachra back into his mouth, and was rewarded with more of it.

And a few words of barely recognizable English. "Please. Peri. Do it. *Now.*"

He almost didn't hear. *Fuck. I can feel my own mouth.* Not exactly… but something was sure as shit rippling along his own length with every pass of his mouth along Fiachra's cock. He didn't want to stop. But he had to.

Wait. No. No, he didn't.

"Hand me the lube."

It took a few tries—Peri's hand was shaking, and

Fiachra apparently wasn't watching what he was doing—but eventually Peri had the top off the tube and his palm filled with the slick stuff. A few quick strokes to his cock were all he thought he could take without exploding, and apparently that wasn't supposed to happen yet, so once he'd readied himself he slid his fingers back into Fiachra and scissored them a few times, until the Fae was cursing again and grabbing the sheets.

"You think this is something?" Strangely, his own laugh sounded a little like Fiachra's. Not quite human. Well, if he had half a Fae's soul, maybe that made sense. As much sense as anything else had so far tonight. "Just wait."

He rocked Fiachra back, just enough to let him slide his knees under that marvelous ass. "You might want to grab a pillow—I think you're going to want to watch this."

"Peregrine…"

The Fae's tone clearly said *move your ass before I move it for you.* Peri shaped a lightning-illumined kiss at Fiachra, then gripped the base of his own shaft and pierced Fiachra's hole, as slowly as he could stand to.

If thunder followed the lightning, Peri didn't hear it. He was too busy trying to remember how to breathe once Fiachra tightened around him. And to focus on what he wanted to do next, which was blow Fiachra's… mind.

"What are you... oh, hot biscuits and sweet Marie..." Fiachra's words ended in a groan, as Peri bent and encircled the head of Fiachra's cock with his lips. "That's not fucking possible."

Peri didn't reply. He couldn't. But he could suckle, taste, tease, play. And work his cock deeper into Fiachra's tight hold at the same time.

Fiachra rocked under him, tilting his hips up. Drawing his thighs apart—with a hint of awkwardness, as if this was something he didn't do often. *No shit.*

"I can't believe you're doing this," the Fae whispered, barely audible over the rattle of the driving rain against the window, the almost-constant low rumble of thunder. "Do you have any idea how sexy you look?"

Peri gave Fiachra the only answer he could. He sucked harder. And Fiachra tasted amazing. Like champagne. He was willing to swear the drops being wept onto his tongue were fizzing.

The deeper he went, the more of Fiachra he took in, the more surreal everything got. Or more real. He couldn't breathe; he shivered with every inch Fiachra let him penetrate, clenched tight each time he swallowed a little more of Fiachra's gently pulsing cock.

Anticipation making the air feel thick. The feeling of something—that insane joy, maybe—building up, ready to release.

The crazy thing was, he recognized the feeling. It was like being on a roller coaster, being drawn up the monster hill at the beginning, the one with the hundred-foot free fall into the abyss on the other side. Feeling the power of the engine, knowing nothing could stop it. Climbing slower, and slower still, knowing that in just a few heartbeats everything was going to stop, and there would be nothing left but the edge. And the fall.

And the prayer, whispered or screamed, that something would catch you. Gravity. Physics.

Love.

"Peri." Fiachra's voice was ragged. "Please. Fuck, *please…*"

Peri could no more resist that plea than he could have sprinted in Falcon's stilettos. He thrust hard, harder; Fiachra's cock slipped out of his mouth, but there wasn't anything he could do about that, not any more. He grabbed the throbbing organ with one hand, pumping in time with his thrusts. Fiachra's cock curved, hardened. A strobe of lightning showed Peri the Fae's hard-muscled body twisted, his hands white-knuckled in fistfuls of the threadbare sheet. He felt Fiachra's cock pulse—felt it in his hand, and in his own aching organ. He heard a wrenching cry.

And then liquid heat sheeted down his spine, pooled in his sac, swelled his cock. He held his breath. Fiachra bucked under him; he cursed under his breath and rammed into the Fae's dark slippery hold—

And fell.

Peri's cry as he came sounded and felt like something breaking. Shattering. White-hot bliss frying every circuit in his brain, every nerve in his body. He couldn't breathe, couldn't see, didn't care.

This can't all be me. It can't. Some of the pleasure had to be Fiachra's. *I'm giving him this… I make him feel like this.*

Which was the only thing that could make what was happening to him even better.

"Peri? *M'anam-sciar?*"

It sounded as if Fiachra's voice was coming from a long way off. Yet there were hands on his back, and they whispered like Fiachra's. *Wake up, lover…*

He blinked, bemused to discover he'd somehow slumped down over Fiachra. And Fiachra's legs had slid off his arms, and were now all tangled with his own. "I'm awake. I think."

213

Fiachra laughed, one hand sliding down to cup Peri's ass cheek. "Feels like you're dreaming?"

"Exactly the opposite." Peri spoke slowly, finding his way through the truth of the words. Lying here, nuzzling into Fiachra's shoulder, he couldn't shake the feeling that he was coming out of a dream. Or maybe taking off a mask was more like it. Taking off a veil. "It feels like you're the first man who's ever touched me."

He felt Fiachra tense.

"Did I say something wrong?" *Please, God, no. Not after everything was just so right.*

One big hand cupped the side of his head and guided him to look into brilliant blue eyes. "You said nothing wrong, *m'állacht*. But this body, these hands touching you—they aren't mine." Lips brushed Peri's forehead. "I'm going to do whatever it takes to hold you myself."

"I'd like that." *Now there's an intelligent observation.*

Fiachra didn't seem to mind Peri stating the obvious. He drew him back down, shifting his weight to make a more comfortable pillow of his shoulder. "I feel like stealing some more time with you. Before..." His voice trailed off as his fingertips played over Peri's shoulder. "Do you mind?"

"I'm hoping I don't come off as that crazy." Smiling, Peri cuddled closer, shivering slightly as the wind lashed rain against the window. "Steal as much as you want."

Chapter Twenty-Five

Janek heard a woman's voice, whispering.

Am I mad, to mistrust a part of my own self?

Not a woman. The bitch.

And the male's voice. Not quite whispering, but not nearly as loud as Janek was used to hearing it.

We're all bugfuck crazy here, or hadn't you noticed?

Maybe he was dreaming. Though if he was, it was the first time in one hell of a long time.

That is no answer.

True.

How was he hearing them both at the same time? Had to be a dream.

You're not mad. But neither is our third face. For once, Janek couldn't hear the male jerking off. **I'm not looking forward to what it has planned any more than you are. But let's face it, things can't go on the way they are much longer.**

There was a low rumbling sound, the walls shaking. The voices stopped. And he was wet.

Fuck. Did I piss myself?

No. The water was colder than room-temperature piss. And there was way too fucking much of it.

Opening his eyes was a fuck-ton of work. As

215

usual, they felt like they were glued shut by whatever the shit was that was oozing out of his pores lately. And once he'd forced them open, he wasn't sure why he'd bothered, because he couldn't see for shit. The fire in the oil drum was out, and the only light in the basement, other than the red glow from his head, came through the window over his head from a streetlight outside. Even that light sucked, because something had blown up against the window on the outside a couple of days ago, and he could hear rain pounding on the glass like some dickhead was training a fire hose on it.

On the glass, and in through the crack at the bottom where the window didn't fit. And down the wall next to the blanket he slept on. Which explained why he was soaked to his rotting skin and lying in maybe an inch of water.

Get up, Meat.

He'd been about to start doing exactly that, but fuck that. Not if the female wanted it as badly as her tone of voice said she did. "Fuck off. You're the one who keeps saying I need a bath."

Get. Up. For once, the male wasn't sniggering.

"Try to imagine how many fucks I don't give about what you want." Janek didn't feel like telling his passenger that he was pretty sure it was going to take something like an hour to haul his ass upright.

It's time for what you *want, Meat.*

"Don't make me laugh." The monster hated water. He remembered that now. All that time in his rocky lair down at Cape Fear, watching the tide come in. Good times.

That was not my intention. The female sounded as if she'd rather be screaming.

216

Janek liked that, so he didn't say anything, just let her fume.

Time to go get what you've been pining for all this time, Meat. The male didn't sound quite as close to losing it. Maybe he just hid it better. ***Your heart's desire.***

Janek couldn't help laughing. Or trying to. Laughing felt like taking a metal file to the inside of his throat. "We've been sitting around on my ass for a year and a half, and now all of a sudden you want me to go out and collect Guaire's head?"

There is a new weakness in the Pattern. The female was back under control. *Attacking now, before its guardians suspect I know of this, is my—our—best chance.*

"Attacking now means trying to get through the fucking ward Dary put up." Whatever enthusiasm Janek had had for the idea of storming Purgatory evaporated. He tried to roll toward the wall, to emphasize the fact that he was ignoring his passenger. But not only couldn't he get up the momentum to roll, he sloshed. Which really did make him need to piss.

Dary's ward reacts to magick. Of which you presently have very little. The pain will be mine. Janek thought he sensed the bitch shudder, and the male took over the convo. ***If you're really lucky, Meat, you won't feel anything.***

"I've had shit for luck for the last year and a half." He was interested. More than interested. But he wasn't going to let his parasite know that. Not until he knew more about what was really going through its half of his head. "Nothing's changed."

Everything's changed. The male was laughing.

217

But not his usual fuck-you laugh. Which meant something, Janek was sure. ***And you need to start hauling ass to Purgatory.***

"I need a fucking boat." Water was pouring in faster than ever. He could hear it running down the wall, splashing on the floor.

You're a big tall guy. The male didn't sound amused any more. ***Just get up and get moving.***

"You really hate water, don't you?"

I have my reasons. The female sounded like she was speaking through clenched teeth. *Move, Meat. You cannot stay here. And no one will be on the street in weather like this.*

And you're going to need all the travel time you can get, the male added. ***You aren't exactly a track star any more.***

Something about the male's tone of voice brought back the end of Janek's dream. If it had been a dream. *"...things can't go on the way they are much longer."*

He was the *thing*. Always had been.

Today is the day, Meat. There was a gloating to the female's voice that Janek was more used to hearing from the male. *You get your wish. Swinging Guaire's head by his lovely long blond hair.*

She sounded like she meant it.

Did that mean anything?

With a groan, Janek rolled over and started the long slow process of levering himself up from the floor. Fucking water. It was half mud, anyway, from the construction next door.

Attaboy.

Janek wanted to throttle the male. Almost as much as he wanted Guaire dead.

He staggered to his feet, leaned against the wall for balance, slipped on the wet concrete and barely caught himself.

Stairs, Meat.

Throttling the female would feel pretty damned good too. Still, he started for the stairs. What the fuck else was there to do?

He stopped at the foot of the stairs, turned, and looked around the room. At the soggy blanket that was his bed. The barrel piled with cold ashes. The stacked crates holding the few things he'd managed to hold on to for the last year and a half.

I'm never coming back here.

He would have given almost anything—if he'd had anything to give other than the Fae knife jammed in his boot top—to know whose thought that was.

Chapter Twenty-Six

"Aren't you going to knock?" Peri ran his free hand through his hair, trying to squeegee some of the water out of it between his fingers. The worst of the storm had blown over by mid-morning, but it was still raining hard enough to make the half-block walk from the Metro station on the corner interesting.

"No need." Fiachra squeezed his other hand.

"But—"

The apartment door swung open, and Peri stared. Fiachra had told him they were going to Conall Dary's apartment, but he hadn't realized that he'd already met Dary. Or at least seen him, usually tucked up against Josh LaFontaine, the owner of Raging Art-On. "Holy shit."

"Good afternoon to you, too." Conall's gaze raked him up and down—and now that he knew what to look for, Peri spotted the strangeness of the redhead's eyes immediately.

"Be nice, Conall." Fiachra was smiling, but somehow he seemed to have become taller when Peri wasn't looking. And menacing. In an incredibly sexy way. "This is all new to Peri."

Conall laughed. "Don't worry, no one here is

crazy enough to mess with another Fae's *scair-anam.*"
He stepped back and motioned Peri and Fiachra into
the apartment.

Peri made it almost to the empty loveseat abutting
the sofa before he stopped to stare again. Everyone in
the room was someone he already knew, by sight if
nothing else. Tiernan Guaire was the owner of
Purgatory, and he recognized the couple on the sofa
beside him as Purgatory regulars. Cuinn, he thought,
and Ryan or Rian or something like that. Though both
of them were wearing a lot more clothes than he was
accustomed to seeing them in. And….

… his boss. "Lochlann?" He was glad his voice
didn't squeak.

Lochlann, one ass cheek perched on the arm of
the sofa, nodded. "Sorry you're getting all this
dropped on you at once."

Peri glanced up at Fiachra, and let himself get lost
in ice-blue eyes and a reassuring smile for a second.
"It's all good." Or it would be eventually. It was a
little intimidating to acknowledge, even if only to
himself, that he was the only human being in the room.

"Have a seat." Conall motioned toward the
loveseat. "I still need a minute to get ready. Which
reminds me, Lochlann, are you going to be able to
handle the ley energy without Garrett here?"

Get ready for what? Fiachra had started to
explain why they'd been called to Conall's apartment,
but he hadn't been very communicative once they had
boarded the Metro. In fact, he'd spent the entire ride
standing next to the door and staring out, with a white-
knuckled death grip on the pole.

Lochlann chuckled. "No problem. Garrett and I

have been up for a couple of hours, in several senses of the word. I'm ready when you are."

"Why don't you start, then?" There was a small table in the middle of the living room, one that looked as if it had been taken from somewhere else and dragged into its present place. The only thing on it was a large hand mirror, one Peri could imagine his grandmother having used. Conall reached out and picked it up, cradling it between his palms. "I'll let you know when we can start with Brodulein."

Dismissed by Conall for the moment, Peri turned back to Fiachra, directly into a kiss. A gentle kiss, but one that managed to conjure up memories of the best hours of last night. And of this morning.

"Ready?"

Peri could feel Fiachra's breath against his lips as he whispered, and the feeling was highly distracting. "I... what am I supposed to be ready for, again?"

Fiachra chuckled, but Peri could feel the tension in his body. "First, Lochlann's going to replenish the living magick I expended at Bobwire, and when I healed you."

"Right, I remember you telling me that part last night. Or maybe it was this morning." Along with Fae History 101 and an explanation of what the Pattern was. All while engaged in mind-blowing foreplay, afterplay, and play. It was a wonder he remembered a word of it. "But what does that have to do with the magic mirror over there?"

"Nothing that I know of—"

"Here, Fiachra, give me your hand." Lochlann's voice sounded odd. And when Peri looked past Fiachra at the dark-haired Fae, he looked strange, too. As if the

222

air around him was almost solid, but flowing like a perfectly transparent liquid. The effect was eerie, and beautiful, and made Peri's eyes ache. "Might as well get this part done."

Fiachra took a deep breath, nodded, and extended his hand. Lochlann gripped it tightly.

And a bunch of shit all happened at once. There was a smell like the air near a lightning strike. Lochlann fell back, missed the arm of the sofa, and landed on his ass on the floor. And Fiachra's body arched, rigid and trembling. His breath came in soft, rapid pants, and he stared unseeing at the ceiling.

"*Fiachra!*" Peri twisted and took Fiachra in his arms.

"Don't touch him—"

"Fuck that." Peri's lips curled back from his teeth at Lochlann's order. But only for a second. After that, he was too busy wrapping himself around Fiachra, holding him with his whole body, to waste time being pissed off.

He felt as if he were holding a live wire, or a racing engine, humming with an unimaginable power. "Fiachra... God damn it, Fiachra, don't you dare. Don't you *dare*...." Over and over. Not letting himself think about what he was telling his lover not to do.

His lover. The cop who'd been sent to arrest him a few days ago. The trick who had walked out on him. The Fae who had saved his life. The other half of his soul. "Don't you dare," he whispered again.

"Are you... always this bossy?" The hard arc of Fiachra's body relaxed fractionally, and his breathing started to slow down. And he was smiling, not so much with his mouth as with his eyes.

223

Eyes were fine with Peri. "This is a special occasion." Ignoring the other Fae huddled anxiously around the two of them, he brushed the backs of his knuckles along Fiachra's cheekbone. His fingers tingled with strange energy. "Don't make me get rough with you." His voice caught on the words.

"Lochlann, what the pestilential festering fuck just happened?" Tiernan got the question out an instant before Conall, who rolled his eyes in apparent irritation at having been cut off.

"I'm not sure." Lochlann had one ass cheek back on the arm of the sofa, and was leaning in to study Fiachra. "The ley energy was acting almost as if our cop wasn't Shared."

Fiachra was relaxed enough by now to be able to extend a middle finger toward the dark-haired Fae, and Peri breathed a quiet sigh of relief. "We're Shared. Count on it." Under any other circumstances, Peri would have considered Fiachra's growl sexy as hell.

"Down, boy." Conall looked as if he got a lot of practice at rolling his eyes. Peri sympathized—people seldom took a twink seriously. "We believe you. But are you all right?—and is your magick replenished?"

Fiachra took one long, slow breath, then another, relaxing more with each one. "Yes to both. Though if it's all the same to everyone, I'd prefer not to do that again for a while."

"A consummation devoutly to be wish'd." Conall grimaced. "And at least a possibility, assuming Brodulein keeps himself to himself for the next few minutes."

"Been binge-watching Shakespeare, Twinkle-britches?"

It was Rian, or Ryan, who spoke, but strangely enough Conall glared at Cuinn. "I told you not to call me that until you can do it yourself. And I wasn't binge watching. Just *Hamlet*. The 2009 version with David Tennant and Sir Patrick Stewart. Thank you very much."

Well, color me confused...

The arch finally left Fiachra's back, and Peri moved with him to settle back into the overstuffed loveseat. Not a piece of furniture Peri would have expected to find in the home of a mythical creature who—according to Fiachra—was the most powerful mage his race had produced in a couple of thousand years. On the contrary, it and the rest of the pieces in the set looked like something the Fae might have picked up at Goodwill, with its 1970's color scheme and worn brocade covering.

But, then, what do I know about mythical creatures' tastes in home decor?

"Rian speaks for Cuinn." Peri could feel Fiachra's breath warm in his ear. It was comforting. And, in an odd way, so was the incredibly ordinary furniture. "They're mated, and they can speak mind-to-mind. And Cuinn's been cursed by a tree spirit, he can't talk, so Rian does it for him."

Screw ordinary.

"Let's go." Conall held up the mirror. "And Fiachra, once I've started, don't speak. One word from you will shatter the whole channeling."

"I hear and obey." Fiachra squeezed Peri's hand, his grip as solid and reassuring as his tone was droll.

The redhead's brows drew together; his suddenly intense expression made him look entirely unlike a

225

twink, and left Peri wondering how old he actually was. Silence settled in around him, almost tangible.

Peri held his breath. No one else seemed to be breathing either.

Conall whispered a few words Peri couldn't make out, and the air around the mirror started to shimmer and swirl. Like fractals made out of soap bubbles. The delicate beauty of it brought tears to Peri's eyes, yet at the same time the shifting light was almost impossible to look at directly. *Can something be* too *beautiful?*

Holding the mirror in his left hand, Conall passed the palm of his right over the silvered surface. Once.

Twice.

The slender hand had no reflection.

Three times.

The mirror gave back Conall's left hand.

Holy shit.

"Here." Conall shoved the mirror into Peri's hands.

Jesus, don't let me drop it. "What am I supposed to do with it?" Peri's hands tingled fiercely, as if he'd slept with them tucked under himself and was trying to shake feeling back into them. He felt Fiachra's hand on his shoulder, and something about the touch helped draw out the pins-and-needles sensation.

"Just hold it up, out here where I can see Fiachra's reflection in it." Conall gestured, and Peri held the mirror out. "Good. I'd do it myself, but I might have other things to deal with in a minute." A muscle twitched in Conall's jaw. "Such as a pissed-off Loremaster."

Peri nodded, not really paying attention. He was looking at Fiachra's reversed reflection in the mirror—

not reversed the way you expected a reflection to be reversed, but the opposite—and then back at Fiachra. *I'm lost here*, he wanted to say. *Surrounded by magic and telepaths and sorcerers, and even you aren't human. What am I supposed to be holding on to here?*

But he didn't say anything.

Fiachra's eyes answered him anyway.

Conall cleared his throat. "*Brodulein. Mastragna. Thogarm'sta mé tú.*"

"Shall we speak English, little cousin? Some here would appreciate the courtesy."

Fiachra's reflection smiled.

***

Fiachra didn't exactly want to look into the mirror in Peri's unsteady hands. Neither did he dare look away.

"As you wish." Conall sounded very much as if he had lockjaw. "I will maintain my channeling as long as you answer our questions truthfully. Lie, and be silenced."

"Yes, of course." The reflection appeared to be fighting a yawn. "And, of course, the one who wears my body is a truthseer. I know my place."

Seeing his reflection speak without him would have been deeply disturbing no matter what it said. Those particular words, however, drove home a truth Fiachra had spent the last 17 years happily ignoring. *The body I live in doesn't belong to me.*

Now he did look away from the mirror. Peri was still staring into it, lower lip caught between his teeth. *Maybe he doesn't care for thieves.*

227

"Then there is no need for small talk." The twitch in Conall's jaw was mesmerizing. And would have been damned funny, under any other circumstances. "Why are you here, and what do you want?"

Fiachra's reflection sighed deeply. "Did it ever occur to you that I might be waiting, with no excess of patience, for someone to get around to asking me exactly those questions?"

"Actually, brother mine, we're pretty sure you're planning to spin us a tale bearing about as much resemblance to reality as the Cloud Rider's buttocks bore to the Water Queen's bird-bath." This from Rian, though it was Cuinn who smirked. "But do go on."

The reflection arched a brow. "Do we have so much time to waste that we can retell children's tales?

The Prince Royal and his consort wore nearly identical stunned expressions. Fiachra wished he dared to laugh.

Judging from the set of Conall's jaw, laughter was far from his thoughts. "Why is it so important for you to get into Purgatory that you would have forced an unShared Fae into proximity with the nexus?"

"Were you sent to destroy it?" Tiernan had been quiet, but now he leaned into the mirror's field of view and fixed the reflection with a glare as keen and cutting as one of the blade-master's knives.

Fiachra's reflection turned. Fiachra wondered if he himself had ever looked so purely disdainful. "I was sent nowhere, *buchal*. My body was ripped from the Pattern, and I had only moments to try to Foresee what awaited me and attempt to arrange circumstances to bring me back to it."

"Quit dodging the question, Loremaster." The

228

owner of Purgatory did not appear at all impressed by Brodulein's second-hand ire. "Are you here to destroy the nexus?"

"What is your stake in this game, kinslayer?"

Kinslayer. Were the stories of House Guaire, the Cursed House, true?

Tiernan went pale. "I'm the guardian of the fucking nexus. And the Pattern. Named as such by you and your devious cohorts. So quit dicking around and answer."

The reflection shook his head. "I am here because this body needs to go back into the Pattern. As soon as it can be arranged."

"Why would you want to do that?" Cuinn again, Fiachra guessed, as there was very little of Belfast in Rian's voice. "Hard to believe you wouldn't want your freedom after all this time."

The figure in the mirror didn't quite choke back a laugh. "You call this 'freedom'? For 17 years, this fragment of my awareness has been unable to speak, barely able to channel, has been a spectator as another male lives in my body, waiting for the circumstances I devised to bring me within range of help. This fits no definition of 'freedom' I have ever heard."

Fiachra felt himself flushing. His reflection, of course, did no such thing.

"You want to go back." Conall's flat tone was pure skepticism.

"Perhaps 'want' is not the best word. But you weakened the Pattern, damaged it, in forcing a path for the ley energy. And the influx of that energy has damaged the Pattern further. I am part of the Pattern, and I am needed to do my part to contain the damage.

But divided as I am, soul from body, I am of little use. I have shaped events, as much as a Loremaster can, to bring my body back here. So I can go home."

"Shit." Conall wielded curse words like a surgeon wielded a blade. "Fiachra, is he telling the truth? Don't speak, just nod or shake your head."

The Loremaster was speaking what a human would undoubtedly call gospel truth. Fiachra nodded.

"How are we supposed to—"

"Wait. Wait just a God-damned minute."

Peri. Iron-tipped talons clawed at Fiachra's gut.

Everyone turned to look at Peri, even the reflection in the mirror. Peri didn't seem to give a damn about any of them but the reflection.

"You talk about 'circumstances' you controlled. 'Events.'" Peri's lips twisted, as if the words tasted bad. "Was I one of your circumstances?" Peri's voice was so tightly controlled it shook. "Are you saying that you—that Fiachra came to Big Boy because I was there? That he saved my life because you needed him to stay with me?" The salt scent of human tears hung in the air. "Did I want to die, all these years, because you needed Fiachra to save me?"

"I… did not intend for matters to play out as they did." The reflection's gaze dropped. "But you are probably correct."

The mirror trembled in Peri's suddenly white-knuckled grip. "You play with humans. We're nothing to you. Our lives, our loves, our pains. Less than nothing."

Not true, Fiachra wanted to shout. Because he knew Brodulein, when he replied, would say the opposite. The Loremaster would speak a Fae's truth—

any Fae other than Peri's *scair-anam*. Or he would lie, and Fiachra would be forced to tell Peri he lied.

The reflection looked up. Ice-blue eyes met Peri's. "My answer to that question is not the answer that matters to you, human."

"No. It isn't." Peri turned to Fiachra, tears still standing in his beautiful dark eyes. "But you can't answer me, can you?"

Yes, I can. Not aloud, though, not without shattering the channeling. Fiachra rested his hands on Peri's slight shoulders and closed his eyes. Felt Peri draw in his arms, the mirror nestled between the two of them. Felt Peri's head come to rest against his chest. *He still trusts me. A little, at least.*

Fiachra needed the silent language the two of them shared, Peri's language of touch. During the hours between storm and sleep, and after waking... surely what he needed to say had been said, somewhere in those intimate moments. Surely he had the words he needed for this.

He stroked open-palmed up and down Peri's arms, cupping his shoulders. Holding him, gently but firmly.

Ask me if I care what any other Fae thinks or feels or wants.

Peri shivered.

Fiachra traced a finger around the curve of Peri's ear. *He speaks a truth any Fae in the Realm would accept. The truth I learned, lived and breathed.* He ran his thumb along Peri's lower lip. *But it isn't my truth. Not any more.*

"Tell me," Peri whispered. "I need you to tell me."

A tear slid down Peri's cheek. Fiachra kissed it away, lips brushing soft skin.

You are my own soul.
You are everything.

***

Conall bit his lip, watching the slight human's shoulders shake. The closest any SoulShared Fae ever came to what humans called empathy was understanding of the bond between other *scair-anaim*. Fiachra had obviously found a way to speak to his human, and Conall was loath to interrupt.

But the Pattern was unraveling, and the body Fiachra had stolen was needed to help knit it back together.

Conall cleared his throat. "We need to finish talking to Brodulein."

Fiachra looked up, his cool stare weighing and dismissing Conall.

Conall pinched the bridge of his nose. "We have plans to make."

Fiachra didn't bother to look up this time. One of his hands rested on Peri's back, and he let two extended fingers convey his reply, a purely Fae gesture.

Conall grimaced. "Ten minutes, damn it. Give us ten minutes."

Fiachra's hand ran slowly down Peri's back. Then Peri spoke, his voice muffled in Fiachra's chest.

"He says you have five."

Chapter Twenty-Seven

"They're coming down the stairs."

Lucien's voice in his headset got Tiernan's attention a few seconds before the heavy black glass doors of Purgatory swung open.

"It's about fucking time you two got here."

Bryce, being Bryce, didn't look terribly impressed by Tiernan's ire. Neither did Lasair, who appeared to be bracing Bryce with one arm around his waist as he cradled his and Bryce's puppy in the other.

"You can take it up with my biggest client, or you can take it up with Amtrak. Your choice, they're equally responsible." Bryce sounded bored. But there was a tightness to his voice Tiernan recognized. And didn't care for, because it was never a harbinger of anything good. "I couldn't take calls for half the afternoon, and there's track flooded between here and New York—that storm you had last night apparently did a number on half the Eastern seaboard."

Tiernan grimaced. They'd wanted to get the errant Loremaster back into the Pattern before the club started filling up, but no one had wanted to proceed without their living *Marfach* detector. Given the way the nexus, and the wards tied into this side of it, tended to go insane whenever the Fae fucked with the Pattern on the other side of it.

"And what's with the dog?" Better to talk about Setanta than about the pale shade of green Bryce was already sporting.

Lasair nuzzled the top of the pup's head. The way he carried on with that dog, no one would ever guess it had the genetic potential to grow up to be an apex predator. "If we tried leaving him at home, he would just have followed us. As it is, he kept Fading to Bryce on the train." Lasair and Bryce shared a smile, one that included the dog and excluded Tiernan.

"Keep him under control when we get started. We can't spare the Faepower to chase him down if he hares off after the *Marfach* again."

"You weren't even there for the first time." Lasair drew Bryce closer. And it looked as if Bryce was leaning into him, just a little. Like he needed the support. Wonderful. "And believe me, a repeat of that *carn d'cac* is the last thing anyone wants—"

"I hate to interrupt." If the whiteness around his lips was any indication, Bryce was actually telling the unvarnished truth for a change. "But can we crank up the tunes and get this party started? The monster's definitely awake. I can't tell exactly where it is, but it's closer than any of us want it to be."

"Come on downstairs. I'll call the others."

***

Peri stood with his back to Fiachra, looking down at the traffic on Eighteenth Street. One slender-fingered hand rested on the windowsill; the human's

234

spine was ramrod-straight, his head barely inclined. There was something strangely familiar about the pose, about the intensity of Peri's focus.

It's Falcon. Standing in Purgatory's cock pit, watching the bears at play, sheathed in teal sequins, Peri had radiated that same don't-touch-me. Falcon's aura opening a space all around him, her, even in the chaos of an orgy.

Fiachra wasn't buying the don't-touch-me. He crossed to the window, cupped his hands around Peri's shoulders. He felt Peri stiffen, then relax.

"You're still angry." His lips brushed Peri's ear as he murmured.

"Sorry." *Not sorry,* the brush of the human's hand over Fiachra's added.

"I'm not sure, but I think you only need to be sorry if you're angry at me."

"What aren't you sure of?" Peri cocked his head, but didn't turn.

Fuck. "I'm still new at this, *m'állacht.* Fae wear their emotions on the inside, there's less need to be careful of them." Not to mention, most of his prior experience dealing with human emotions had been acquired in Homicide, and ran the gamut from terror to bereavement, with the occasional side order of murderous rage. None of which were any help to him at the moment.

Peri's soft laughter let Fiachra breathe. "Okay. I'm not angry at you. So I guess I'm not sorry after all."

Fiachra buried his nose, and hid his smile, in Peri's soft blond hair. "So what is it? Brodulein?"

"Not really. I was pissed off at him at first. And

I'll never be happy about having my head fucked with. But at least I understand now why he did what he did. It was an emergency, he was panicking, he was desperate. And it doesn't sound like he had a hell of a lot of control over the shape his plans took."

"He didn't. From what I understand, the more the Loremasters control one thing about a transition, the more everything else about it tends to get fucked up." Fiachra's hands slid down Peri's arms, wrapped around him, drew him close. It was strange, this wanting another close all the time. Strange and wonderful. "So if it isn't Brodulein…"

Peri turned and came into Fiachra's arms, with a sigh so deep his whole body shook with it. "It's the rest of the Fae. Including my boss." Slender hands slipped around Fiachra's waist. "I'm not sure they've given any thought to anything beyond getting the Pattern fixed. I didn't hear anything about you getting your body back."

Fuck my navel. "That's why you were so angry with them when we left?" He had just been thankful to be able to escape the bickering of a master mage and a Loremaster on fine points of metamagickal physics. And to have another few hours with his *scair-anam.* "Not because of how they felt about what happened to you?"

Peri turned his head to rest his cheek against Fiachra's chest. "I doubt what Brodulein did to me even showed up on their moral radar. But I can kind of understand that, now that I've had a chance to see what they're like, how they think. There's no real reason they should care about humans, other than their own SoulShares, especially right now when their whole world is at risk." Peri's grip tightened, warm and surprisingly solid for such a slight human. "But they should care about you. You're one of them."

"Sometimes that's the most dangerous thing to be."

***

Is it time yet? Should we wake him?
You sound frightened.
If you are not *afraid, your brain is as dead as our host's.*

Janek wasn't asleep, slumped against the dumpster behind Raging Art-On and listening to the monsters in his head bicker. Neither was he awake, strictly speaking. He'd given up trying to figure out what the fuck he was just after sunrise, right around the time the monster had driven him out of hiding to go play in traffic. He hadn't been in full control of his body as he lurched across H Street. He didn't think the monster had been, either.

At least none of the cars had hit him. No fucking way he wanted that. He was pretty sure the monster wouldn't have let him stop moving even if his legs had been run over by a fucking semi.

Ever since, the act of walking had been like playing a pirated copy of a first-person shooter. The controller didn't work for shit, the video lagged the fuck out, and he would have ragequit hours ago if he'd had the option. He'd had to slam into the dumpster in order to stop moving, and he'd left a couple of his remaining teeth on the metal edge of the bin on his way to the concrete.

Janek O'Halloran was finally, irrevocably, officially out of options.

237

Chapter Twenty-Eight

"Which genius decided to put the Secret Entrance to the Inner Sanctum right behind the bar?"

Bryce ignored the way Tiernan's eyes rolled, as the Fae held the door—and its concealing channeling—open to let him and Lasair through. The pain gripping his gut made his ass even surlier than the Fae of Purgatory considered normal for him. And he hated needing Lasair's support for something as simple as walking down a flight of stairs, even though his SoulShare was doing his best to make the arm around Bryce's waist look like nothing but the simple gesture of affection it had started as.

"Nobody thought to ask me about the arrangement when they built the place back in 1962. I had to take things as I found them. " Tiernan followed the two of them down the stairs, then pushed past them to cross to a second door at the back of the little basement storeroom. This door's lock, unlike that of the door upstairs, was aglow with magick, and more magickal light boiled out from under the door. "I'd have to have the whole fucking place rebuilt to put in a new entrance or move the bar." He studied the lock, and the froth of light, with an arched brow. "Though there are days I wouldn't mind. This way of doing things is a pain in the ass."

"Did you just admit I had a point? No, no, please don't bring my comfortable world crashing down around my ears by acknowledging it."

Lasair's low laughter in Bryce's ear more than made up for the bird Tiernan flipped him. Then the inner door swung outward, spilling both magickal and normal light out into the storeroom. The Fae stepped back and ushered Bryce, Lasair, and Setanta in with a gesture several orders of magnitude more grandiose than necessary.

Bryce had only been down to the nexus chamber a few times. Actually, calling the cramped, crowded space a "chamber" was vaguely ridiculous. The main piece of furniture was a black leather settee, on which Cuinn lounged with Rian kneeling astride him. Lochlann and Garrett stood between the head of the settee and the bare concrete wall, leaning into one another, and Conall and Josh did the same at the foot. Kevin stood next to the door like some kind of sentry; Tiernan eased the door closed and joined him, stripping off a leather glove and lacing his crystal fingers with the lawyer's.

Bryce would have been jealous as fuck of every couple in the room, once upon a time. And would have ruptured himself trying to demonstrate that he didn't give a damn, because it would have been stupid to be jealous of them for having something he knew he'd never have, something his personality would never win him and all his family's money couldn't buy him.

Then Lasair had given him a soul. And love.

And now he was going to help this collection of

Fae and humans try to keep two worlds from falling apart at the seams. For no reason other than because that was what a decent person would do under the circumstances. *Or a decent person in training.*

Tiernan, meanwhile, was studying the floor, and the magickal energy swirling over it. If he, Bryce, a mere human, could see the currents of raw magickal power, they had to be fucking spectacular to a Fae. "Good job getting the ley energy under control, Conall."

"You call this under control?" Lasair didn't sound convinced. He did, however, sound incredibly sexy—most of the other Fae had lost the distinctive accent they'd brought with them from the Realm. But not Lasair. His accent alone could almost make Bryce forget the crawling in his gut.

"I didn't do anything." For the first time Bryce could remember, the twink mage sounded nervous. "It just settled down a few minutes ago. On its own."

Bryce had heard stories of the way Conall had faced down the *Marfach.* More than once. Nervousness did not bode well. "Is there any chance at all that that isn't a bad sign?"

Conall didn't exactly ignore him. "Maybe we should get started. Just in case."

Tiernan nodded. "Just give me a few minutes to clear out the club. Also just in case." He Faded.

Bryce slumped against the wall, trying to focus on his SoulShare's warm breath in his ear, and Setanta's gentle insistent nuzzling. Not the part of his gut that was feeling the call of a monster.

Canaries in coal mines had an easy job…

***

Tiernan took form in his office, then let himself out and made his way through the crowd to the bar. At least most of Purgatory's patrons still had their clothes on—*if this had happened on a Friday or a Saturday, we might have had problems.*

"What's going on, boss?"

Instead of answering Mac immediately, Tiernan switched his headset back on and swung the mic down from behind his ear. "Lucien, need you at the bar."

It was interesting, watching the crowd part in front of the bouncer. Lucien wasn't tall, but he was broad, and had a presence that made potential troublemakers decide elsewhere was a good place to be. "You rang?"

Tiernan had had most of the afternoon, while waiting for Bryce's train, to come up with a cover story. He leaned in over the bar, beckoning Mac and Lucien closer. "I've just had a call from Washington Gas. Their computer's showing a gas leak somewhere on this end of the block. Probably not serious, but they're suggesting we evacuate. Just to be on the safe side."

Mac nodded; Lucien was already looking around, sizing up the crowd, heading out into the milling bodies. "The usual 'cops in the house' drill?" Mac ducked under the pass-through, staggered a little as he put weight on his artificial leg, caught himself.

"Yeah, but move people a little farther off than you usually do. Half a block would be good."

"Should we check Raging Art-On and Big Boy, too?"

241

"Nah, I called them, they're already clearing out."
Not quite true, but close enough for Fae—Lochlann
had closed the massage parlor an hour ago, and Josh
had sent Terry home on some pretext or another at
about the same time. "Now go."

"What about you?"

"I'll be along." Tiernan started back for his office.
"Just need to clear a few things up first."

***

"What do you really look like?" Peri's words
were partly muffled against Fiachra's chest.

"I can't believe you haven't asked me that
before." Fiachra twined his fingers through Peri's hair.
It was more than a little ridiculous, how reluctant he
was to answer. Peri wasn't a Fae, didn't have a Fae's
prejudices, had never heard the word *adhmacomh* and
wouldn't give a shit if he had. Yet he didn't want to
answer.

"It was kind of a silly question, up until now."
Peri laughed softly, working one arm between
Fiachra's back and the sofa, holding him awkwardly.
"I mean, I can see you. But if this goes the way it's
supposed to, you're going to be different. Aren't you?"

Fiachra nodded. "Brodulein's body is pretty
damned close to the Fae ideal. Mine... not so much."

"You don't want to talk about it."

Fiachra brushed a thumb along Peri's cheekbone.
So far as he knew, no Fae had ever been rendered
speechless by a human's beauty. But, then, no Fae had
ever loved Peregrine Took Katsura.

Loved. Damn.

And he was sure no Fae had ever been as afraid as he was of losing a lover, by becoming a stranger.

He took a deep breath. "My hair is dark brown. Not quite as dark as Lochlann's. My skin is darker than normal for a Fae, too. Think Latino, you'll get a pretty good idea. And my eyes... well, smoky quartz. If I remember right, it's been a while since I've seen them."

"Jesus." Peri's embrace tightened. "I bet you're heart-stopping."

"Not to other Fae." Pushing aside the fear made plenty of room for old bitterness. "They repeat old stories, and call my line names that imply we're descended from tree spirits. And their trees."

Peri's head came up at this. "Trees?"

Fiachra nodded tightly. "Supposedly it happened a long time ago. Millennia. But Fae genetics don't work quite like human. One interbreeding between *Gille Dubh* and Fae, thousands of years ago, would be enough to produce dark Fae children all the way up to today."

"You believe the stories?"

He's curious. Nothing more. No taunting, no air of smug superiority. "Maybe. I don't know." He rested a cheek against Peri's soft hair. "But it's hard to get comfortable with the idea after you've had to kill a male for telling your sister he had trouble getting the pine tar out of his pubic hair after he lay with her."

Peri's dark eyes—even darker than Fiachra's own—widened, and it was a few seconds before he found his voice. "Are you sure you want your body back?"

Was he?

Was he ready to risk becoming a stranger to half of his own soul, for the sake of being *adhmacomh* among his own kind?

For the sake of holding his SoulShare, as himself?

"I will neither eat, nor drink, nor sleep, until I see you with my own eyes and touch you with my own hands. *Tseo mo mhinn ollúnta.*" *This is my solemn vow.*

No turning back, now. He was Oathbound.

Chapter Twenty-Nine

We should move. Now.
Why the rush?
I am having difficulty sensing Meat.

Meat wasn't having any difficulty sensing the monster. Janek was more awake now than he'd been in weeks. Maybe it was the very last of his adrenalin, finally kicking him in the ass. One final shot at Guaire, just a few minutes away.

No question, it was his last shot. He knew. He'd overheard enough of the monster's pissing and moaning to know its plans for tonight included ditching its ride, once he'd gotten them through the wards Dary had put up around Purgatory. He was pretty sure there was nothing he could do to stop that from happening.

And frankly, as long as he went out swinging Tiernan Guaire's head around by the hair, he was good with that. As badly as he wanted to make the monster in his head suffer, the way it had made him suffer for the last fucking year and a half, he'd run out of time.

His zombie life reminded him of boiling frogs, summers on his uncle's farm, when he was a kid. First you wrecked their legs or their backs, so they couldn't go anywhere, and then you dropped them in the water over the fire. And then you waited for the water to boil. Sometimes it had been boring to watch, when the frogs were too broken, or too stupid to notice what was going on. But sometimes it had been funny, that moment when the little shits realized they were being cooked.

Funny, until he was the fucking frog.

Being cooked at last was going to be a mother-fucking relief.

Wake up, Meat.

The only thing worse than the bitch ordering him around was the bitch begging. Janek grunted and started pushing himself to his feet. It was a slow process.

Hurry.

"Shut the fuck up." If anyone had been around to listen, Janek doubted they would have understood a word. But talking to the *Marfach* bugged the shit out of it. Which still made it worth doing.

Staggering upright, he leaned against the dumpster while he got his bearings. The back door to Raging Art-On was diagonally across the narrow alley.

Are you ready, Meat?

Janek felt a rush of something that was almost excitement. He wasn't sure whether it was because shit was finally about to get real, or because the bitch sounded ready to piss herself. "Hell yeah."

Maybe not expecting to live through the night gave him an advantage. He didn't have anything left to be afraid of.

He stumbled across the alley, slamming up against the door. One-eyed depth perception sucked sweaty orangutan balls.

There was a low sound inside his head. Not a growl, more like a slo-mo avalanche. Only the rocks were alive, and made of pain. And the avalanche formed words.

EARN YOUR LIFE. OR I WILL TAKE IT FROM YOU.

Janek hurled himself at the door. Again. Again. Anything to make that cunt biting noise stop.

The door gave way with a crash.

The screaming inside his head, male and female, started even before he hit the floor. As he fell in slow motion, through the fucking Fae wards. As his blood caught fire, as the flesh crisped from his bones.

His eye told him there was no fire. His eye fucking lied. He groped for it with thick fingers, to gouge it out.

The bitch howled. The male shrieked and gibbered.

The abomination... laughed.

Nothing to be afraid of, my ass.

Janek slammed his head into the floor, over and over again. The floor slick with brown blood, gritty with pieces of bone and broken teeth.

FEED ME, the pain grated.

Brilliant, blinding flare of hideous red.

Nothing.

Chapter Thirty

With the house lights up, the bar lights off, and the sound system shut down, Purgatory was unrecognizable. Fiachra would have been quietly amused at the way Peri held his hand and stuck close to his side as the heavy black glass doors swung closed behind them, if he hadn't been preoccupied with a serious case of nerves himself.

At least Brodulein wasn't being chatty, despite their proximity to the nexus. *He's probably as nervous as I am.*

"Where are we supposed to go?" Peri wasn't quite whispering, but the way the empty space swallowed up the sound of his voice, he might as well have been.

"Conall said the door's behind the bar—there." Fiachra debated ducking under the pass-through for all of half a second; he raised it and led Peri through. A door stood ajar at the end of the bar; he eased it open and hurried down the stairs, around a jog at the bottom.

Light shone through a second door, which likewise stood open a crack. "Fiachra? Peri?" On the far side of the door, Conall sounded just as distracted as he had on the phone a few minutes before. Maybe more so.

"No, it's Tegan and Sara."

Peri barely smothered a snicker, and Fiachra squeezed his hand. *I made you smile,* m'állacht. *That's well, then.* "Are you ready for us?"

"Probably not. But that's par for the course." Fiachra could practically hear green eyes rolling. "Give me a second to slip into someone more comfortable. And then do me a favor and just stand in the doorway for a minute, until I get a sense of how the nexus is going to react to you."

"Hurry the fuck up, would you?" Fiachra barely recognized Bryce's strained, twisted voice. And it obviously wasn't directed at him. "I have no clue what just happened, or what the bloody suppurating asshole's going to do next, or how long we have until it does it."

"Point taken."

What the nether hell is he talking about?

"Ready." This time, the voice was Josh's baritone, though there was something of Conall's tenor to it. "Peri, you first. Move off to the side and leave room for Fiachra."

Peri nodded and squeezed Fiachra's hand. Then he let go, pulled the door open, and stepped into the inner room.

"All right. Fiachra, Brodulein. You're up."

***

Lucien eased Mac down into a semi-sitting position on top of a battered metal newspaper dispenser, ignoring the Purgatory patrons milling around. "Shit. I thought you were doing better today."

"So did I." Mac's face was almost as gray as his hair. He shifted his thigh, gingerly, apparently trying to find a position that didn't cause him pain. Trying and failing. "Son of a *bitch*."

Lucien's hands balled into fists. He could handle anything. Anything at all. Except seeing Mac hurting. "Let me go over to the coffee shop and get you some water. And then you take a special." Mac's 'specials' being completely fucking illegal morphine, courtesy of one of Purgatory's regulars. Because Doc Jaime, who had still been in diapers when Mac had been 'in country', wouldn't prescribe opiates for anyone who had served in 'Nam. The morphine was a last resort, but from the sick sheen of sweat on Mac's face, he was definitely in last resort territory.

"Oh, *fuck*." Mac's eyes went wide, showing white all the way around the blue. "My meds—they're in my cubby, under the bar."

"*Osti de marde*." Lucien's uncle's repertoire of curses were also a last resort.

"Do you kiss your mother with that mouth?" Mac's smile was tight, but at least he was smiling. For a second.

Lucien bent and kissed Mac's temple. "Hang in there. I'll be right back."

***

Neither eat, nor drink, nor sleep...
This is it.
Fiachra stepped into the doorway, and froze in

response to Josh's hand signal. The human stood at the foot of a black leather chaise, staring fixedly at the floor in front of him, while a small bronze-winged dragon swooped in circles around his head.

The rest of the gray-walled windowless room was almost too crowded for Fiachra's liking—a Fae's genuine claustrophobic reaction only kicked in when he was in an enclosed conveyance, but given a choice, he would also avoid small enclosed spaces full of people. Or Fae. Which this definitely was. Cuinn was stretched out on the chaise, with Rian kneeling astride him, gentle erotic touches readying him to tap into the ley energy. Lochlann and his human, Garrett, were all wrapped up in one another, leaning against the wall near the head of the chaise, Garrett obviously preparing Lochlann for the same thing. Tiernan and Kevin stood to the left of the door; Kevin was still in the act of drawing Peri gently to the side, out of the way. Just for a second, Fiachra's gaze locked with Peri's. The look felt like a touch. A kiss. Strength.

Lasair and Bryce were on the floor to the right of the door, the Fae sitting on the floor with his back against the wall and the human lying with his head in the Fae's lap. Bryce's face was white as milk and shining with sweat, his dark eyes like holes burned with a hot poker.

Bryce drew a long, shuddering breath. "I don't feel it." His hand played over his side, as if he were trying to palpate something under the skin, in the same spot where the air had been warped and twisted last time Fiachra had seen the human, back in Greenwich Village. "If you're going to do anything other than look studly, now would be a good time."

One of Josh's eyebrows went up, in exactly the same way Fiachra had seen Conall's do more than once. He didn't rise to Bryce's bait, though. "GentleFae, if you'd be so good as to shield yourselves and your humans. There's going to be Realm-based timeslip going on in a minute, once we expose the Pattern."

"What does that mean?" Peri's voice was slightly distorted, behind a crystal lattice of light that sprang up around Tiernan, Kevin and himself as soon as Josh/Conall spoke. Peri, too, was pale. Fiachra wished he could take his *scair-anam*'s hand.

"Anytime the Pattern interacts with the human world, there's a certain amount of time distortion. It'll affect anything magickal nearby that isn't shielded, and I wouldn't be surprised if that includes a Fae soul housed in a human." Josh/Conall glanced from one couple to the next, nodded. "All right. Fiachra, one step forward."

Fiachra obeyed.

Cuinn's back arched so hard Rian was nearly thrown from the chaise. At the same time, a brilliant circle of light sprang up from the floor around the chaise, a beautiful whirlpool of white light touched with red and green and blue, its edge just short of Fiachra's toes.

"The Pattern knows he's here." Rian's arms went around Cuinn as he spoke, supporting the Loremaster; it was Cuinn who turned to face the others. "And it's calling the prodigal home."

Josh/Conall was cursing, softly, in an interesting mix of human languages and *Faen*, and glaring at the maelstrom in the floor, which was starting to be shot through with veins of what looked like lightning. "If he touches the nexus, he's going to fry. And maybe take the rest of us out with him."

"You think you have problems?"

Everyone turned to stare at Bryce.

"The monster's awake."

Chapter Thirty-One

Meat!

The enormous body sprawled in the corridor jerked. Again and again.

Stop screaming. Nobody's home.

I. Refuse. To give. Up. Each utterance was punctuated with another convulsion.

Do you really want to wake up the—

FOOL.

Fuck.

I HAVE FED, AND FED WELL. WE CONTROL THE HUMAN'S BODY NOW. Low grinding laughter filled the empty space. *WE MERELY REQUIRE... PRACTICE IN ITS OPERATION.*

Janek's body lurched, rolled, fetched up against the wall. A hand scrabbled, a leg bent. Suddenly it was on its knees, swaying, tilting. The iron sole of a boot clanked against the floor. Slipped. Clanked again. Pushing against the wall made balance easier.

Meat was a tall son of a bitch.

Shut up.

DOWNSTAIRS. NOW.

The sidewalk outside the tattoo parlor was deserted, so there were no witnesses as the shared body staggered through the open door to Purgatory. The stairs required concentration, but there were no distractions, and the wall provided all necessary support. Black glass doors loomed before the eye Meat had so thoughtfully left open, and gave way before the former bouncer's body with a soft whisper of hydraulics.

Where the fuck is everyone?

Neither of the *Marfach*'s other two personalities deigned to answer the male, but their body managed a puzzled frown as it did a three-sixty. Even Meat's dulled senses made it plain that the nightclub was empty.

Is it a trap?

"Holy shit."

The three brought their body around so they could glare at the human straightening up from behind the bar. Short, bald, bulging with enough muscle that he probably could have arm-wrestled Meat to a standstill back in the days when Meat had been alive, the male appeared not so much terrified as nauseated. Even when confronted with the crystal-headed corpse that was all that was left of Janek O'Halloran, in all its glory.

That, at least, was easily remedied. If there was one thing the *Marfach* had learned about humans during its tenancy in Janek's body, it was the ease with which they could be taught to fear.

The human bolted for the end of the bar, sending bottles and barware and tubs of ice clattering to the floor. Janek's body lunged forward, but was too late to stop a hinged section of the bar from crashing down onto its outstretched hands.

The female snarled, the scorpion hissed. But the male laughed. ***"I almost felt that, you pathetic little piece of shit."*** Of course, most of Janek's lower lip had been left behind on the edge of the dumpster, along with his front teeth, so M's, F's, and especially P's were largely impossible.

Not that it mattered. The section of bar flew up as easily as it had crashed down, and the human's ill-advised attempt to brace it with his body meant that his face got in the way. All three laughed at the crunch of cartilage, the spray of blood from the human's nose. The female tried to make Janek lick the blood from his face.

Idiot. We don't have time for that.

Ignoring the gore in the middle of his face, the human stepped back as far as the shelves behind the bar would let him. His head went down, his shoulders bunched, ready to charge.

Again the male laughed, both at the human's insane bravado and the scorpion's attempt to flex nonexistent tail muscles and sting. There was just enough room to bring Janek's knee up into the little human's balls, then plant the heel of his hand in the middle of the ruined face and smash the human's head back against the bottle-covered wall, pinning him there as glass rained down around them.

He is still trying to hit us. The female was trying to sound bored, but there was no hiding the way the human's blood made her pant with excitement.

Oh, for fuck's sake. It was true, the human had no concept of when to quit. Even gasping for breath, half blinded by his own blood, and pinned to the wall, the burly son of a bitch was still trying to put his fists up. ***We have shit to do.***

Meat's hand reached up and grabbed a bottle that was about to slide off the edge of a broken shelf. Fingers like sausages closed around the neck of the bottle and brought it crashing down. The human's bald scalp split, from forehead to crown. He sagged silently to the floor, almost taking Janek's body down with him before they could make it let go.

IGNORE HIM. WHERE IS THE DOOR?

***

I've got you, I've got you, easy...

Rian's thought cut through the clamor in Cuinn's head, and the feel of soft lips on his bare torso was pure relief. The mute Loremaster drew in one deep, unsteady breath, then another, letting his Prince's caresses draw the tension from him. And simultaneously feed his arousal, which was a tricky pavane to dance but which gave him the strength to stand up to the shouts being funneled through the ley nexus.

Testing, testing, is this fucking thing on? Cuinn tried to direct his thoughts toward the Pattern, letting his hands do the job of thanking his bondmate properly. *We're out of time for games, in case you hadn't noticed.*

We hear you, youngest brother. Dúlánc's voice rose over the noise and quieted it.

Cuinn hoped there was at least time for a quick sigh of relief, because he couldn't help one. *We have your truant.*

Rian was repeating his words, and Dúlánc's, aloud, for the benefit of everyone else, and Cuinn shaped a quick kiss before continuing. Twinklebritches was the go-to Fae for anything having to do with the workings of the great nexus, but Cuinn was the rump Demesne's best contact with the Pattern. And if the damned *daragin* had damaged that connection, Cuinn would have had to seriously consider going out and playing with matches and gasoline.

Focus, Cuinn. *Brodulein wants to go home, and we'd love to send him back to you, but the motherfornicating nexus won't let him through.* Which was putting it mildly, the damned thing was starting to look like a 2-D version of the twister from The Wizard of Oz and the hair was beginning to stand up on Cuinn's arms. *It's acting like he isn't Shared.*

He might not be.

I beg your pardon?

"I most certainly fucking am," Fiachra added. Any other time, Peri's concurring blush would have been the cutest thing since kittens.

I heard that. And Dubhdara's soul is Shared, yes. The ancient Loremaster sounded slightly put out. *As is his body. But the essence of his body is here in the Pattern. Brodulein's body has not been part of a true Sharing, and the nexus may well be rejecting it.*

Cuinn's jaw dropped. *Fuck me till I glow.*

Rian didn't bother to pass that observation along to the others.

Dúlánc didn't need a translator, unfortunately. *I doubt we have time for that, either.*

Cuinn thought the other Fae was amused. Hoped so. *Any chance of you having something useful? Like a plan?*

Something of one, yes. Yes, he was definitely

258

hearing amusement. *Has your inclination to follow instructions increased at all in the last few centuries?*

***

Mac. Have to... get to... Mac.

Some instinct told Lucien not to groan. Not to move. Just opening his eyes took pretty much everything he had. And even when he'd managed to open them, one of them wasn't working. Probably full of blood, from the warm wet feel of it.

The other one worked, though. He wished to fuck it didn't.

He hadn't recognized Janek O'Halloran at first. No wonder—the last time he'd seen his predecessor as Purgatory's bouncer, the *gros criss de tas de marde* hadn't smelled like a whale carcass on a shit-wagon, none of his face had rotted off, and half his head hadn't been made out of glowing red glass.

He couldn't remember whether Janek had been talking to himself then. If he had, he probably would have been easier to understand.

Crazy-zombie-Janek was looking for something. Whatever it was, Lucien hoped he didn't find it. If he didn't find it, he might go away.

And then he, Lucien, might stand a chance of living until someone came and found him. Assuming the club didn't blow up first. Though he hadn't smelled gas, when his nose worked.

It took a second for Lucien to realize the sound coming out of the Janek-monster was laughter. One of his, its, bloated hands rested on a section of the wall behind the bar. The air seemed to be swirling around the hand, turning dark, like smoke.

Concussion. Great.

The monster was laughing harder now. And the smoke, or whatever it was, was being drawn into its hand. Sucked in, like through a straw. Where it had been, was...

...the open door to the basement storeroom.

Hadn't that door always been there?

Why didn't I see it?

Why didn't I miss *it?*

Zombie-Janek said something. It sounded like "*AT LAST.*"

It sounded like death. Dragged screaming over hot coals and frozen cinders and broken glass. Screaming in pleasure.

Lucien shuddered.

The zombie turned.

"Not dead yet?"

The iron-soled boot came down.

Chapter Thirty-Two

"Ready for you, Lochlann."

Peri stepped back to let Lochlann and Garrett squeeze between him and the whirling disk of light set into the floor, to meet up with Josh. And Conall inside Josh.

If he were going solely by what he saw, Peri would have to assume he was witnessing the early stages of what was likely to become a seriously raunchy party. Arousal helped Fae work magick, Fiachra had explained to him in the course of the long afternoon. And every Fae with magick to contribute to the plan outlined by the Fae on the other side of the Pattern had someone working very hard to be sure he was ready.

No, 'working' was the wrong word. The air was thick with a power Peri couldn't begin to comprehend, energy that could be life or could be death and could apparently go either way on a whim. Yet somehow, in the middle of all that, every male in the room was pushing back against the impersonal force with the tangible power of a very personal love.

Garrett dropped slowly to his knees in front of Lochlann, eyes closed, tongue teasing the tip of an erection poking out from the waistband of Lochlann's trousers. Josh gripped himself through his jeans, his throat working, whispering 'baby' and '*d'orant*' and '*dar'cion*'. Rian trailed kisses across Cuinn's chest and throat, kisses that left fire in their wake. Lasair wrapped himself around the prone Bryce and answered his human's every faint moan with a slow, hot kiss. And behind the crystal lattice Tiernan had erected around himself and Kevin and Peri at Conall's direction, Kevin dropped kisses in the palm of Tiernan's hand, held that hand to his cheek, a hand made of living crystal.

Peri and Fiachra were the only ones who stood alone. Fiachra stared at the center of the deadly whirlpool of light, the pulse pounding in his throat his only movement, fear coming off him in waves Peri could feel shivering on his skin. And Peri felt as if his own heart were trying to beat outside his chest.

"Fiachra..." He could barely whisper.

Yet his SoulShare heard him. He turned. Smiled. Shaped a kiss.

"Let's do this." Josh nodded to Lochlann, who rested the hand that wasn't gripping Garrett's blond curls on Josh's shoulder. An eddy of the whirlpool curled out, circled Lochlann's feet, flowed up Lochlann's body and down his arm, into Josh. "Check your wards one more time, gentleFae." The odd combination of Josh's baritone and Conall's tenor was now even more distorted, almost as if it were coming from under water.

The request gave Peri precious seconds. Time for a few more words.

"I love you. Whatever happens."

262

Fiachra's smile made Peri's knees threaten to buckle.

Josh gestured, and a hole slowly opened in the center of the whirlpool. The hole looked black at first, in comparison to the color-shot brilliant white of the nexus. But it wasn't black, not entirely. It was laced through with intricate gleaming strands of what looked like wire, silver and blue, in an ever-shifting design. It was the other side of the nexus—the Pattern, the barrier between the Fae Realm and the human world.

"Hurry." Josh was sweating, his outstretched hand trembling. "I'm not sure how long I can hold this."

Fiachra went pale. Just as he had earlier in the long afternoon, when Rian had translated the voice setting out what he was going to have to do to send Brodulein back into the Pattern and regain his own body.

"You need to transit the Pattern again, to retrieve the body you left behind here."

The silence seemed to suck all the air out of the room.

"What does that mean?" Peri finally asked. "You've already done it once, right?"

Fiachra took Peri's hand, stroked the back of it with his thumb.

The pain is indescribable, the touch said.

"Most Fae who try don't survive even once," Lochlann replied softly.

"Brodulein says good-bye." Fiachra's voice was tight. "And he'll be what help he can from the other side." Then he turned to Peri, and just for a second Peri thought he caught a glimpse of exquisite dark eyes, smoky quartz. "Wait for me, *m'állacht*. I won't be long."

"I'm not going anywhere. Believe me."

Fiachra faded to transparency, and then to nothing, as Peri watched. Then, as quickly as he had vanished, he reappeared over the dark empty space at the heart of the whirlpool, his gaze locked on Peri's.

"Cuinn," Josh said softly, in a voice almost indistinguishable from Conall's.

Cuinn nodded and closed his eyes. The energy swirled up and around him, poured out of him, became a rush of wind. Wind like a hammer, driving downward.

Fiachra vanished in an instant. His scream lingered.

Then it, too, cut off. Where the Pattern had been, at the heart of the nexus-light, there was nothing. Less than nothing. Even nothing would have been something.

Bryce struggled to lift his head out of Lasair's lap. "What the fuck is that?"

"Frozen timeslip," Rian whispered. "They're stopping time for Fiachra. To give him a chance." Rian's expression as he looked at Cuinn suggested he had no idea what he was saying and wished his partner would explain.

Before anyone could enlighten anyone any further, the nothing exploded. Silently, rushing outward, leaving Peri shivering as if he had just run through a curtain of cobwebs.

"Is everybody all right?" Josh's voice shook only a little less than his outflung arm. "Did your wards hold?"

"They're all good." Rian replied gently, the richness of his accent more Belfast than Fae. "And I think you're supposed to be letting go now, *draoi ríoga*."

Even before Josh/Conall could react, the swirling energy in the floor reversed its direction and started pouring into the space in the center. Then he lowered his hand, and the flow became a torrent. One with no outlet; Peri had to shade his watering eyes, then look away from the eye-searing glare.

He didn't see the second explosion. But he felt it, like a scalding wind.

And he heard it. The wind carried a scream. Like the street outside the Guard House.

Fuck blindness.

The maelstrom was gone, faded to a glow in the floor. And a body lay curled in the center, next to the chaise. Dark-haired, bronzed skin. Motionless.

Everyone stared.

Everyone but Peri. He hurled himself at the ward Tiernan had thrown up. It shattered around him. He staggered, caught himself, then fell to the floor beside Fiachra. He gathered the unfamiliar head into his lap, wrapped his arms awkwardly around sun-darkened shoulders.

Unfamiliar? No. This man, this male, this Fae, had carried him out of Bobwire, had healed him and held him as he wept and made love to him in a way no man ever had.

"You made it," he whispered. Gently he brushed back dark hair from a forehead the color of dark honey.

Everyone was staring at him. He could feel it. Feel them.

Fuck them all.

"Wake up." He kissed Fiachra's forehead. "I'm sorry, I suck at the Prince Charming thing. But *please*—"

The chamber door crashed open, narrowly missing Lasair and Bryce.

In the doorway stood a pale woman in a clinging scarlet gown, black hair falling down her back. Her slight smile showed serrated fangs; her eyes glowed the red of infection.

"Your deaths will be swift."

All around the room, Fae and humans stood, sat, or lay transfixed.

The woman changed, in the blink of an eye, to a man. One with stinking, matted brown dreadlocks, dirt ground into every pore of skin so filthy it was impossible to tell its color, fingernails and toenails like mad yellowed growths of horn, and a dripping hard-on the size of a baseball bat. And the same fangs and dead red eyes.

"I have other things to do. A world to destroy."

Peri held Fiachra tighter, hunched protectively over him. He owed his *scair-anam* his life. Be damned if he was going to run out on the bill. Tears burned in his eyes, dropped onto Fiachra's cheeks.

Eyes of smoky quartz blinked open, tried to focus.

The sounds from the doorway made Peri's stomach wrench. The intruder was a monster now, all jaws and swirling opal eyes and dripping green ichor hissing in acid puddles on the concrete floor.

"IN YOUR OWN MINDS, I PROMISE, YOUR DEATHS WILL GO ON UNTIL I GROW TIRED OF THEM."

***

There are not words for how fucked we are.

Cuinn hadn't recognized the woman, or the man. And he knew he'd never seen anything like the obscenity filling the doorway—he'd still be in therapy for the nightmares if he had. But no Fae who had survived the final battle with the *Marfach* could ever forget that voice.

What do you need me to do?

In that instant, Cuinn an Dearmad loved his bond-mate, Rian Aodán the Prince Royal of the Demesne of Fire, with an intensity that would have left him weak-kneed had he been standing. *Keep on doing what you do so well*, dhó-súil. *I have to keep that thing away from the Pattern, no matter the cost.*

The scorpion-thing in the doorway shuddered, became the woman. Something about her was naggingly familiar... Cuinn vaguely remembered stories that had sprung up over the millennia, stories that the *Marfach* had once had a body. Stories he'd known to be false, and had paid little attention to.

Stories the monster had apparently heard. And enjoyed.

Maybe that's why we can see it.

"Stand aside, brave guardians." The woman smiled, baring saw-edged fangs. "Your wards can no longer stop me, and any other magick you turn against me will only feed me."

Cuinn turned his thoughts to the Pattern. *We have a situation here.* An understatement. If Conall's wards, structured after those binding the Pattern itself, were useless, any ward he himself could put up would have all the stopping power of wet tissue paper. *Any suggestions?*

Dúlánc's voice was almost unbearably calm. *Water worked the last time.*

To imprison it. Not kill it. Besides, we don't have any.

The woman stepped forward, her hand outstretched toward the swirling nexus. No. Toward Cuinn, sitting in the middle of it. And toward Rian.

"Perhaps I will feed first."

Cuinn's snarl was silent. *I will eat the living flesh from the hand that touches my bond-mate.*

"Elemental blood must be—"

The *Marfach*'s body jerked, shuddered. Turned to face Tiernan.

What the—

"No one goes fucking anywhere until I get Guaire's head," the *Marfach* snarled.

Chapter Thirty-Three

Conall gaped. He couldn't help it. He suspected Josh needed a moment, too. *Janek's still in there somewhere.*

Tiernan deliberately moved a shaken Kevin out of the *Marfach*'s path, then manifested a gleaming crystal knife from the living Stone of his hand. "You've been waiting to try for me for a hell of a long time, asswipe. Was it because your keeper didn't give a shit what you wanted?" The blade-dancer's smile was the coldest thing Conall had seen in a very long time. "Or no, wait, could it possibly because you're stone fucking dead?"

It was interesting—and terrifying—to watch the woman bellow with what could only be Janek's rage.

"He's buying us time." Rian was barely whispering, and Conall suspected—hoped—he was channeling Cuinn.

"Any thoughts on what we should do with it?" He kept his own voice—Josh's voice—just as low. Fae hearing would have no trouble with it. Of course, neither would the *Marfach*'s. Hopefully, the Noble's nearly unparalleled talent for being irritating was working to their advantage.

The *Marfach* took one lurching step toward

Tiernan. Another. It never completely changed form, but hints of the man and the obscenity flickered around the woman's form like ghosts. Of the particular ghost apparently driving it, though, there was no sign.

Tiernan stepped to one side, drawing it away from Kevin. "So come try me, you putrefying half-brained pile of foaming dogshit."

Interesting choice of invective.

Inside their shared head, Josh made a sound like a choked laugh. *Keeping Janek's attention, I'm sure.*

Rian hissed softly to get Conall's attention back. "The Loremasters say it's susceptible to water," he whispered, once Conall managed to turn away from the bizarre dance. "That's how it was trapped at the last, in the Sundering."

Helpful. But not enough. "Trapped. Not killed."

"It can't be killed. Not by the likes of us. And trapped would be a distinct improvement over the present situation."

"You have a point."

The *Marfach* charged Tiernan. Tried to. It was fighting for every step. Fighting against itself, as if it fought a headwind. Enraged. Tiernan kept himself barely out of its reach, his grace and speed in doing so a silent taunt.

The sight would have been laughable, if the monster at war with itself were anything other than a force that had once come within a few heartbeats of destroying a world.

If it has its magick back... and if Janek lets it use it...

"Now would be a good time to do something, Twinklebritches."

Conall grimaced. "I can't touch it directly with

270

my magick, it would climb the channeling like a rope and suck me dry—"

The *Marfach* roared and lunged. Tiernan jumped to one side, and the female stumbled and smashed into the concrete wall. The Fae blade-master pivoted and drove his crystal knife up between its ribs.

Everything blurred with the monster's howl. Including the monster. Suddenly it was the naked male, and the knife which had been between the ribs of the shorter female now stuck out of its lower abdomen. Until the knife flared, turned a viscous glowing black, and melted into the monster's flesh.

"Fuck me oblivious," Tiernan murmured, calmly manifesting a new knife as the creature turned on him.

Bryce struggled to sit up, brushing off Lasair's supporting hands.

Oh, fuck no, Josh murmured. *He can't try to siphon the* Marfach *again. It'll kill him. It damn near did last time.*

Peri gathered Fiachra close, kissed him gently. Fiachra's eyes were open, his gaze going from his *scair-anam* to the nightmare on the other side of the room. His legs twitched, as if he were trying to ready himself to move. To attack.

I know what I have to do.

"Tiernan. Get it away from the Pattern."

"You don't ask much, do you?" Tiernan's glance around the cramped room full of Fae and humans was more eloquent than anything he could have said. Yet he didn't hesitate. He positioned himself between the *Marfach* and the swirling nexus, crystal knife in crystal hand. "Come on, *bodlag*, get with the program, I don't have all fucking night."

271

The male shook its head, and for a split second Conall thought of bulls, and bullfighting, and a toreador's suit of lights with its flashing crystals. Then he stopped thinking and held his breath, as Tiernan slowly cross-stepped toward the open door. *If it doesn't follow him...*

The male snarled and padded after the Fae, hands outstretched and flexing. One step. Another. It crouched.

Now.

The channeling itself was child's play. Literally. A smaller version of the *laród-scatha* that sprang into being around the *Marfach* was a channeling a Fae might create for a child in the Realm, a sphere with no outside, only an inside, to hold a dragon-fly or rainbow-wing to be brought home as a pet for a day. Tiernan had crafted one to hold the tiny piece of the *Marfach* Kevin had dug out of Bryce's gut. Now a much larger one confined the entire monster.

For a few seconds.

"I can't hold it for long. Get out. Everyone."

"How do you propose to get the humans out, Red? Your toy is blocking the door, and they can't Fade."

At least Cuinn wasn't making Rian call him Twinklebritches. "I'm going to force-Fade everything in the *laród-scatha.*"

"Erm... that includes the doorway, or hadn't you noticed that? And a goodly chunk of load-bearing wall. And the ceiling. And hopefully not Tiernan."

"Thanks for thinking of me." Tiernan's voice was oddly muffled by the magickal barrier. "I'm clear. Do what you have to do, Conall, I'll try to brace things from this side long enough for everyone to get out."

"You heard the Fae." It sounded strange, even to Conall, to hear his normally easy-going partner's voice speaking in the curt, clipped tones he, Conall, used when preoccupied with a channeling. "Get ready to move your asses. And those of your *scair-anaim*, if necessary." He could feel the *Marfach* fighting the field inside the *laród-scatha*, trying to touch the magick that formed it. "Someone help Peri with Fiachra."

"I've got him."

To Conall's utter astonishment, Peri already had the *adhmacomh* Fae on his feet and was bracing him, with a good deal more strength than Conall would have thought he had.

Never underestimate a twink, Josh informed him, with a hint of laughter. *Are you ready to do this,* d'orant?

More than ready.

Closing his eyes, he felt Josh's embrace. His kiss. His touch. The power of Fae arousal, and the inconceivably greater power of the SoulShare bond. He reached out and gathered in the energy of the great nexus, let it flood him. Transformed it to living magick. Held it balanced there, in his own being, kept apart from Josh's too-human flesh, while he chose a destination for the monster. *Water... a water prison...*

Conall gestured. The magick thundered out of him in a brilliant torrent to envelop the *laród-scatha*. Brightened.

Everyone, Fae and human, averted their eyes.

The *Marfach* struggled. Screamed. The scream made Conall want to rip his ears off and set fire to them. But the channeling held. Gritting his teeth, he bore down.

273

The *laród-scatha* vanished. So did a perfectly spherical chunk of the storeroom.

Conall released the power of the nexus—and staggered, Josh barely catching them both.

The building groaned around them, a low rumbling sound.

The circumference of the space where the sphere had been was quickly shot through with light, the shining clear light of living Stone. But cracks spread through the ceiling, and the floor, widening as they watched, faster than the Stone could chase them.

"Move." Tiernan's voice was hoarse. "No telling how long this is going to hold."

Conall waited until the last Fae and human—Lasair and Bryce, the latter's eyes wide with astonishment and his hand palpating his side in a manner suggesting he was looking for something he wasn't finding—had cleared the entrance before bolting himself, practically treading on Bryce's heels. Maybe the human couldn't hear Purgatory's protesting bones, but he sure as hell could.

"What the *fuck*?"

Tiernan's raw shout all but dragged Conall the rest of the way up the stairs. And he, along with everyone else, stared in shock at the wreckage behind the bar. Everyone but Lochlann, who pushed his way through the crowd and dropped to his knees in the middle of a sea of broken glass beside a fallen human.

If Conall had been asked to identify the human by his facial features, it would have been impossible. He needed Lucien's broad shoulders and impossible biceps to recognize the bouncer. His face had been smashed, repeatedly, to the point where it was barely recognizable as a face; his head had been split open, also more than once.

"Jesus, don't make me have to tell Mac." Kevin was pale, clutching at the bar to stay standing. "Jesus fucking God, it would kill him."

"He's alive." Lochlann cradled the battered face between his hands. "I'm not sure how, but he is." He looked up at Kevin, then at the rest of them, his aquamarine eyes vivid in the shadows. "I'll take care of him. You all get the hell out."

"I'll stay." Garrett went to his knees beside his *scair-anam*, shaking his head as Lochlann opened his mouth to protest. "You'll need me for the healing, and you may need help getting him out of here."

"*Move!*" Tiernan barked. And everyone, including the humans, heard the building creak.

They all raced up the stairs, onto the street. All but Conall, who brought Josh to a stop on the stairs and slipped out of his body. "Go." He waved Josh on, leaning against the wall, panting, listening.

"Like fuck." Josh's reply was almost amiable. He took up station on the step below Conall, putting himself between the Fae and the building's imminent collapse.

"I think the wrong one of us is called 'impossible'."

"I just take lessons from a Fae."

The black glass doors at the bottom of the stairs swung open. Lucien's massive arms were draped around the shoulders of Lochlann and Garrett; his bald head hung between them, bloodied but intact, and his feet dragged on the ground.

"Coming through." Garrett was gasping for

breath, and his face was pale under his mop of blond curls. The groan of stressed metal punctuated his words from below ground.

And from above it.

"Shit, the whole thing's coming down!"

Josh herded them all up the stairs and into the growing dusk.

And they all felt the ground shudder under their feet as Purgatory fell.

Chapter Thirty-Four

"Wait." Mac grabbed the back door of the ambulance before it could swing closed, and before Tiernan could get a hand on it. "I want to ride with him."

"You family?" The paramedic who had been about to close the door didn't sound hostile, just abrupt. As if she was in a hurry. Which she and her crew definitely were, and a damned good thing. Lochlann said there was no physical reason why Lucien was still unconscious. Maybe human doctors could figure something out.

"No." The ex-Marine looked as if fear for his partner had aged him ten years in the last ten minutes. And he could barely stand, besides—*fuck, we have to make him let Lochlann look at his leg, humans are so fucking obstinate.*

The paramedic shook her head. So did the one crouching over Lucien in the ambulance. All that was visible of the bouncer were the soles of his feet. "You can follow along behind, he's going to George Washington University Hospital."

"How the hell am I supposed to—"

"Hold on."

Tiernan didn't recognize the voice. He barely recognized the Fae it belonged to. The blond giant he and the others had been dealing with was back in the Pattern, assuming the body swap had worked the way it was intended. This male... the new Fiachra, or the original... well, Tiernan supposed he could get used to six inches shorter, swarthy, dark-eyed, with dark brown hair falling around his shoulders and a mouth that looked like at least six kinds of sin.

Clothed, too, fortunately for everyone with *scair-anaim* milling around. Tiernan figured they had Conall and a quick channeling to thank for that.

The Fae's dark gaze fixed the paramedic at the ambulance door. Her eyes slowly unfocused. Once he was satisfied with her reaction, he gave the same treatment to the guy in the back of the ambulance.

When they had both quieted, he spoke, so softly Tiernan would have sworn only another Fae could make out the words. "Mac has every right to ride with his partner to the hospital. And you'll explain that to anyone at the hospital who might question his right to be there. Are we clear?"

"Clear."

"Clear, sir."

Tiernan whistled under his breath. "Useful gift you have there."

"It's been known to come in handy." Fiachra's jaw set. "It's a good thing Brodulein decided to leave it with me."

Fiachra stepped back, his arm going back around Peri's shoulders as the paramedics helped Mac into the ambulance. Almost as if he wanted to disappear, and only his SoulShare's presence kept him anchored.

The doors slammed shut. As the ambulance slowly pulled away from the curb, the other SoulShares gathered around to watch the vehicle out of sight. Most of the Fae, Tiernan suspected, were trying as hard as he was not to shudder at the thought of being shut up, helpless, in a moving conveyance.

"Should I follow them, give Mac a hand at the hospital?" Kevin's hand on Tiernan's shoulder was the cure for pretty much everything ailing the Fae at the moment. "Or are you going to need me here?"

"You might as well go, Mac's going to need help and I don't have a fucking clue what we need here yet." Someone had fetched sawhorses from the under-construction dance studio and used them to block off the entrance to the club. Tiernan was trying to ignore the creaking noises coming from said studio. "I'm sure the city's going to send someone out to inspect, but I have no fucking idea when that's going to be."

"I'll Fade-walk down and have a look at the damage. In a minute." Conall was leaning against Josh, nearly lost to view in the larger man's brightly-inked arms. "I need to recharge from the nexus anyway, if I can. There's no telling when anyone but me is going to be able to get back down there."

"Excuse me."

Peri wasn't asking to be excused. Not at all. In fact, going strictly by facial expressions, he'd managed to grab five Fae quite effectively by the short hairs in the space of just two words. *Damn, Falcon. School is in session.* Tiernan cleared his throat. "Yes, Peri?"

Peri glanced up at Fiachra. Tiernan couldn't quite make out the exact look exchanged by the dark Fae and the porcelain twink, but there was no mistaking the way they were standing. As if each were half of the other. SoulShares. *They are one smoking hot couple.*

279

"I'm taking Fiachra home. Now."

***

Peri let the door swing closed behind him, locked it by touch as he looked around.

"Are you… in here?"

After everything he'd been through in the last few hours, everything he'd seen, he wasn't sure why he was having trouble accepting the possibility that the lover who had pleaded claustrophobia and vanished apologetically from their shared taxi had actually teleported—Faded—to Peri's apartment, the way he'd said he would.

Maybe my brain just has to draw a line somewhere. For a while, anyway.

The door to his bathroom opened and Fiachra came out, a Sebastian the Crab towel wrapped around his lean hips and his hair still damp from the shower.

Peri couldn't breathe.

Fuck drawing lines between what he could and couldn't believe. Any line drawn this side of what a sane person could wrap his mind around would exclude beauty like Fiachra's.

It took him a minute to realize that Fiachra hadn't moved, and was watching him. Warily.

"It's me."

It wasn't the voice Peri knew. Yet it was.

"I know."

He reached out for Fiachra's hands, and for a second he was terrified that his hands were going to be outstretched forever. That Fiachra wouldn't take them. *Please. Please.*

280

The Fae's hands were cool, still damp from the shower. "I'm sorry. I just couldn't stay in the taxi another minute."

"You told me about the claustrophobia." *And why am I talking?* He tugged on Fiachra's hands, harder when the Fae didn't budge. "Fiachra, what's wrong?"

"Your bathroom."

Peri waited.

"The mirror."

"Oh." He stopped waiting for Fiachra to come to him. Instead, he moved closer, slipped his arms around a waist leaner and harder than the one his hands remembered. "How long has it been? Since you'd seen your real self?"

Fiachra shrugged, a tight quick movement. "I lost track of time after I Faded. At least a hundred years, I'm guessing. And then another 17 in Brodulein's body." He put his arms around Peri; even the embrace felt tense. "I wish—"

"Wish what?" Peri tilted his face up to Fiachra's. He didn't have to tilt it nearly as far as he was used to. And his breath caught again. *Maybe I should just give up trying to think. For now.*

Another shrug. Was he only imagining this one looked a little less painful? "When I woke up, after the transition... I didn't want to see what I looked like. I wanted to hear it. From you." Fiachra rested his cheek against Peri's hair with a soft sigh. "I'd rather see myself through your eyes."

"I can do that." A smile crept across Peri's face. "If you really want me to."

***

Fiachra let Peri lead him through the living room, down the narrow hall, past the breath of humid air from the bathroom, into the bedroom. All in silence.

I wanted this. I Oathbound myself for this.

Yes. But one chance look at his new face, new body—his old face and body—in Peri's bathroom mirror had revived a life more than a century old. And with Peri still in the taxi from Purgatory, and unable to help him put the past where it belonged, he might as well have been back in the Realm, with nowhere to hide from the taunts ringing in his ears.

Adhmacomh, wood-bodied. *Craobód,* twig-dick. Bark-haired, stub-rooted, leaf-muncher. And the host of insults reserved for his sister and his mother. Petty, all of them. Vicious, but intended only to wound, not to destroy. To make absolutely clear that he and his kin were less than Fae.

The wounds hadn't gone away when he Faded. Or when he miraculously obtained a body with none of the failings other Fae had so meticulously categorized.

And as deep as the old wounds went, they were still easier to contemplate than his alien, utterly unFae fear of rejection.

A gentle hand rested on his chest. Dark eyes—even darker than his own—looked up into his. "Are you okay?" Peri asked softly, slender fingers tracing over Fiachra's chest. *You're so far away,* those fingers added.

Fiachra brushed Peri's blond hair back from his forehead. *I'm here.* "Tell me who I am, *m'állacht*."

***

282

Peri tugged at the towel wrapped around Fiachra's waist, holding his breath until it fell away. He stepped back and sat down on the bed, drawing Fiachra to stand between his parted thighs. Funny, the way he was trying not to look down. *I'm saving it. Like opening a present.*

Instead of looking, he touched. His hands knew exactly what they wanted, skimming over hard abs and the ridges that formed a V, leading his hands exactly where they wanted to go. Not so much because he wanted to discover Fiachra's new body—he did, desperately—as because he wanted to make Fiachra's new eyes unfocus with pleasure, hear his lover's new voice go hoarse and dark with need.

I want him to feel the touch of the real me. A man who gives pleasure because he wants to, not because he's paid to and not because he has to.

Where was this coming from?

Peri suspected this new Peri Katsura had been born while looking into Conall's magic mirror. Hearing Brodulein's promise, with Fiachra's truthsight to confirm it—knowing no one was pulling his strings any more, that his feelings were his own.

He knew what he wanted. *Who* he wanted.

"Well?"

Fiachra's smile robbed Peri of what breath he had left. No one should look as perfect as the Fae—and no one who looked so perfect should ever look so uncertain.

"Come here." Peri slid back into the middle of the bed, grabbing Fiachra's hand and pulling him along until the Fae toppled onto him, laughing.

Hells yes. That's what I want.

283

"I'm not sure this is fair." One of Fiachra's hands wound itself into Peri's shirt. "You're still dressed." Fae and human legs made a sweet tangle on the bed, dark and pale twining.

"It's perfectly fair as far as I'm concerned." Peri rolled to lie atop Fiachra, only realizing how odd that felt once he'd done it. "I'm supposed to be doing the looking." He worked his forearms under Fiachra's shoulders, and stifled a groan as the Fae's legs wrapped loosely around his thighs.

"So what do you see?"

The tightness of Fiachra's voice caused a large lump in Peri's throat, one he had to swallow a couple of times to get rid of. And then, finally, he looked. Really looked.

"Your eyes...." He bit his lip. "Dark. Not brown, more like smoke. Warm. Beautiful." He worked his fingers into thick dark hair. "Your hair isn't quite black. Not like mine would be, if I didn't bleach it."

"I like your hair." Smoky eyes brightened with Fiachra's smile.

Peri couldn't resist kissing Fiachra's nose. "I love your nose. I've always had a thing for noses that didn't look like they were apologizing for taking up space."

Fiachra chuckled. The sound lit Peri from within. "Thank you for not calling it 'proud' or 'magnificent.'" Laughter faded back to a curve of the Fae's lips. "What else do you see?"

He couldn't just look. He didn't even want to try. He kissed his way along Fiachra's jaw, down his throat. "You taste like... I don't know. Like the wind. When I'm standing someplace wild, open." Gently he nipped at Fiachra's collarbone, slid down the Fae's body just enough to let his tongue play over lightly-furred pecs.

"My skin?" That note of hoarseness Peri wanted edged Fiachra's voice.

But Peri wanted more than just a note. "Beautiful." He couldn't help laughter of his own. "I must really want to eat you, because everything I think of when I look at you is either food or drink."

"That works just fine for me."

The edge was still there in Fiachra's voice, but so was delight. The first notes of a joy Peri remembered watching, remembered feeling, and wanted to revel in again. His teeth closed gently around Fiachra's nipple, then bit down harder when the Fae gasped. "Cinnamon, I think." He laved his tongue over the sharp peak, and then over the ridges of muscle rippling over ribs. "And I've seen honey almost this color, I think. Dark amber honey."

"Fuck." Fiachra was laughing again. Peri had heard the old Fiachra laugh—had been completely entranced by his first tastes of Fae laughter—but it had been nothing, compared to this deep, rich sound. "Fae get epically shit-faced on honey."

"You don't have to worry about eating yourself." Peri could feel his cheeks growing hot, but he didn't care. "I'll be happy to do that for you."

"That does it." Fiachra's growl wasn't all that different from his laughter. Lower, darker, and with a delicious edge to it. "Out of the clothes. Now."

Peri couldn't breathe properly. By the time he'd shucked his T-shirt and wriggled out of his jeans, he was light-headed.

Fiachra had raised himself up on his elbows, and

was watching Peri through a tumble of dark brown hair, with a smoldering intensity that made him shiver. The Fae was hard already, and getting harder, his cock curving proudly up from a nest of tight curls, wide and wine-dark.

"That's yours, *m'állacht.*" Fiachra's voice slid across Peri's skin like velvet. "Tell me what it tastes like."

Peri swallowed hard and knelt between Fiachra's legs, reaching out to cup the Fae's shaft between his palms. The sight of his own pale hands against Fiachra's darkness, the soft skin over hard heat, started a familiar sweet heaviness in his own groin, as Fiachra fell back onto the mattress. And he could feel an echo of his touch along his own length, a tingle of remembered joy like champagne, just under his skin.

He wants to know what he tastes like... Wrapping his hands around the base of Fiachra's shaft, Peri bent and slid the head between his lips, teasing the smooth flesh with the tip of his tongue, probing the weeping slit. And he groaned, delighted, as the slit wept a familiar effervescence.

Fiachra's head came up. "What is it?" One dark brow sketched an arc.

"You still fizz." Peri laughed, low in his throat. "It's so good…"

Fiachra rested one hand over both of Peri's, squeezing them more tightly around his cock. "Brodulein must have been Demesne of Air, too, or at least had the lineage—"

"I don't want to hear about Brodulein." Peri was surprised by the tinge of jealousy edging his arousal. "He got in on action that should have been all yours."

Peri licked, a long slow stroke up as much of Fiachra's cock as he could get at.

"I was there, too." The smile was gone from Fiachra's voice, replaced by something else. Something Peri couldn't identify, something that roughened the Fae's words and wrapped like a hand around his throat. "For all of it. But thank you." Dark faceted eyes closed; when they opened again, the pure jolt of emotion in them nearly rocked Peri back onto his heels "Thank you for seeing me."

Oh, God. "You were afraid I *wasn't* going to see you. In this body."

"I still am."

***

Fiachra hadn't realized it was possible to feel more naked than he had felt when Peri tugged the towel from around his waist.

Adhmam d'agla, 's'na rílacha lat. Confess your fear, and it rules you.

And what Fae had ever let himself be ruled by fear of rejection?

He'd managed to forget the fear, for a few precious minutes. It had fallen silent, listening to Peri describe his every quality that had once been scorned, as something beautiful, something worthy of a most unFae love.

Silence was fragile, though, and easily shattered. One mention of Brodulein had been enough to bring his fear roaring back.

Peri frowned. "You're afraid? Still?" He let go of Fiachra's shaft and leaned forward, settling his body over Fiachra's, working his arms under Fiachra's torso, holding himself up on his elbows. Deep brown eyes were only inches from his own; feathery golden blond hair brushed his forehead.

"I shouldn't be. It's not a Fae thing. Most feelings aren't." The soft caress of Peri's hair was the equivalent of a wordless murmur, gentle comfort. "Fae don't know how to love. But you taught me how. Fae don't share. But you shared your truth with me, trusted me with it. Maybe the hardest truth of your life." Fiachra took a deep, unsteady breath. "And I was afraid that was all going to be gone, along with the body that held you when you wept."

"Dear God." Lips brushed Fiachra's forehead. "And yet you went through with it."

"The Pattern needed Brodulein back. And I… I needed you to see *my* truth."

Suddenly, Peri smiled, like sunlight cutting through mist. "You've seen Falcon."

"Yes." Only once, but those few seconds were branded into Fiachra's memory.

"Is she a stranger?

"Hell no. She's you. And she's beautiful." An understatement. Falcon was every bit as exquisite as Peri.

Peri's kiss was gentle, and thorough, and sweet, and left Fiachra completely without breath. "So if you can see that, why are you so surprised I saw the real you through the Brodulein mask?

Fiachra tried to answer. And he failed.

He saw me.

He sees me.

"Of course I see you," Peri whispered.

He loves me.

He cupped Peri's face in his hands. *"Bei mé tú a'ecáil g'deo."*

"What does that mean?"

Fiachra kissed Peri's eyelids, gently. Like a benediction would have been, if Fae had gods to bestow blessings. "I will see you forever."

Peri blinked hard; water trickled down his cheeks, scented with salt. "If that's what you want. Yes. You will."

Delicately, Fiachra tasted his human's tears with the tip of his tongue. And he smiled. They tasted like joy.

Slowly, Peri returned the smile. "I just had a thought."

"Thinking is overrated. Stop." Fiachra nibbled Peri's chin, along his jaw.

Peri riposted, nipping Fiachra's lower lip. "Remember when Lochlann gave you back the energy you needed for your magick? And he said it was like you hadn't Shared?"

"Yes. Are you sure you aren't tired of thinking yet?" His tongue soothed where he'd nibbled, eliciting a groan from Peri.

"Maybe your body—Brodulein's body—actually hadn't. Shared, I mean."

Peri's killer eyelashes were not helping Fiachra stay focused. On anything, that is, except how he wanted to feel them fluttering against the soft skin in the hollow of his hip. "Interesting thought." He leaned heavily on the *thought*, arching a brow.

Peri blushed. Adorably. "Sharing is a soul thing, right? Whatever that is, whatever that means. Between souls."

"True..."

"So... maybe we need to Share again? Just to make sure we get it right?"

Peri's downcast gaze was almost shy. Almost.

Taking a deep breath, Fiachra ran a finger slowly up Peri's chest and throat, then used it to draw him in for a kiss that lasted as long as a Fae's patience. "Will you top, *m'állacht*?" He curled out his tongue, stroked Peri's lower lip. "I want to watch you watch me."

"Jesus." The word stuck in Peri's throat, and beads of sweat stood out on the human's porcelain brow. He shifted his weight, his hands unsteady as they glided back down Fiachra's torso, pausing to flick manicured nails over the Fae's nipples. "Show me— show me how you like to be touched."

Fiachra arched his back up into Peri's hands, eyes already going heavy-lidded. *Scair'ain'e*, the act of SoulSharing, changed a Fae, opened doors to new emotions and new sensations. New was good. But it was also good to see that a Fae's talent for seduction survived *scair'ain'e* intact.

Peri's hands didn't stop; the human sat back on his heels, and stroked Fiachra's thighs, fingers sketching a mesmerizing study of light on dark. Fiachra's shaft rose once more, curving back up toward his abs, dripping clear fluid onto the muscles, where it danced like water on a hot griddle before disappearing. He shifted his legs, trying to encourage more of the stroking.

I can't believe you're letting me touch you like this, the human's hands whispered, teasing the insides of Fiachra's thighs before moving back to grip his cock.

"You believed it well enough last night." Raising himself up on one elbow, Fiachra reached for Peri with the other hand, tousling his hair, stroking his cheek, teasing at his lips.

"I think you're going to have to convince me all over again. Every time you let me touch you like this." Peri's grip tightened, and Fiachra's hips came up off the bed.

"Oh, fuck," Fiachra breathed, shaking his head to clear out the little white lights clustering around the edge of his vision.

"That's the idea." Peri's smile might have been angelic, except that based on what Fiachra knew of that particular myth, any angel who looked like that could expect to fall in short order. Then the human bent his head, encircled the dark engorged head of Fiachra's cock with his lips, and bathed the tip with his soft tongue, and any theoretical resemblance to anything angelic went straight out the window.

"If you do that suck-and-fuck thing you do again," he gasped once he had his breath back, "take notes. Because you may be discovering a whole new way to break a Fae, and the knowledge might come in handy someday."

Peri's laugh sounded more like Falcon's. Or what Fiachra imagined Falcon's laugh would sound like. Imagining made him even harder.

"I don't want to break you. Not yet, anyway." Peri watched his hands slide up and down Fiachra's cock, swirled the balls of his thumbs in the liquid at the tip. "I'd much rather play with you." Peri was panting now, and apparently unaware of the fact, so intently focused he was on the magick he was working

291

with his hands. "Until I can't stand to play any more... and figure out something else to do."

Breathing was a language, too, a wordless one. Peri's soft, rapid breaths, catching hard in his throat when the backs of Fiachra's fingers passed over his nipple. Fiachra's slower, hoarser, unsteady sighs, turning to faint groans as his hand curled around Peri's cock to fondle the silk over ivory of it. Stroking again and again. Peri's hips rising and falling, pistoning into his hand. Dark stubble around the base of Peri's cock tickling the side of his hand.

"Oh, shit." Peri breathed. "Do we have any lube left, after last night?"

"I think so." Fiachra fumbled blindly behind himself, under the pillow. He couldn't, didn't want to, take his eyes off Peri.

Bei mé tú a'ecáil g'deo.

His fingers closed around the crumpled tube; he twisted off the cap and let it fall, lost in the twisted sheets, and handed the tube to Peri.

"Damn. I don't want to stop touching you." Peri ran the tip of his tongue around suddenly dry lips as he squeezed the scented gel into his palm and stroked himself briskly. "Raise up—"

Fiachra needed no second invitation. He hadn't needed the first one, but the quiver of need in Peri's voice made his cock jerk and swing heavily to the side as he grabbed his thighs, raised his legs up, offered himself. "Do it—"

They both cried out as Peri worked his slick shaft in. Fiachra shivered with a sudden unexpected pleasure as Peri's sac fell against him, warm and heavy. Once again Fiachra could feel Peri's pleasure, somehow—not just his human's caressing hand, though sweet blinding fuck that was amazing too. No, he felt what Peri was feeling. Lust, and awe, and wonder. And pure delight.

And a need to orgasm, the sheer power of which could potentially drop a charging rhinoceros.

My need or his?

It didn't matter. Grabbing fistfuls of the sheet, Fiachra bore down, clenched, worked the length buried in him. Reveled in the fullness. And in the way he could feel it when Peri curved and hardened and—

ohfuckyes—

Jet after jet filling him. Peri's beautiful eyes wide, staring, unseeing, his body quivering in tight rhythmic jerks Fiachra could feel in his own body like a taut string being plucked. Bliss, as pure and bracing as glacier melt. And Peri's hand clamped around the base of Fiachra's aching, throbbing organ, as tight as any cock ring, keeping him from coming.

Forcing him to wait, so he could finish the Sharing.

As deft as Peri's grip was, though, Fiachra almost didn't make it. Peri was still shivering with aftershocks when Fiachra grabbed his upper arms and pulled him forward, urging the slender male to straddle his hips and glancing around for the discarded tube.

Peri shook his head, closing his hand around the wrist of Fiachra's grasping hand. "No. I want to feel you without." His smile as he looked down at Fiachra was a whole night's intimacy. "Just take it slow."

Slow? Fiachra started to laugh. Then Peri raised up, just enough to let the head of Fiachra's cock brush his puckered entrance. Reached down with an

293

unsteady hand, bracing his swollen shaft. And slowly, so fucking slowly, lowered himself, sucking in a long shuddering breath. Not stopping until Fiachra felt the tight grip of the human's ring, right where his own engorged cock rose from its nest of dark curls.

"Your turn." Peri rested his hands on Fiachra's chest, fingers splayed out, pale against russet skin. "Or maybe it's mine."

Fiachra's fingers sank deep into Peri's ass, bracing him. He sank down into the mattress—felt Peri tremble—slammed up into him, his sac already tightening at the sound of his human's cry. Again, and again, and once more—

It was the lightning storm, all over again. White-light bliss and a roar of magick unbound; deafened by the thunder and losing himself. And finding himself.

No. Not finding himself.

Being found.

Peri had fallen forward, and was holding him. Not just with his arms, but with his whole body, clasping him closer every time his spent shaft forgot it had just been spent and pulsed between their bodies. *Am I enough?* his body whispered. *Can I be enough?*

Fiachra stroked Peri's soft pale-gold hair. The gesture felt awkward, but it was an awkwardness more precious to the Fae than any treasure out of legend.

Always. You will always be enough.

Epilogue

September 10, 2013

Peri raised his free hand to knock on the door of suite 203, but lowered it again before Fiachra could shake his head. "I'm learning." He grinned as Fiachra squeezed his hand. "Slowly but surely."

The door to the suite swung open onto chaos. Well, not quite chaos, but a great many Fae, and their respective human partners, in a fairly small space. One had to admire the space, though. Peri had never been inside the Hotel Colchester, the place Lochlann and Garrett called home—none of his outcall clientele had been high enough rollers to afford the boutique pocket hotel. The furniture all looked like it was named after French kings, except for the large plasma screen television jammed in between the dining room sideboard and what looked like an antique garderobe, looking rather uncomfortable with the company it was keeping.

"I've never seen brocade on walls before," he whispered to Fiachra.

Whisper it might have been, but it was enough to interrupt whatever Conall had been saying to Rian, and turn all heads in their direction.

"Have trouble finding the place?" Lochlann nudged Tiernan with a foot. "Make room, Your Grace."

"*Sús do thón*," the blond Fae replied. But he and Kevin slid over, opening up space enough for two on the impossibly plush carpet. "Not that I'm ungrateful, healer, but if we're going to do this again, we're going to need a bigger space than your en suite."

"Hopefully, next time will be in Purgatory." Rian, the young Prince, sat forward in a deep white-on-white brocade loveseat, one hand resting on Cuinn's thigh, as Fiachra eased himself down to the floor and Peri made a place for himself between his legs. "And as long as we're all here, let's begin—Tiernan, when are we likely to see that happy day?"

"I wish I had better news." Tiernan grimaced. "The city inspector did her final walk-through yesterday, and she says the whole building's going to have to come down before Ishkhan can start with the reconstruction."

"Raging Art-On and Big Boy, too?" A muscle in Josh's jaw jumped, and Lochlann didn't look any happier. Both the tattoo parlor and the massage parlor had been closed since the night of the *Marfach*'s banishment.

"No. That's what good news I have. It turns out the parlors and your apartment are actually part of a separate building." Tiernan waited for the murmurs to die down. "When Purgatory was built, and the spaces over it, the contractor connected the building with the one next door, and unless you looked at the plans you'd never know. And the damage to Purgatory is entirely too fucking thorough, but it's also a lot more localized than you'd think."

"So what's to be done next?" Rian's hand tightened on Cuinn's knee.

Peri had noticed, most Fae preferred to be touching their SoulShares if possible. On the thought, he stroked Fiachra's palm with his thumb, and didn't need to look to sense his *scair-anam*'s answering smile.

"I've been discussing rebuilding plans with Ish. He's pretty sure we can reopen by New Year's Eve, if he can get a demolition crew started next week."

"Most of you will need to get at the nexus long before New Year's." Rian and his consort traded a long, unreadable look. "And we can't be that long away from the Pattern, not with things as they are."

"One step ahead of you, Highness, at least when it comes to the nexus." Lochlann nodded to the pierced and inked Prince. "I can still call the ley energy—the collapse didn't cut that off. And between Conall and Fiachra's special skills, we should be able to make sure the demolition workers clear out the nexus first—and either don't notice anything, or don't remember noticing anything, until we have a new nexus chamber built and hidden."

"One that's fucking easier to get at," Tiernan added. "There's a silver lining to all this."

Peri felt Fiachra tense beside him when his name was mentioned. His name and his new gift. His SoulShare didn't particularly enjoy fucking with people's thoughts; he'd done it to make Russ Harding and the rest of D.C. Vice forget about tall blond Fiachra and the whole clusterfuck that had been August. But even that much use of his talent had brought back memories, he'd said, memories of what had been done to Peri.

And Lucien.

Peri didn't realize he'd blurted the bouncer's name aloud until everyone turned toward him. He cleared his throat. "Where is he? *How* is he?"

Back when he was first encountering a room full of Fae focused on, well, Fae problems, Peri would never have imagined he would see those Fae looking crestfallen at the reminder of a human's plight. But this particular human had fallen while trying to stop the monster that was out to destroy their world. Maybe that mattered.

"He's at Evergreen Manor, a rehabilitative care facility up in Palisades." Kevin was the one who finally answered him. The lawyer had the look of a man who was missing out on sleep; Lucien's partner was an old friend of Kevin's family, or so Peri thought he remembered hearing. "Showing no sign of waking up."

"Which makes no fucking sense." Lochlann's expression was calm, but Peri couldn't help noticing that his hands were balled into fists. And Garrett was snaking an arm around his waist and resting his head on the healer's shoulder. "I healed him before we even left Purgatory. And I checked him again in the hospital. There's not a damned thing wrong with him."

"You can't heal magickal damage."

Peri actually hadn't noticed Bryce, sitting on the edge of the en suite's lavish bed with Lasair and Setanta. But yeah, Bryce would know about that limitation on the healer's abilities. Peri and Fiachra had been told what Bryce suffered at the *Marfach*'s hands, and about the showdown with the monster in Washington Square Park that had nearly killed him.

Conall, too, needed cheering from his human partner. "That's a possibility. And believe me, I've thought about it. But magick only left the nexus chamber twice. Once when Fiachra got his body back, and once when the Loremasters warped time when he went through the Pattern. The first got us the three, maybe four faces of the *Marfach,* but there's no way it could have done physical damage to anything. And the temporal distortion..." Conall grimaced. "Only unshielded magick could have taken any harm from that. Of which there wasn't any around, other than in Fiachra himself and the motherhumping *Marfach*, which apparently just sucked it down as an *hors d'oeuvre*."

"Lucien's getting the best care in D.C." Kevin plowed a hand through his hair, apparently not caring that it made him look like he'd just fallen out of bed. "And Mac's pretty much living out of the chair next to his bed."

"Is there anything else we can talk about, Highness?" Tiernan wrapped an arm around Kevin's shoulders and pulled him close.

Rian shrugged. "I've been avoiding the issue of what the feck's going on with the Pattern, not the least because the Royal consort here doesn't seem to want to discuss it..." He dug an elbow into Cuinn's ribs.

Cuinn gave Rian another one of those looks, long and measuring. The Prince sighed, and when he spoke again, most of the Irish was gone from his voice. "He says to tell you all, I asked for it. Brodulein's back in the Pattern, but he's not able to help as much as he'd hoped. The Pattern is still weakening. Breakouts of magick, like the one in Central Park and the one over the lesser nexus in Greenwich Village, are happening all over the world. No way to be sure how often. And we can't afford to let any go unguarded. Not with the *Marfach* still out there somewhere. Speakin' of which," Rian added in his own voice, "Conall, where the feck *is* the *nascód ar más'cranách*?"

"Somewhere under the Antarctic ice. That's the best I could do for a water prison on such short notice. And your command of *Faen* is improving daily, Highness."

Rian whistled under his breath. "Remind me never to piss you off."

"I'll do that." Just for a second, when he laughed, the red-haired mage was pure jailbait, the way he looked most of the time when he wasn't channeling magick or talking about magick. "I can sense where the breakouts occur, but I'm going to need Lochlann's help when I need to channel enough magick to erect the only kind of shield I have left that can stop the bastard. And for me to do that, and for him to help me do that, we need Josh and Garrett. Neither of whom can Fade."

It was Tiernan who broke the silence.

"Gentlemen, gentleFae, one way or another it sounds as if we don't have very long to figure out how not to be fucked."

***

This is your fault. The female sounded like she was trying hard not to scream.

Janek laughed. Of course, he wasn't running their shared body, so the only place anyone heard it was inside their shared head, but that was fine with him. "Fuck that. If you'd given me what you promised me, instead of fighting me, I could have had Guaire's head and you could have sucked up to the big glowing tit in the ground, no problem. Karma's a bitch."

Shut up, Meat. The female's teeth ground together.

Janek kept grinning, hidden away where no one could see him. "I heard once that if you were trapped inside a spherical mirror, it would drive you crazy."

Shut up, Meat.

The male manifested, and closed everyone's eyes. Which was probably a good thing. Janek suspected the story might have been true, and he didn't want to find out first hand. Even though the thing they were trapped in wasn't really a mirror, it reflected whoever was running the body at any given time, when it wasn't showing them a whole fuckload of nothing much except weird glowing plankton. And if he really squinted hard, when someone's eyes were open Janek thought he could make out a glimmer of deep blue light. Somewhere a hell of a long way off, and over their heads. Maybe a crack in the ice. Maybe not. The ice went on fucking forever. They'd been here long enough for him to figure that out.

"Why don't you just suck all the magick out of the trap and make it go away?"

The male made a noise like he wanted to spit. But there wasn't any place for the spit to go, so he coughed and swallowed instead. ***Because then we'd be trapped in the water, under a shit-ton of ice.***

"Yeah, but you're immortal, what the fuck do you care?"

301

WATER COULD BIND US, EVEN BEFORE WE HAD A BODY.

Janek could feel the obscenity trying to curl up around itself, to keep from touching the walls of their bizarre prison. The little bugs that made up its tail made chittering noises like something straight out of the kind of horror movie you only watched once and then smashed the fucking television you watched it on.

NOW WE ARE DOUBLY IMPRISONED.

Janek wondered when the *Marfach* had stopped being an "I" in its own head and started being a "we".

And he wondered what else had changed in that blast from the Pattern.

"You could die."

SHUT UP. MEAT.

Over their head, the great ice shelf groaned; a sound deeper and more painful than bone grinding on bone.

And not quite as cold as hell.

Undertow
(SoulShares Seven)

Prologue

August 16, 2013 (human reckoning)
Domhnacht Rúnda, *The Realm*

Rhoann corkscrewed lazily down into the shadowed depths of the gorge, his body parting the crystal water, his gleaming gray fur as slick as skin. He wouldn't be able to stay down long, not in his seal body; salmon was better for exploring the deep places, or mer-form. He didn't need to breathe when he wore those bodies; he was free to spend hours, days, tracing the caverns underlying his bottomless mountain-bracketed refuge. But he wasn't truly exploring; after all the long centuries, he knew every inch of *Domhnacht Rúnda*, the Secret Depths. He was simply reveling in his Element. And for the enjoyment of the caress of water, there was no sweeter form to wear than that of a selkie.

Rhoann Callte.

Rhoann froze. The water spoke his name. It had never done that before.

Perhaps if he dove deeper, it would stop. The light around him went from aquamarine to tourmaline to emerald; he skimmed near the face of a submerged cliff, honeycombed with tunnels.

Rhoann Callte.

The voice was female. Something like his mother's. He thought. But it had been many years since he had heard Miren's voice, except in dreams. And the water had never spoken with her voice. His mother had been a Water Fae, but not an elemental.

He dove deeper, into colder, darker water. But his lungs were starting to hurt. He drew in the magick of the water, and shifted; fur became scales, gills pierced the skin of his throat. Everything around him blurred, colors became bluer. The cooler water of a tunnel beckoned him, and his salmon form darted inside.

Rhoann Callte. Rhoann Lath-Ríoga. Tá thú toghairm.

The words caught him. Like a fisher's hook sunk deep under his jaw, only without the pain Rhoann had always imagined the true fish of his mother's stories would have felt. He thrashed, he fought; his rainbow scales clouded the water around him until the words pulled him free from his refuge and into the open water.

Thou art summoned.

Helpless to resist the call, he rose. But as he rose, he called on the magick once again, wrapping it around the salmon's form and willing his shape to change once more. He rose toward the surface, fluking with his gossamer tail and powerful violet-and-blue lower body; his arms and webbed hands trailed beside his Fae torso, until the power of the Summoning demanded that they, too, drive him upward.

304

His faceted tourmaline eyes were wide with fear, as the light brightened around him. His life depended on staying hidden. Miren had spent a lifetime's magick ensuring that the Secret Depths would never be found, would vanish from the memory of all living Fae.

If you are found, they will take you. He had never needed to ask who 'they' were. His father's people, the Water Royals. Fae loved their children with a ferocity unknown to any other species in truth or legend. And if Rhoann's Royal father had ever learned of his existence, that love would have torn him from his mother's arms.

The sunlight dazzled on the water over Rhoann's head. He thought he saw a figure on the shore, leaning out, trailing fingers in the water.

Rhoann was an impossibility, a bastard. Only Royals among the Fae pair-bonded, so only a Royal's child could be legitimate or illegitimate. And a Royal simply could not bear or father a bastard, because Royals only bonded with other Royals. Elementals to others of their own kind.

Yet Rhoann existed, child of a union violating one of the only taboos Fae knew. And his mother loved him, as only a Fae mother could. And she had hidden him.

Until now.

Rhoann's head broke the surface of the water; his tail melted away, he gasped air into his lungs. He tossed wet blond hair out of his eyes, treading water as he looked around for the source of the voice that had summoned him. His whole body trembled, waiting for the moment when he would be free of compulsion, free to dive.

"Rhoann. Please, don't fear me, I mean you no harm."

The female knelt on a rock jutting out from the steeply-sloped shore of the lake, her fingertips trailing in the water. Red hair spilled over her shoulders, which were pale and slender and lightly freckled; she wore a lilac gown of raw silk, its skirts fanned out in a circle around her feet. Rhoann supposed she was beautiful; surely her eyes were kind, and her smile gentle.

But she knew his name, she had dragged him bodily from his hiding place, and her beauty made her no less dangerous. "If you meant me no harm, you would not have called me by names no one knows, and you would have left me where I was."

The female looked away. Looked down, at her fingers dancing in the water. "There are no secrets from the Loremasters, though we ourselves are as forgotten by time as you are forgotten by reason of your mother's arts."

Magick fanned out from the female's fingertips, pouring into the water in an intricate pattern of barely visible silver-blue knotwork. So this was the net which had caught him. "The Loremasters are stories."

"And you are not even a story, Rhoann Half-Royal. Yet you are real."

"Who are you? And how do you know me?"

"I am Aine."

A name out of legend, but looking nothing like the warrior mage of his mother's stories. Though appearances—especially Fae appearances—deceived.

"The Loremasters have always been able to see anything touched by magick, anywhere in the Realm." Aine cupped water in her palm, let it trickle between her fingers back into the bottomless lake. "And your mother poured so much magick into your protection, she made herself nearly mortal. We knew of you since the moment of your birth."

Rhoann felt a tightness in his throat. "Then everything she did to hide me, everything she lost, was for nothing."

"No." Aine reached out to rest her free hand on Rhoann's shoulder. He flinched back, and she let her hand drop with a sigh. "She kept you safe—you would never have been in any real danger from your father's people, but you also would never have known the solitude you love."

"The risk of that loss was danger enough." Rhoann tried to ease back, away from the shore. He could not. "And my solitude is no more."

It had been a guess, but he knew the truth of it when Aine looked away again.

"I am... sorry." Aine watched her fingertips play in the cool water. "But you have a gift, and the exile Demesne in the human world has need of it. Or so the other Loremasters in the Pattern have Foreseen."

Rhoann stared, not even bothering to blink away the cold lake water trickling down from his blond crest into his eyes. "My understanding of other Fae is that 'sorry' is a word they learn but never use. And as for the rest, I understand none of it. You may have need of me, but I have none of you."

"Rhoann—"

He tried to push off from the shore, his toes barely able to grip the stones. But Aine's magick would not release him, and he cried out in frustration. "Let me go!"

She would not. She reached out, instead, this time touching Rhoann's shoulder—

—and overbalancing as he pulled away, falling face-first into the water with a startled cry.

Her gown soaked through, her chemise likewise. She struggled, her legs tangled in swaths of wet silk, her eyes wide with panic. Grey-blue eyes, beautiful, like the *Rúnda* when a storm threatened. Her eyes, and the rest of her, sank below the surface of the lake.

Instinctively, Rhoann dove, wrapped an arm around the mage's waist, and bore her to the surface, holding her face out of the water to let her breathe. She gasped for air, clinging to Rhoann with one arm, using her free hand to clear the water from her face.

Rhoann watched her in silence for a while. "Did you do that on purpose?" he asked at last.

"Did I..." Aine's laugh was breathless. "I suppose I can see where you would think so. No, I was clumsy. After 2000 years as a disembodied soul trapped in a matrix of magick, my balance is chancy. And may remain so for a while." She smiled, reaching down under the water to try to tame her tangled, floating skirts. "But even accident may be turned to serve a purpose."

"I... don't understand."

She twisted in Rhoann's arms, bracing her arms on the rock from which she had fallen; vaulting up out of the water on a surge of magick, she turned again to sit neatly on the stone. Neatly but for the water pouring from her skirts. "Now I know for certain you are a healer. You showed me compassion."

Rhoann's jaw clenched. He could not move away, but he could turn away, and he did. "If you came here for

308

my healing gift, then leave. It's useless. You should have known that." *If you truly know everything,* he wanted to add. But that would have sounded petulant. Childish.

A hand rested gently on his shoulder. "You speak of your mother."

Rhoann nodded once, curtly. Miren had spent her magick making the *Domhnacht Rúnda* safe, crafting a home for the two of them to share and filling it with what they would need. And then she had severed her tie to the land, so she would not draw magick from its dwindling supply to replace what she had spent. She had made herself a mortal Fae. And had died as no Fae had ever died, of an illness. In the arms of the son who should have been able to heal her with a thought, with the simplest of channelings for any other Water Fae.

"We know of her. And we saw your tears. But your gift is not useless merely because you could not save her. Your gift is rare, the ability to sense and heal damage done by magick alone."

Rhoann grimaced. His mother had been gone less than thirty years. Barely a heartbeat, as Fae reckoned time. Her loss was still an ache, one this female's reminders were doing nothing to ease. "My so-called gift comes from my half-Royal blood, my elemental nature. It works only in water."

"Better there than nowhere at all."

So you think you have found some use for me?"

The hand on his shoulder urged him to turn. Against his better judgment, treading water, he did so. And was greeted with a smile, but a real sadness as well. "I have recently come from the human world. There are Fae there, and they battle our race's most ancient enemy. With humans at their sides."

309

Rhoann would have darted away, but now the hand on his shoulder prevented him. The thought of a world full of unknown Fae, the world in which he lived, was foreign enough. Another world, full of humans? "I might know compassion, at that. Because I feel sorry for them."

Aine's laugh was light, as if it flew on its own wings. "Fae and humans on the other side share souls, the effect of passing through the Pattern."

Rhoann grunted. "This has nothing to do with me."

"Oh, but it does."

The touch on his shoulder turned into a caress, the kind his mother would have given him. For the first time, Rhoann wondered how old Aine was. Old enough to be a mother, surely. Much older, if she was actually the Aine from his mother's stories. Impossibly old. "They have some need of me."

"Yes." Something, perhaps the edge to his voice, made Aine study him curiously. "One of the Loremasters recently returned to the Pattern—the portal between the worlds—after spending some time in the human world. He reports that two among the exiles have sustained magickal hurt in their war against the *Marfach*. Damage that no one can heal."

"Then let them come to me. Somewhere that is not here." Rhoann turned away from the curiosity, the kindness, in the storm-grey eyes. "I will heal them, if you ask it of me." *And ask me no more. Leave me in what is left of my peace.*

"That will not work." Aine sighed. "For your sake, I wish it would. But Brodulein's case was... unique, to say the least. The Pattern only allows travel one way, into the human world."

310

She expects me to leave the Realm. Forever. And she has the power to force me.

"Rhoann."

Rhoann wondered if Aine could still see wherever magick was found. If she could see into his soul. Surely, she looked as if she saw Rhoann's fear and pain. The seeming was more deception, most likely. "You have netted me, you will do as you will."

"I would not force you." Aine pushed a strand of wet auburn hair off her face. "But the Fae and humans of Purgatory have become... dear, to me." She spoke slowly, considering her words, as if not quite sure of their meaning, or how well they suited her truth. "And the Loremasters in the Pattern have cast a Foretelling. They agree, there are two in the human world who will be whole only with your help."

The Loremasters were ancient stories, and Foretellings were lore more ancient still. Stories told by a name out of legend, who had lured him from the depths of the *Rúnda* like a siren, and who proposed to tear him from the only home he had ever known and send him on a quest to battle an enemy even myths spoke of as myth.

But what choice did he have, now that the refuge for which his mother had spent her life had been shattered by a warrior mage?

"Tell me what I must do." It was hard to force words past the lump in his throat.

Aine's smile eased the ache in his chest a little, despite his fears. "I will bring you to the portal between the worlds, and send you through, as prepared as I can make you. And I will do my best to send you where you will be found by the ones who need you.

311

Though I cannot promise precision, that has never been how the Pattern works."

"Will it hurt?"

"Yes." It was as if something came between Aine's face and the sun, casting her features into shadow. "But not forever. Half of your soul will go ahead of you. When you find it again, it will wear human flesh, and you will be a SoulShare. And shared pain is lessened. This is not a Fae truth, but one I have learned from the exiles."

Rhoann shuddered. It had been years since he had seen so much as another Fae. And someday he would be forced to intimacy with a human.

"We should go, then. Before I change my mind."

Rhoann. Brother.

This time it was the lake that called to him, the cool depths, clear as air. Calling him neither *Callte*, hidden, nor *Lath-Ríoga,* Half-Royal. Water calling to water, nothing more.

Rhoann would never feel that touch, or hear that voice, again.

Glossary

The following is a glossary of the *Faen* words and phrases found in *Hard as Stone, Gale Force, Deep Plunge, Firestorm, Blowing Smoke,* and *Mantled in Mist*. The reader should be advised that, as in the Celtic languages descended from it, spelling in *Faen* is as highly eccentric as the one doing the spelling.

(A few quick pronunciation rules—bearing in mind that most Fae detest rules—single vowels are generally 'pure', as in ah, ey, ee, oh, oo for a, e, i, o, u. An accent over a vowel means that vowel is held a little longer than its unaccented cousins. "ao" is generally "ee", but otherwise diphthongs are pretty much what you'd expect. Consonants are a pain. "ch" is hard, as in the modern Scottish "loch". "S", if preceded by "i" or "a", is usually "sh". "F" is usually silent, unless it's the first letter in a word, and if the word starts with "fh", then the "f" and the "h" are *both* silent. "Th" is likewise usually silent, as is "dh", although if "dh" is at the beginning of a word, it tries to choke on itself and ends up sounding something like a "strangled" French "r". Oh, and "mh" is "v", "bh" is "w", "c" is always hard, and don't forget to roll your "r"s!)

313

a'bhei'lár　　　lit. "to be the center"; an extremely charismatic person

ach　　but

adhmacomh　　wood-bodied. An insult.

adhmam　　admit, confess

a'gár'doltas　　vendetta (lit. "smiling-murder")

agean　　ocean

agla　　fear(n.)

állacht　　　beautiful. Can be used to describe persons of any gender.
　m'állacht　　my beauty. Fiachra's pillow-name for Peri.

amad'n　　fool, idiot

anam　　soul
　m'anam　　my soul. Fae endearment.
　n'anamacha　　their souls

aon-arc　　unicorn
　asiomú　　'reversal-vengeance'. The act of making oneself crave whatever is being done to one as a punishment, thereby turning one's punisher into one's procurer.

asling　　dream

314

batagar   arrow

beag   little, slight

blas   taste (v. imp.)

bod   penis (vulgar)

bodlag   limp dick (much greater insult than a human might suppose)

bragan   toy (see phrase)

briste   broken

buchal alann   beautiful boy

cac   excrement

ca'fuil?   Where?

carn   pile

ceangal   (1) chains

ceangal   (2) Royal soul-bonding ceremony in the Realm (common alt. spelling *ceangail*)

cein fa?   Why?

céle   general way of referring to two people
    le céle   together (alt. form *le chéle*)
    a céle   one another, each other

chara   friend

cho'halan   so beautiful

chort-gruag   "bark-hair". Derogatory way of referring to a dark-haired Fae

coladh   sleep

cónai   live

craobód   twig-dick. Insult, occasionally lethal.

crocnath   completion
     m'crocnath   my completion. One of Cuinn's pillow-names for Rian

croí   heart
     Croí na Dóthan   *Heart of Flame*, the signet of the Royal house of the Demesne of Fire

Cruan'ba   The Drowner. Name given to the *Marfach* by the Fae of the Demesne of Water.

Cu droc!   Bad dog!

cugat   to you

cúna   aid, assistance

daoir   1. beloved; 2. expensive

d'aos'Faen   Old Faen, the old form of the Fae language. Currently survives only in written form.

dara-láiv   lit. "second-hand". Euphemism for masturbation.

dar'cion   brilliantly colored. Conall's pillow-name for Josh.

dearmad   forgotten

deich   ten
   deich meloi   ten thousand

derea   end

desúcan   fix, repair

dhó-súil   fire-eyes. One of Cuinn's pillow-names for Rian.

dóchais   hope (n.) (alt. spelling dócas)

dolmain   hollow hill, a place of refuge

doran   stranger, exile

d'orant   impossible. Josh's pillow-name for Conall.

draoctagh   magick
   Spiraod n'Draoctagh   Spirit of Magick. Ancient Fae oath. Or expletive. Sometimes both.

317

draoi   teacher

dre'fiur   beloved sister

dre'thair   beloved brother

dubh   black, dark

dúrt me   I said

dúsi   Wake up (imp.)

ecáil   will see
    a'ecáil   I will see

eiscréid   shit

Elirei   Prince Royal

fada   long (can reference time or distance)

Faen   the Fae language. *Laurm Faen*—I speak
Fae.
    as'Faein   in the Fae language. *Laur lom
as'Faein*—I speak in the Fae language.

fan   wait (imp.)

fiáin   wild

fiánn   living magick

fior   true

flua   wet

fola   wounded, injured

folabodan   Fae sex toy. Derived from *fola,* injured, and *bod*, penis

folath   bleed

folathóin   bloody asses

fonn   keen, sharp

fracun   whore
Comes from an ancient Fae word meaning "use-value"—in other words, a person whose value is measured solely by what others can get from him or her.

ful-claov   blood-sword; a magickal weapon usually formed from the channeler's own blood

galtanas   promise

gan   general negative—no, not, without, less
    gan derea   without end, eternal

gaoirn   wolves

g'demin   true, real

g'deo   forever

g'féalaidh   may you (pl.) live (see phrases)

g'fua   hate (v.)

g'mall   slowly

grafain   wild love, wild one. Lochlann's pillow name for Garrett.

halan   beautiful

impi   I beg

laba   bed
    as a'laba!   (Get) off the bed!

lae   day

lámagh   hot (v., p.t.)

lanan   lover. Tiernan's pillow name for Kevin, and vice versa

lanh   son

laród-scatha   mirror-trap. Essentially a magickal ball with no exterior, only a mirrored interior.   And the sweet revenge of all of us who failed solid geometry in high school.

lasihoir   healer

laurha   spoken (see phrases)
    related words—*laurm,* I speak; *laur lom,* I am speaking, I speak (in) a language

lobadh   decayed, rotten

lofa   rotten

mac   son, son of
    mac'fracun   son of a whore

madra   dog

magarl   testicles (alt. spelling *magairl)*

ma'nach   mine

Marfach, the   the Slow Death. Deadliest foe of the Fae race.

marh   dead

marú   kill

Mastragna   Master of Wisdom. Ancient Fae title for the Loremasters.

milat   feel, sense

minn   oath
    mo mhinn   my oath

misnach   courage

nach general negative; not, never

né not, is not

n-oí night

'nois now

ollúnta solemn

onfatath infected

orm at me

pian pain

prácháin crows

rachtanai addicted (specifically, to sexual teasing)

Ridiabhal lit. "king of the devils", Satan. A borrowed word, as Fae have neither gods nor devils.

rílacha (it) rules

rinc dance
    rin'gcatha gríobhan "labyrinthine dance". A euphemism for Fae sexuality
    rinc-daonna "human dance", a game of teasing and sexually overloading humans
    Rinc'faring the Great Dance, an annual gathering of hundreds of Fae light-dancers
    rinc'lú little dance

rochar   harm (n.)

sallacht   extremely stubborn

saor   free

sasann   we stand

savac-dui   black-headed hawk, Conall's House-guardian

scair'anam   SoulShare (pl. *scair-anaim*)
   m'anam-sciar   my SoulShare
   scair'aine'e   the act of SoulSharing
   scair'ainm'en   SoulShared (adj.)

scian   knife
   scian-damsai   knife-dances. An extremely lethal type of formalized combat.

scílim   I think, I believe

scol-agna   lit. "school of wisdom", school for children with high magickal potential

sibh   you (pl.)

slántai   health, tranquillity
   slántai a'váil   "Peace go with you". A mournful farewell.

s'ocan   peace, be at peace

spára   spare
  spára'se   spare him

spiraod   spirit

súil   eyes
    sule-d'ainmi   lit. "animal-eyes", dark brown eyes

sumiúl   fascinating, beguiling. Lasair's pillow-name for Bryce

sus   up

s'vra lom   I love (lit. "I have love on me")

ta'sair   I'm free (exclam.)

thar   come (imp.)
    Thar lom. Come with me.

thogarm'sta   answer (imp.)

Tirr Brai   Folk of Life. Living beings with magickal essence.

t'mé   I'm

tón   ass (not the long-eared animal)

tón-grabrog   ass-crumb (of the clinging variety)

torq   boar

tráll   slave

tre   three
    Tre... dó... h'on...   Three.... two... one...

tréan-cú   strong hound. Lasair's nickname for Setanta, his blind runt Fade-hound puppy

tróhi   fight (imp.)

tseo   this, this is (see phrases)

turran'agne   mind-shock, the effect on a Fae of magickal overload

uiscebai   strong liquor found in the Realm, similar to whiskey

veissin   knockout drug found in the Realm, causes headaches

viant   desired one. A Fae endearment.

Useful phrases:

...tseo mo mhinn ollúnta.   This is my solemn oath.
G'féalaidh sibh i do cónai fada le céle, gan a marú a céle.
"May you live long together, and not kill one another."
A Fae blessing, sometimes bestowed upon those Fae foolhardy enough to undertake some form of exclusive relationship. Definite "uh huh, good luck with that" overtones.

bragan a lae "toy of the day". The plaything of a highly distractible Fae.

Fai dara tú pian beag. Ach tú a sabail dom ó pian I bhad nís mo.
You cause a slight pain. But you are the healing of more.

Cein fa buil tu ag'eachan' orm ar-seo? Why do you look at me this way?

Dóchais laurha, dóchais briste. Hope spoken is hope broken.

Bod lofa dubh. Lit. "black rotted dick." Not a polite phrase.

Scílim g'fua lom tú. I think I hate you.

S'vra lom tú. I love you.

Sus do thón. Up your ass.

D'súil do na practháin, d'croí do na gaoirn, d'anam do n-oí gan derea.
"Your eyes for the crows, your heart for the wolves, your soul for the eternal night." There is only one stronger vow of enmity in the Fae language, and trust me, you don't want to hear that one.

Lámagh tú an batagar; 'se seo torq a'gur fola d'fach.
"You shot the arrow; this wounded boar is yours." The equivalent *as'Faein* of "You broke it; you

326

buy it." Often used in its shortened form, "*Lámagh tú an batagar.*" (or "*Lámagh sádh an batagar*" for "they shot." It's probably only a matter of time before some Fae in the human world, taking his cue from "NMP" for "not my problem," comes up with "LTB."

Tá dócas le scian inas fonn, nach milat g'matann an garta dí g'meidh tú folath.
    Fae proverb: Hope is a knife so keen, you don't feel the cut until you bleed.

G'ra ma agadh.   Thank you.

Tam g'fuil aon-arc desúcan an lanhuil damast I d'asal. G'mall.
    "May a unicorn repair your hemorrhoids. Slowly." One can only imagine….

Magairl a'Ridiabhal.   Satan's balls.

Se an'agean flua, a'deir n'abhann.   The ocean is wet, says the river. The pot calling the kettle black.

galtanas deich meloi
    "promise of ten thousand." A promise given by a Fae, to give ten thousand of something to another, usually something that can only be given over time. Considered an extravagant, even irrational showing of devotion.

Támid faoi ceangal ag a'slabra ceant.   We are bound by the same chains.

Né seo a'manach.   This isn't for me.

mo phan s'darr lear sa masa   my favorite pain in the ass

Dúrt me lath mars'n   I told you so

Bual g'mai, aris.   Well met, again.

An'Faei a ngaill, ta'Fhaei an tráll.   The Fae who needs(, that Fae) is a slave.

lasr, s'oc as fola
    Flame, frost and blood. A Fae oath, a little milder than the ones involving hearts and eyes
        and wolves and suchlike.

Do dalat-serbhisach.   "Your saddle-servant." The equivalent of "at your service." Usually sarcastic.

Fan lel'om. Bh'uil tú ag'eistac lom?   Stay with me. Do you hear me?

An-bfuil tuillt aige a'hartáil? Nó an-bfuil sé a'fracuin?
    Is he worth saving? Or does he only have use-worth?

Sé ar'chann de dúnn.   He is one of us.

Ca' atá tú a'rá?   What are you saying?

Ní fed'r lom an'uscin lat.   I can't understand you.

328

Tá cúna saor in asc is'daoir.   Free aid is the dearest.

A'buil gnas le lom ar-gúl.   Fuck me backwards.

A'buil gnas le leat a's a'madra dúsigh tu suas leis. Fuck you and the dog you woke up with.

Blas mo thón.   Taste my ass.

Sasann muid le chéle.   We stand together. Unofficial motto of the Demesne of Purgatory.

Tá'siad marh.   They're dead.

draoi ríoga   royal wizard (actually Irish, rather than *Faen*, Rian's title for his court mage)

Bei mé tú a'ecáil g'deo.   I will see you forever.

329

About the Author

Rory Ni Coileain majored in creative writing, back when Respectable Colleges didn't offer such a major. She had to design it herself, at a university which boasted one professor willing to teach creative writing: a British surrealist who went nuts over students writing dancing bananas in the snow, but did not take well to high fantasy. Graduating Phi Beta Kappa at the age of nineteen, she sent off her first short story to an anthology that was being assembled by an author she idolized, and received one of those rejection letters that puts therapists' kids through college. For the next thirty years or so she found other things to do, such as going to law school, ballet dancing (at more or less the same time), volunteering as a lawyer with Gay Men's Health Crisis, and nightclub singing, until her stories started whispering to her. Currently, she's a lawyer and a legal editor; the proud mother of a budding filmmaker; and is busily wedding her love of myth and legend to her passion for m/m romance. She is a three-time Rainbow Award finalist.

Books in this Series by Rory Ni Coileain:

Hard as Stone: Book One of the SoulShares Series

Gale Force: Book Two of the SoulShares Series

Deep Plunge: Book Three of the SoulShares Series

Firestorm: Book Four of the SoulShares Series

Blowing Smoke: Book Five of the SoulShares Series

Other Riverdale Avenue Books You Might Like

The Siren and the Sword: Book One of the Magic University Series
By Cecilia Tan

The Tower and the Tears: Book Two of the Magic University Series
By Cecilia Tan

The Incubus and the Angel: Book Three of the Magic University Series
By Cecilia Tan

The Prophecy and the Poet: Book Four of the Magic University Series
By Cecilia Tan

Spellbinding: Tales From Magic University
Edited by Cecilia Tan

Mordred and the King
By John Michael Curlovich

Collaring the Saber-Tooth: Book One of the Masters of Cats Series
By Trinity Blacio

Dee's Hard Limits: Book Two of the Masters of Cats Series
By Trinity Blacio

Caging the Bengal Tiger: Book Three of the Masters of Cats Series
By Trinity Blacio

Made in the USA
Las Vegas, NV
14 February 2021